W9-ASW-519

PRAISE FOR THE NOVELS OF RUTH GLICK
WRITING AS REBECCA YORK

"Action packed . . . and filled with sexual tension . . . a gripping thriller."
—*The Best Reviews*

"A steamy paranormal . . . danger, shape-shifters, and hot romance. The best of everything. Brava."
—*Huntress Book Reviews*

"A compulsive read."
—*Publishers Weekly*

"York delivers an exciting and suspenseful romance with paranormal themes that she gets just right. This is a howling good read."
—*Booklist*

"Mesmerizing action and passions that leap from the pages with the power of a wolf's coiled spring."
—*BookPage*

"Delightful . . . [with] two charming lead characters."
—*Midwest Book Review*

"Rebecca York delivers page-turning suspense."
—*Nora Roberts*

"[Her] prose is smooth, literate, and fast-moving; her love scenes are tender yet erotic; and there's always a happy ending."
—*The Washington Post Book World*

continued . . .

"She writes a fast-paced, satisfying thriller."   —UPI

"Clever and a great read. I can't wait to read the final book in this wonderful series."   —*ParaNormal Romance Reviews*

Don't miss these other werewolf romantic suspense novels from Rebecca York

KILLING MOON
*A PI with a preternatural talent for tracking
finds his prey: a beautiful genetic researcher
who may be his only hope for a future . . .*

EDGE OF THE MOON
*A police detective and a woman who files a
missing persons report become the pawns of an
unholy serial killer in a game of deadly attraction . . .*

WITCHING MOON
*A werewolf and a sexy botanist investigate a swamp
steeped in superstition, legend, and death . . .*

CRIMSON MOON
*A young werewolf bent on protecting the environment
ends up protecting a lumber baron's daughter—
a woman who arouses his hunger as no other . . .*

SHADOW OF THE MOON
*A journalist investigates a sinister world
of power and pleasure—alongside a woman
who knows how to bring out the animal in him . . .*

NEW MOON
*Unable to resist his desire for a female werewolf,
a landscape architect will have to travel
through two dimensions to save her—
and earth—from the wrath of her enemy . . .*

Books by Rebecca York

KILLING MOON
EDGE OF THE MOON
WITCHING MOON
CRIMSON MOON
SHADOW OF THE MOON
NEW MOON
GHOST MOON

BEYOND CONTROL
BEYOND FEARLESS

GHOST
MOON

REBECCA YORK

BERKLEY SENSATION, NEW YORK

THE BERKLEY PUBLISHING GROUP
Published by the Penguin Group
Penguin Group (USA) Inc.
375 Hudson Street, New York, New York 10014, USA
Penguin Group (Canada), 90 Eglinton Avenue East, Suite 700, Toronto, Ontario M4P 2Y3, Canada
(a division of Pearson Penguin Canada Inc.)
Penguin Books Ltd., 80 Strand, London WC2R 0RL, England
Penguin Group Ireland, 25 St. Stephen's Green, Dublin 2, Ireland (a division of Penguin Books Ltd.)
Penguin Group (Australia), 250 Camberwell Road, Camberwell, Victoria 3124, Australia
(a division of Pearson Australia Group Pty. Ltd.)
Penguin Books India Pvt. Ltd., 11 Community Centre, Panchsheel Park, New Delhi—110 017, India
Penguin Group (NZ), 67 Apollo Drive, Rosedale, North Shore 0632, New Zealand
(a division of Pearson New Zealand Ltd.)
Penguin Books (South Africa) (Pty.) Ltd., 24 Sturdee Avenue, Rosebank, Johannesburg 2196,
South Africa

Penguin Books Ltd., Registered Offices: 80 Strand, London WC2R 0RL, England

This is a work of fiction. Names, characters, places, and incidents either are the product of the author's imagination or are used fictitiously, and any resemblance to actual persons, living or dead, business establishments, events, or locales is entirely coincidental. The publisher does not have any control over and does not assume any responsibility for author or third-party websites or their content.

GHOST MOON

A Berkley Sensation Book / published by arrangement with the author

PRINTING HISTORY
Berkley Sensation mass-market edition / May 2008

ISBN: 978-0-425-22245-4

BERKLEY® SENSATION
Berkley Sensation Books are published by The Berkley Publishing Group,
a division of Penguin Group (USA) Inc.,
375 Hudson Street, New York, New York 10014.
BERKLEY SENSATION and the "B" design are trademarks of Penguin Group (USA) Inc.

PRINTED IN THE UNITED STATES OF AMERICA

10 9 8 7 6 5 4 3 2 1

GHOST
MOON

PROLOGUE

THE TWO WEREWOLVES were out for blood and too inexperienced to think of death—their own or the other's.

They had fought over a flirtatious little brunette, and neither one of them was willing to say she was just a temporary whim. So they met in a patch of Maryland woods, far from the haunts of men—each prepared to rip the hide off the other.

They had driven in separate cars to the dueling grounds, neither one of them bringing a second because this was a very private affair.

Back into the mists of time, the adults of the Marshall clan had trusted no one besides their life mates. Certainly not their fathers or brothers or cousins. They were all alpha males, all leaders of their own pack. And the only individuals admitted to that pack were their wives and children.

But neither had yet reached the age of bonding. And neither of them knew how to control the rage that flared in the animal portion of their spirit.

So they pulled their cars into the woods, then went to

separate thickets to strip off their clothing and say the ancient chant that changed them from man to wolf.

Neither of them understood the words. They only knew the ritual had been passed down from father to son through the ages.

Then they trotted into the clearing that they had selected and faced each other, eyes blazing and muscles tensed. One of them howled, then the other, before they began to circle—looking for an opening.

At the beginning, someone might have backed down. Yet pride and the violent instincts of their kind outweighed good sense. One sprang, knocking the other to the ground, and the fight was on.

They rolled across the forest floor, each trying to score a bite that would punish the other enough to make him back off.

Then one lost all sense of proportion and went for his opponent's throat, his teeth sinking through thick fur into vulnerable flesh. And when he felt the other combatant go limp, he raised his head in alarm, then took a quick step away from the shaggy form sprawled on the ground.

His cousin lay still, blood gushing from his neck, his expression as astonished as that of the wolf who had taken the fateful bite.

The attacker stepped back, saying the ancient chant in his mind, feeling his muscles and tendons contort as he changed from wolf to naked man. Ignoring the wounds on his shoulders and ribs, he knelt beside the injured animal.

"Caleb, Jesus. I'm sorry. I didn't mean . . ."

His cousin raised dull eyes. His jaws moved, and his face contorted, and then he, too, made the transformation from wolf to man.

He lay breathing shallowly, then tried to push himself up, before falling back against the blood-soaked leaves, his fingers clawing the ground.

"Jesus," Aden repeated, fear leaping inside his chest. "We've got to get you to a doctor. We can say . . . an animal attacked you."

But it was already too late. The life in his cousin's eyes flickered, then went out.

Aden looked around wildly, wondering what the hell he was going to do.

His heart pounding, he went back to where he'd left his clothes and swiftly pulled on his khaki pants and long-sleeved shirt.

It struck him, then, that he had killed a man. Well, a were-wolf. His cousin. He had heard whispered tales in the family of werewolves who had disappeared over the years. Caleb lived alone, the way they all did before they bonded with a life mate. And his job took him away from home for long periods of time. It might be days, weeks before anyone realized he was missing. And there was nothing to tie his disappearance to his cousin.

Still, it seemed wrong to leave his naked body in the woods. So he retrieved Caleb's discarded clothing, dressing him in his jeans and shirt before pulling on his shoes and socks.

As he worked, his mind churned, making feverish plans. He'd have to drive the abandoned Ford somewhere else. Maybe he should push it off a cliff into the river. That might be the best option. Or maybe not.

Well, he didn't have to figure out that part yet. But he'd better not drive too far, because he'd have to race back here in wolf form and . . .

Bury the body. He couldn't leave the evidence. Or could he? What evidence was that, exactly? That a man had been killed by an animal in the woods.

He shuddered, and a surge of family loyalty made his throat tighten. He might have killed another one of the Marshall men in a stupid fight, but he wouldn't abandon him out here in the open—to be torn apart by forest animals.

He gritted his teeth. He had come out here roaring mad over a woman who wasn't important. And now he was reaping the consequences.

CHAPTER
ONE

QUINN HAD COME through the portal between the worlds six times now, into this strange place—the Maryland woods.

She took a deep breath of the air. It smelled different. In her universe, she would have caught the tang of wood smoke. Here, underlying the scent of pine trees, she detected exhaust from automobiles and smoke from factories—even this far from the city called Baltimore, so unlike anything in her world.

She had been there a few times, riding in a car with Rinna and Logan Marshall. Although they were both werewolves, they were very different from each other. Rinna was from Quinn's world. Logan was from this universe, where few people had the psychic talents that were so important to the lives of Quinn's people.

Rinna and Logan had both taught her so much. Enough to get around here. She had a driver's license, Social Security number, and credit cards. They were of no use back in Sun Acres, the city where she had lived for the past nine months.

But here, they were a necessity. Logan had even given her driving lessons, although she wasn't very good at it yet.

She rubbed her arm, where an adept had removed the slave mark from her flesh. She was a free woman now. Yet she carried heavy obligations. And she must hurry.

After taking a moment to orient herself, she went to the green plastic storage bin that she had hidden in a tangle of raspberry brambles. Inside was modern American clothing. After removing a T-shirt and jeans, she stood for a moment, sending her mind outward, searching the woods for danger. In this place, it always felt like someone was watching her, yet when she looked around, she saw nothing.

Putting the feeling down to her own uneasiness, she pulled off her leather tunic, the cool evening breeze tightening her nipples. With a shiver, she snatched up the bra that Rinna had told her was part of a modern woman's clothing here and wrestled it into place. Again she looked around, seeing no one but still feeling like someone was spying on her.

Determined to shrug off the unsettling feeling, she reached for the T-shirt.

It was tempting to keep on her own leather pants, but she knew they would look primitive in twenty-first century America. So she shucked them down her legs as rapidly as she could before donning silky panties.

When she followed them with the worn blue jeans Rinna had given her, she breathed out a little sigh.

Next she exchanged her sandals for socks and running shoes.

After bundling up the clothing and hunting knife from her own universe, she took out a fanny pack and hooked it around her waist. Inside were her ID cards—and a Sig Sauer. Logan had taught her gun safety and marksmanship, but she still hated the power of the weapon.

When she'd returned the plastic box to the tangle of brambles, she started toward the Marshalls' stone and wood house, using a rough trail through the thick underbrush. It was a familiar route, but this time she came to a place where loose dirt and boulders had tumbled down a cliff, blocking her path.

She stopped, running a hand through her sun-streaked hair as she considered climbing over the mess. But if the rubble shifted, she could get hurt. And out here, there was no one to help her. So she reversed directions, taking an alternate route.

She reached a small clearing in the woods and started forward, then stopped short, her nerves tingling.

Sometimes she could sense other people's emotions. And this evening the ability was working strongly.

Her eyes strained to penetrate the shadows. Although she saw nothing, she knew there was some presence hovering here. Waiting for *her*.

Waves of deep pain beat at her, pain and a gnawing hunger. Not for food.

Shuddering, she took a quick step back, ready to turn and flee. But before she could escape, the air around her rippled, as though a portal had opened in front of her.

A portal to her world?

Impossible.

Portals didn't just spring up at random times and places. And as far as she knew, nobody here could open one. A group of trained adepts from her world had to cut a slice in the membrane that separated one world from the other. At least that was the way she had pictured it. Cutting with a sharpened psychic talent instead of a knife. And it took the energy of more than one person to do it.

When the air stopped shimmering, she breathed out a little sigh. The sigh turned into a scream when a man's strong arms grabbed her from behind. But the scream was cut off by a large hand clamping over her mouth.

CHAPTER
TWO

QUINN GASPED AND tried to twist away from the man who held her. She knew it was a man, because she could feel a masculine body pressed to her back—and feel his arm across her middle, just below her breasts.

Unable to break free, she kicked backward, trying to inflict some damage. But she couldn't make contact with his legs.

Although he held her in place like a giant restraining a troublesome child, when she looked down, she saw nothing.

And that was more terrifying than catching a view of a powerful opponent. As the horror of her plight slammed home, her heart skipped a beat and started up again in double-time.

She had called him a man. But she couldn't see him. Not because he was hidden. There was *nothing* to see. Yet she felt the substance of his energy body and knew that his grasp was stronger than that of any mortal.

He wasn't human. Couldn't be human. And a feeling of desperation made her redouble her efforts to get away. Arms and legs pumping, she jabbed and kicked at the air, even though she knew that to best a demon or ghost or whatever

this supernatural being was, she needed cunning, not physical force.

As her strength ebbed, she wondered how she had gotten
caught by this creature. Truly, she hadn't expected anything
like this in Logan's universe.

Fighting the impulse to keep struggling, she forced her
shoulders, arms, and legs to relax. And when she did, she
thought she heard a ghostly sigh.

"Turn me loose," she said softly, a plea not a demand.
Maybe that would work.

"Not yet."

Because she hadn't expected an answer, hearing any
words at all gave her as much of a shock as her captivity.

His voice was deep and resonant and just a little rusty,
like a man who hadn't spoken in a long time.

"Who are you?"

"I will not hurt you," he answered softly.

"Turn me loose," she repeated.

"You'll run."

He had that right. But she wasn't going to agree—not out
loud.

With nothing to lose by trying to gain his confidence, she
closed her eyes and leaned back against him.

"What do you want from me?" she said, hearing the
strained quality of her own voice.

"I want . . . company."

"Why?"

"I have been here a long time."

The way he said it had her fighting empathy, yet she
answered, "Other people must have come through these
woods."

"Yes. But they cannot feel me or hear me the way you
do."

What luck! Her psychic talents had gotten her into this
trap.

Was her captor a ghost? Or a demon? Or something else?
She wanted to know, but she was afraid to find out.

While she was silently debating her options, she felt him
stir, felt his hold on her change subtly.

One arm moved upward to press against her breast. While she was reacting to that, she felt the fingers of his other hand stroking her cheeks, then her jawline in a pattern that could have been soothing—or sensual.

Then the feel of his fingers on her skin was replaced by his lips. His invisible body hunched as he slid his mouth gently along the line where her hair met her face. And he sighed as he found the curve of her cheekbone.

"Your skin is so soft. Like silk."

His voice had turned almost dreamy. Was this her chance to pull away?

She shouldn't let this opportunity go—when his guard was down. If it was down.

But her resolve faded as she caught the woodsy scent of him and felt his lips travel to her neck. Her earlier fear was replaced by a buzzing in her brain . . . and a tingling along her nerve endings.

"Don't," she managed.

"Why not?" he asked, his mouth moving against her neck, then sliding lower, to her collarbone. His lips were warm on her skin, his breath exciting little tingles of sensation.

His breath? Warm? How could that be possible?

The question drifted through her mind and right out again. He was standing behind her, so that his mouth couldn't reach hers, even when she arched her neck and threw her head back.

"You're beautiful. I love your hair." He ran his fingers through the locks she had grown out recently. "Your little nose. And your sensual lips." As he spoke, he touched each feature he mentioned.

He still seemed to be behind her. Could he really see her face? Or was he talking about the view of her when she'd first walked into the clearing?

A thought struck her, and she stiffened.

"What?" he murmured.

"Were you watching me undress?"

"You gave me a wonderful view of your body. But not all at once. First your breasts. Then that sweet dark triangle at the top of your legs."

She felt her face heat.

"I was too far away to touch you."

"But not too far away to make those rocks block the path!" she accused.

He chuckled, his voice rich and deep. "That wasn't easy. But I did it."

"Why?"

"Each time you came from . . . the other place, I tried to get you to notice me. But you were too far away to hear my voice—or feel my touch."

The finger at her lips stroked back and forth. "Open for me."

She struggled to resist. But somehow he had bent her to his will. After a few moments, she did as he asked, and his finger slipped inside her mouth, tenderly playing with her inner lips and, sliding along the line of her teeth, arousing currents of sensuality that pulsed through her.

In some corner of her mind, she was shocked at what she was doing—allowing herself to respond to him on such a basic level.

Yet she had stopped fearing him. He was no devil. Or if he was, he knew how to give a woman pleasure. Was he an incubus, trapped here in this patch of woods? That would explain the effect he was having on her.

Or was she simply so starved for a relationship with a man that she welcomed the attentions of a phantom?

She tried to stiffen her resolve. Even if she was needy, she shouldn't allow him this access to her body. Yet what choice did she have? He was stronger than she was. And he wanted this contact.

She dragged in a breath, her legs turning shaky so that she swayed as though she were fighting a strong wind blowing through the forest.

He pulled her more firmly against his invisible body, and she knew that he was aroused. At least she felt what seemed like an erection wedged against the top of her ass.

Rationalizations tumbled through her mind. He had her under his control. This was not her fault. She was helpless to keep him from doing whatever he wanted.

Even if he had once been a man, he was more than that now. More powerful. More commanding. Sexier.

Maybe he sensed her response to his power, because he increased the intimacy of the contact, his hands sliding to her breasts, weighing them in his hands, pressing and kneading, his fingers circling around her hardened nipples but not touching them.

"Please." She wasn't sure whether she wanted him to go on—or stop.

No, that was a lie. She knew exactly what she wanted him to do.

And so did he. His fingers tightened the circles barely brushing the sides of her raised nipples, wringing a cry from her. In some corner of her brain, she realized he didn't have to slip his hand under her bra the way a mortal man would have. His knowing touch was simply there, his fingers circling then plucking at her with the practiced skill of a man who knew how to arouse a woman.

She felt the blood rushing hotly through her veins, felt her breath sawing in and out of her lungs as physical sensations spiraled out of control.

"You like that."

She didn't answer. She didn't have to. He understood very well what he was doing to her.

With the arrogance of a conquering male, he slid one large hand down her body, cradling her thigh and then gliding inward toward her sex. As her response leaped to meet his touch, a measure of sanity returned to her mushy brain.

If this kept up, he was going to make her come—and maybe he was doing it to give himself more power over her mind and her body.

As he'd aroused her, her fear of him had receded. Now it surged up again. And in that moment of terror, she summoned the strength to wrench herself away. Or maybe he had let his guard down.

Freedom was a shock. She hadn't expected to escape, so she lost her footing and tumbled forward, landing in a pile of leaves a few feet from where she had been standing.

She tensed, waiting for him to come down on top of her. He chose not to. And she breathed out a grateful sigh.

As the night air cooled her heated flesh, she sat up and looked around, trying to find him.

"Damn." It was a mild curse, yet it carried a wealth of emotion.

She zeroed in on the place from where the voice had emanated. "Stay away from me."

"I won't force myself on you."

You already did, she thought. Well, at the beginning. Then she'd been a willing participant.

The light was starting to go, but she still focused on the place where it sounded like he was standing. Could she see something? A flickering in the air? Like when she'd first sensed him?

In her world, children with psychic talents went to special schools. And in one of her classes, the teacher had taught a series of lessons on ghosts. Not just in theory. The instructor had summoned several apparitions. She remembered how they had looked. A few had taken human form. Most were not substantial at all, just a disturbance or a ripple in the air. Of course, for the safety of the students, they had been benign ghosts. Although few of the children could communicate with them, Quinn had been able to talk with some. But that was years ago, and she hadn't done it again, until now.

"What are you thinking?" the phantom asked.

"If you were me, wouldn't you think this was a strange situation?"

"Yes. It is for me, too. But I won't hurt you."

"Why?"

"I have my honor." He made a derisive sound. "Honor! That's how I ended up dead."

"So you *are* a ghost." she said, glad of the confirmation.

"What else would I be?" he shot back.

She didn't bother to educate him on the other possibilities. Instead, she asked her own question. "And when you were alive, what was your name?"

"Caleb Marshall."

Her breath caught. Marshall. The same last name as Logan and his brothers and cousins. Could that be a coincidence? Or was this one of the werewolves in his family?

That might be true. She had sensed hidden power in this being. Was she sensing a werewolf as well as a man?

Or was he lying to her? Had he picked up the name from her mind? Because he was actually a demon bent on controlling her.

If so, why was he still standing a few yards away?

Her mind supplied an answer. Because he'd changed tactics, and he was trying to get her to drop her guard.

She hated looking for hidden meaning in everything he said. But she couldn't help herself. She could be in danger. Even if he'd kissed and caressed her, he could turn on her at any moment.

"What are you—besides a ghost?" she asked.

"The guardian of this place."

"What does that mean?"

"I . . . protect the animals."

"And how long have you been here?"

CHAPTER
THREE

CALEB FELT A rush of frustration as he considered the question. He didn't know the answer!

For a long time, anger had kept him here. He hadn't even known what he was angry about. But he knew that he couldn't let his soul slip into eternity.

Then memories had started coming back to him, little by little.

First he'd recalled the fight. He and Aden had come here—each bent on teaching the other a lesson. They had changed to wolf form and rolled across the forest floor, both of them trying to inflict damage.

In the middle of the battle, Aden had broken the unspoken rules and gone for his throat. He remembered the hot pain. The blood draining out of him. His terrible weakness—and then the darkness where he had clung to some kind of existence that he couldn't even describe.

His first memories had been of his own death. Only that. It was like someone had taken a knife and cut a big, gaping hole in his consciousness. Then other recollections came stealing back into his mind. All of them dark.

His mother's sorrow over the death of a baby girl. The

death of his older brother—when he'd first changed from man to wolf. Caleb's own dread of that first transformation.

Finally, he'd remembered something good—the family celebration after his first transformation, when he'd made it through to the other side. Not long after that, he and his father had started to fight, and he'd known it was time to move out. He'd found a broken-down little house near the woods and made it livable. And when he was home, he prowled the forest at night in wolf form.

The memories had been like a dream—of someone else's existence. At first he had waited here through endless loneliness, watching the seasons change and the forest creatures live their lives. Then he realized he could make this patch of woods a place where hunters were afraid to venture. He couldn't speak to them, but he could give them a bad feeling about stopping here—and keep them from shooting the animals for sport.

He glanced at the woman's expectant face, knowing she was waiting for his answer. It was strange to be talking to her. Stranger still to touch her and feel her reaction to him.

That connection made him give her the truth. "I cannot answer you. Time . . . passes. The world changes. I have been here for a long time. I know that much."

He watched her take that in, watched her come at the question from another angle.

"Do you know what year you died?"

He hadn't thought about the year in a long time. But it came to him. "1933."

She nodded, then supplied an answer. "That was seventy-five years ago."

"Ah." The number sent emotion sweeping through him. Yes, that was a long time. Longer than most men lived.

How many things had changed in the world? Did they still have bread lines? What about people fleeing the Dust Bowl? Did everybody still listen to the *Jack Benny* show on the radio? Were the New York Yankees still losing to the Washington Senators?

She cut off his silent musings with a question. "How did you end up here?"

He raised one shoulder. "I fought with one of my cousins. He killed me, and he buried me here."

She winced. "And you're a werewolf?"

Surprise jolted him. That was something they kept in the family. "How did you know?"

She hesitated for a moment, then said, "I sensed it."

"Yes. You have senses that most other people do not possess."

She nodded, then asked another question. "Why are you still on earth? I mean, why haven't you . . . gone on?"

He hesitated, wondering how much he should say.

"First, I stayed to avenge my death. Then I saw that I could make this place a haven for the forest creatures."

She went back to what he had first told her. "The wolf who killed you has to be long dead."

"Maybe he had sons."

QUINN pushed herself to her feet and dusted leaves off her jeans and shirt, facing the spot where Caleb Marshall's voice came from. Now she thought she saw the dim simulacrum of a man. Was he becoming more solid while she watched?

As she stared at him, she could add details. He was tall—perhaps six feet, with dark eyes and dark hair cut short. His nose was strong. His jaw conveyed stubbornness or maybe aggression. He was wearing jeans and a long-sleeved blue shirt, which she had to assume he'd been wearing when he'd been buried.

In 1933 in this universe, men's clothing hadn't looked so different than it did now. Or to put it another way, his dress was closer to what men wore here than what they wore in her world. Except for his shoes. They might have been athletic shoes, but they had strange, high tops that disappeared under the legs of his jeans.

She gave herself a mental shake. She shouldn't be standing here evaluating Caleb Marshall's clothing. She had to escape from him. For more than one reason.

Taking a step back, she said, "I have to go."

"Why?"

"A woman's life depends on my mission," she answered. As soon as she said it, she was sorry she'd put it that way, since she was talking to a man who had already crossed that boundary.

"A woman from that . . . other place?"

"Yes."

"So you say."

"Why would I lie?"

"To get away from me." He appeared to shift his weight from one foot to the other. "What is the place where you come from?"

"It's hard to explain."

When he stood silently staring at her, she answered, "All right. A universe parallel to this one."

He answered with a harsh laugh. "You expect me to believe that?"

"Being a ghost hasn't given you more knowledge about the universe? You didn't . . . go to an astral plane or something like that?"

"Astral plane? What is that?"

She struggled to remember the lessons she'd learned in school. "It's a place of the mind and spirit—outside the physical world. Living people can sometimes go there to meditate. And there are other beings there—spirits."

He flapped his arm in what looked like exasperation. "No. I have been *here* the whole time. In this forest."

"And you saw me come . . . out of a cave."

"Yes. I know you didn't go in there. But you came out. Then later you went back in and vanished."

"Yes, I crossed over from my world—and went back there."

"*This* is the world."

"There are others. Only a thin . . . wall separates them, if you know how to find it."

She considered how much to tell him about her friends, Zarah and Griffin. She'd met Zarah when they were both slaves, and the other woman had been sent to spy on Griffin, a powerful council member in Sun Acres.

But everything had changed soon after they'd come to the

city. Griffin had ended up freeing them both—and then he'd
married Zarah. Now he was under attack by another council
member: a man named Baron, who wanted to rule alone.

Griffin was prepared to fight him, but not to put his wife
in danger. So he'd had his most talented adepts open a portal
from his world to this one, and soon Quinn would bring
Zarah through.

Trying to convey her sense of urgency, Quinn spoke from
her heart. "The woman I'm helping is with child. Her husband has enemies, and he sent me to find a place where she
will be safe until the crisis is over."

"Why you?"

Raising her chin, she said, "I'm her best friend. Both of
them trust me to bring her to safety. And they know I have
the skill and the courage to do it."

She waited with her heart pounding, wondering if he
would accept that.

Finally, he said, "I hear the truth of that in your voice.
And I have seen your courage for myself."

"Thank you."

She would have sworn she heard him swallow hard.

"You can go—if you promise to come back and see me
again."

"If I can," she answered, wondering if she was telling the
truth. He had frightened her. Touched her. Stirred something
inside her that was better left unstirred. At least with him.

When she started to take a step away, he held her with his
gaze. "Tell me your name."

"Quinn."

"That's not a woman's name. Women have names like
Helen or Betty or Doris."

"Where I come from, my name is fine!"

"All right, Quinn. Go. Before I change my mind."

HE was the one who vanished.

One moment she was standing in the forest talking to the
ghost of Caleb Marshall. Then he was gone. To his grave?

She shuddered. It was a disturbing notion.

She hated to think of him as a dead man in his grave. And maybe there was a different explanation for where he had come from. If he'd simply flickered into existence, then disappeared from the scene just now, maybe he was only "here" when he wanted to be.

She shook her head and backed away from the clearing where they'd been talking, then made a circle around the area, finding her way back to the trail that she had used previously.

There were places like this in her world. But around Sun Acres, much of the land was empty of life and littered with ruined buildings that had been destroyed in wars over a hundred years ago. And forests near the city had been cut down for wood to heat houses and cook food.

She hadn't known much about the history of her universe when she'd come to Sun Acres. That wasn't something they'd taught in school. Maybe because most people were too busy surviving to worry about history.

But Griffin had access to books and journals that ordinary people never saw. He had let her read some of them, and she knew that life had been very different before the turn of the previous century.

The change was precipitated by a man named Eric Carfoli, who had come to a place called Chicago, for a "World's Fair." Logan had told her they had had the same fair in his world, only nobody named Carfoli had been there. In *her* world, the man had said he could create psychic powers, and people had flocked to his tent.

And when they emerged, many of them did have abilities that they'd never dreamed of.

Some could read the future. Some could move objects with their minds. Some could look into the private thoughts of other people—or communicate mind to mind over long distances. And some had acquired the ability to change from human to animal form.

They'd been excited about their new talents and eager to use them. But the people without the powers had feared them and killed many of them. And in the end, the two sides had lined up against each other and fought fierce battles.

When the fighting was over, the land was in ruins, the place called the United States of America was destroyed, and the people who were left banded together for protection in walled cities like Sun Acres.

That was how strong men had declared themselves nobles and taken power. And how some previously free people had been forced into slavery. It had also created a world where men had asserted their domination over women.

Quinn broke from a stand of trees and saw a light flickering ahead of her. An electric light. In her world, it would have seemed like magic. You flipped a switch, and the room filled with brightness. You didn't need oil lamps or candles. Or fireplaces for heat. And you didn't need slaves with psi powers to run equipment like ovens or water pumps—the way she had done.

This side of the portal was different. In so many ways. There were a few people with psychic abilties, but not enough to be a problem for the rest of the population. And in truth, many people didn't even believe in those powers. Which was why a family where the men changed to wolf form could keep their secret hidden.

EVERYBODY has secrets. And his were bigger than most because there was so much at stake, Colonel Jim Bowie thought as he looked out the window of his quarters onto the parade ground of the military compound. Not a standard U.S. Army installation. No, this was Flagstaff Farm, and he had built the facility from scratch—after inheriting the property and a small fortune from his late wife.

God rest her soul. She'd died in a fatal car accident five years ago. An accident he'd arranged, because he'd needed her wealth more than he'd needed a wife.

With her money and his know-how, he was preparing his men for a mission so secret that he hadn't spoken of it aloud.

He ran a hand over the close-cropped gray hair on his head. Prematurely gray. He was still in his prime. He trained every day along with his troops. He could still climb a thirty-foot rope and scramble over an eight-foot barrier almost as fast as his fastest recruit. And he could beat any of them on the firing range. Ordnance had always been his specialty.

Not that he was competing with them. He wouldn't allow himself or them to see it in those terms. But staying in top physical condition was part of leadership.

Superb intelligence and careful planning were even more critical—when it came to the task he'd assigned himself, the most important thing he had ever undertaken in his life.

It had been in the planning stages for month—years, even. And now he was very close to the big day.

Everything was in place, but he had one nagging doubt. A soldier whose behavior seemed a little off. And until he was sure of the man, he would wait to inform the squad of the up-coming mission.

AS Quinn drew closer to Logan and Rinna's house, she mar-veled once again at the way their home sat isolated in the woods. It was the perfect place for a werewolf, yet it would be so vulnerable in the badlands outside Sun Acres.

Rinna lived here now. She had come through a portal the year before. Quinn had found her six weeks ago—much the same way she'd found the ghost—by sensing her presence.

Although Rinna had been shocked to see someone from her own world, she'd been quick to offer her hospitality, once Quinn had made it clear she wasn't there to try and drag Rinna back. But Quinn couldn't help feeling like she was imposing, maybe because she wasn't used to much kindness in her life.

As she approached the house, she went still. She could see Logan and Rinna through the window, standing close, their arms around each other. They looked like they might be heading for their bedroom. A flare of heat shimmered through Quinn's body as she watched them. She had been aroused in the forest. Now, seeing this couple so obviously in love brought her own arousal back.

She clenched her fists, feeling like a voyeur. Again.

It was like being around Griffin and Zarah. They were so much in love that they didn't always think of how other people would react to their displays of intimacy.

Living with them made Quinn all too conscious that she had no one. Was that why she'd responded with such heated passion to a ghost? Because she wanted a man of her own?

But he was not a man, she reminded herself. And there was no future with him.

As though Rinna knew she were being watched, she raised her head and peered into the darkness. Then she patted her hair with her hand and stepped away from the window. A moment later, the front door opened.

"Is someone there?" Rinna called.

Quinn scuffed her foot against the ground. Glad of the dark, she said, "I'm sorry. I think I came at a bad time."

Logan joined his wife, his voice hearty. "Quinn! We were wondering when you'd be back. Is Zarah with you?"

"Not yet."

"Come in."

She took a breath and let it out before stepping inside.

"How are you? How are Zarah and Griffin?" Rinna asked.

"They're fine. But he wants to send her soon. I'm here to make sure everything's okay."

"We have a room all ready for her. Do you have the photograph?"

"Yes." Quinn unzipped the fanny pack and removed the small camera that Logan had given her. She'd followed his instructions and taken several digital photos of Zarah. She and Griffin had been amazed at the likeness. They'd seen old photographs, but never of anyone they knew.

Logan ran through the images Quinn had taken. "We can get started on a driver's license for her. We've already got a birth certificate that says she was born in a little town in Pennsylvania, where the records were wiped out in a fire twenty years ago."

"That's good."

"Sit down and relax. Did you have any problem?" Rinna asked.

She hesitated. She wanted to ask about Caleb Marshall, yet she was afraid that she'd get an angry reaction from Logan. Certainly, a relative of his had killed Caleb. But who? His great-uncle? His second cousin? His grandfather?

Rinna picked up on the hesitation. "What happened?" she demanded.

"A . . . landslide."

Rinna winced. "I'm glad you weren't hurt."

"No. It didn't happen on the way. The rocks and mud must have slid down a hill a few days ago. Or a week. I couldn't tell. But it blocked the trail, and I had to go another way."

"Lucky you didn't get lost."

"I have a good sense of direction."

Rinna nodded. "Let's go into the family room. I've been collecting tapes and DVDs that will give you a better understanding of our world."

Our world. She said it so casually, like she had completely transferred her life to this place. Rinna had been born a slave. And Quinn had become one when her city was conquered by its neighbors. She and Rinna were both free now. But their lives had taken very different directions. Quinn doubted that she could ever fit in here. Or would a strong bond with a husband from this world make the difference?

Husband. Why was she thinking about that? Was she planning to marry a ghost?

Rinna was still talking. "And tomorrow, we can go down to Washington, D.C. I want to show you the Capitol and the Washington Monument. Then we can go into the Smithsonian Museum complex. I'm sure you'll love Air and Space. And the Arts and Industries Building. And you've got to see the IMAX. It's a movie theater with a five-story-high screen."

Quinn dragged her mind back to the conversation. She had read about those places and wanted to visit. But she also felt guilt. About neglecting to mention Caleb Marshall.

"Are you hungry? Can I get you a snack?" Rinna asked.

"Can I help you?"

"No. You relax. I know you had a tiring journey."

"It wasn't that bad."

In the great room, Logan used the cable recorder to bring up something called *The View*, and Quinn watched in dumb fascination as a group of women chatted about topics only men would have discussed in public in her world. The commercials were just as enlightening as the show. She had never seen so many products that people could buy.

Rinna set out cut vegetables and a delicious sauce and also little sandwiches of turkey and ham.

Trying not to seem too greedy, Quinn helped herself.

THE next day, Rinna was as good as her word. The three of them drove down to the capital of the nation, and Quinn was more amazed than any of the other gawking tourists as she took in the sights. It was a beautiful city. An open city. And obviously a place of power.

They ate at what Logan called a tapas bar, which had a menu full of dishes that the three of them could share. They each picked something that sounded good. And Logan added several more plates of food, which they passed around, sampling meatballs, artichoke salad, a wonderful paste called hummus, and a selection of different kinds of olives.

It was all a strange experience for Quinn—not just because of the difference between this world and hers. In her life, she'd encountered few people who wanted to please her or entertain her. She'd spent her early years studying hard in school. And when she'd graduated, she'd started working for the benefit of others.

Suddenly, two people were devoting themselves to showing her things she would enjoy, even if it had a serious purpose: getting to understand this culture.

They went back to the city twice more, and each day she felt worse about hiding something from her friends. She should tell them about Caleb. But it had gone too far, she told herself. How was she going to explain him now?

Then came the nights. She could fill her days with new experiences. But when she climbed into bed, Caleb Marshall haunted her in a way no living man ever had.

Back in her world, Griffin had said he would find her a husband. But she knew that his search wasn't going well. Since she had been a slave, probably none of the nobles wanted a woman of such low status. And what if Griffin found her a merchant or someone from one of the guilds? Would he be a man she could love?

Griffin had said she didn't have to abide by his choice. But then what? Was she dooming herself to a life without a mate?

So what was she planning—to choose Caleb Marshall instead?

Too bad he wasn't alive. Yet he was still one of the strong, sexy, aggressive Marshall men, and she knew she should talk to Logan about him.

She shuddered. More importantly, she should warn him that the ghost might be dangerous. But he hadn't done anything bad yet, so she kept the knowledge of him to herself, feeling guilty and disloyal.

Each night, her roiling emotions kept her up for hours. But finally she would fall asleep—and dream about Caleb.

She would wake in a sweat, her nipples tight and her woman's parts throbbing. In her dreams, she was aroused, but she never reached the point of satisfaction.

CALEB sat in the darkened forest with his knees bent and his back propped against his favorite oak tree. He had watched it grow from a sapling to a mature adult, towering in the forest. And he thought of the tree as a friend. Once he'd been friends with an orange-striped cat. Or, it had seemed that the animal could sense him. It came back to this patch of woods again and again, and sat staring at the spot where he stood. But maybe that was just an illusion. Maybe it had come here because it found the hunting good.

One day, he'd realized it wasn't there anymore. And it had never come back. He thought it was dead, and he hoped it hadn't met a painful end.

That was when he'd started trying to make the forest safe for the animals who lived there. He knew he had scared hunters away with the little ghostly effects he could produce, like making the leaves rustle or the air colder. And he had even managed that landslide that had made Quinn change her route through the woods.

Quinn was the first person he had made contact with on a personal level—he guessed because she had sensitivities that few people here possessed.

He moved his back against the tree trunk. It was strange that he could feel the bark. Had he felt anything so solid like that before?

He wasn't sure.

But he knew he had started becoming more aware of—everything—after Quinn had first stepped into a shaft of sunlight filtering through the trees. And he had known that she came from some unreachable place.

He had followed her progress through the woods. A woman of medium height with slender curves, an elfin face, and long, sun-streaked hair. He had sensed that he could communicate with her—if she would only come closer. But she had taken a trail that was too far from this spot.

And the farther he got from his grave, the less real he felt.

His grave!

He hated to think about that place. About the skeleton that must be lying there now.

Pushing away that image, he turned his mind back to Quinn. She had awakened a hunger inside him, so he'd schemed to get her close enough to touch.

And when he'd touched her, he'd experienced a jolt of physical sensation that had almost knocked him off his non-existent feet. When she'd struggled against his hold, he knew he couldn't let her go. Not yet.

As he remembered those moments, sensations came rushing back to him. The feel of her woman's body in his arms. The weight of her small breasts in his hands. The gentle curve where her hips flared out from her waist. The dart of pleasure that had traveled through him when he'd stroked his fingers across her nipples.

He had felt his cock grow stiff, and he had marveled at the sensation. He remembered sexual pleasure. He'd had his share of bed partners in life, since a werewolf before he found his mate was a magnet for women.

Could he join his body with Quinn's? Probably not. But he thought he could give her the ultimate pleasure. If she would only come back to him.

She had said she would come here again. But she hadn't. And he knew days had passed because he'd seen the sun come up and go down three times.

Panic seized him. Somehow he had the terrible feeling that if he didn't bring Quinn back here now, he would lose his chance. Standing, he sent his mind outward, calling her back to him.

CHAPTER
FOUR

QUINN WOKE WITH a start—a summons ringing in her head. Not words, but a steady humming sound that pounded through her brain with a terrible urgency. Lurching up, she looked around, then leaped out of bed and stood in the dark on unsteady legs.

She was alone. But she whispered, "I'm coming."

There was no answer, only the buzzing inside her head.

After dressing quickly, she made a fast trip to the bathroom, then debated what to do. Neither Rinna nor Logan had come out of their bedroom, and she decided it was best to let them sleep. But she knew they would worry when they woke and found her missing, so she wrote a note and left it on the kitchen table.

Then she slipped out of the house, shivering a little in the early morning air. The gray light that came just before dawn gave her enough illumination to see. And a run through the forest quickly warmed her up. She headed back the way she'd come, her total focus on the job she'd agreed to do.

She was sure the urgent message had been sent by Draden, one of Griffin's most trusted men, and a powerful psychic. Before she'd left Sun Acres, Griffin had arranged for a way to summon her quickly. If he needed her in a hurry, he could have Draden reach out to her—even across the doorway between the worlds.

Under ordinary circumstances, it wouldn't have worked, because she didn't have Draden's abilities. To forge a link between them, the adept had given her several treatments that tuned her mind to his.

But on each trip away from Sun Acres, she needed a "booster." And, even so, she was never able to hold a conversation with the adept.

This time, the message was blurred around the edges. She closed her eyes, trying to focus. The summons wasn't as clear as she had expected. But she knew her duty.

"I'm coming," she repeated, hoping he was picking up her answer.

As she hurried toward the portal, a deep male voice stopped her in her tracks.

"You came back to me," he said, his tone warm and sure.

Caleb.

"No," she breathed, knowing that she had made a mistake. She should have skirted this part of the forest, but as soon as the summons had come, she had been totally focused on getting back to her own world. Raising her head, she looked around, trying to see the ghost as she had done last time, but failing to make out anything visual.

"I called you, and you are here."

His words made her head spin. He was the one who had called her? She closed her eyes, trying to figure out what had really happened.

She hadn't counted on Caleb's confusing the issue. A half hour ago, she was sure Griffin had instructed Draden to summon her. And she still had to assume that Griffin needed her urgently.

"You have to let me go."

"No. You came to me."

Before she could answer, she felt the air ripple. And then he was with her. The way he had been before.

Not a man. But with so many of the attributes of a man.

Last time he had stood behind her, the front of his body pressed to her back.

This time, he was facing her. She could smell the appealing woodsy scent that she remembered from before—and see a tall, lean man who seemed to be partially hidden by mist.

He took a step toward her, then another, until he was right in front of her. When he reached for her, she tried to push against his chest, but his hands cupped over her shoulders, holding her in place.

"Let me," he murmured.

"No." She got out that one syllable of protest. She was here because she had urgent business on the other side of the portal between the worlds.

But conscious thought evaporated as the warmth of his body sank into hers.

Warmth? How was that possible? How much of this was she making up?

Her eyes fluttered closed, and as she shut out the world, the feel of his body came into sharper focus.

He was real and solid and very sexy. And if she kept her eyes closed, he seemed entirely alive.

She wrapped her arms around his waist. He felt warm and muscular. And her own body fit against his so perfectly. As she pressed more tightly to him, the compression of her breasts against his chest was the most erotic thing she had ever felt.

She tipped her head up in invitation, sighing her pleasure when he rubbed his mouth against hers.

At the same time, he reached down, enveloping her small hand with his large one while he pressed his mouth more tightly to hers. She marveled at the firmness of his fingers— at the calluses she felt just below them. And, at the same time, at the softness of his lips.

"Open for me," he murmured against her mouth as his hand squeezed hers.

She did. And the rich taste of him flooded through her.

She forgot why she was here, because suddenly she had been transported to a place and time she had never imagined— with a man as real and solid as one of the forest trees.

Greedy for more of him, she opened fully, so that he could stroke his tongue along the sensitive inner curve of her lips.

Then he was kissing her deeply, lustily, like a man drinking some exotic wine.

Her head spun, and she hooked her hands over his shoulders to steady herself, the intensity of her own need almost spiraling out of control. And it seemed to be the same for him as his hands moved urgently over her, stroking her hair, her arms, her shoulders.

She made a sound low in her throat, and she knew he took it for an invitation.

He eased far enough away to cup his hand around her breast, holding her gently in his palm, fueling her need as he molded her shape to his desire.

Her nipples beaded to tight points of sensation that begged for his touch. And he was glad to accommodate her.

Shifting, he stroked his fingers across the tip, and she moaned into his mouth as she instinctively moved her hips, pressing herself against his erection.

"You're too tall," she heard herself say.

He chuckled and moved the two of them backward. She went with him, keeping her eyes closed because she didn't want to break the spell.

But she knew he had propped his back against a tree trunk and splayed his legs so he could bring her center against his cock.

"That's so good," she whispered.

His answer was another low chuckle.

She was already so aroused that there was no room in her mind for anything besides erotic thoughts.

Would he undress her? Would he make love to her? Here in the forest?

As if he caught her thoughts, the hand at her breast moved downward and pushed up her T-shirt. Because the band at the bottom of the bra was made of something stretchy, he could push that up, too.

She felt the cool morning air on her breasts. And then he bent to her, and the breeze was replaced by his hot mouth.

"Oh!"

He leaned her back over one of his strong arms so that he could move his head from one breast to the other, licking her nipples, making them tighten even more before he closed his lips around one and sucking strongly.

Her sexual experiences had been many years ago, with a boy named Brandon she thought she loved. Those were some of the best memories of her life, and she had held them close to her heart. What she and her first lover had done had been very, very good. But Brandon had not been Caleb Marshall's equal. The sensation of his mouth on her nipple was exquisite, and the pleasure spun out of control when he used his free hand to tease its mate between his thumb and finger.

She cried out and moved her hips frantically against him as heat surged through her body.

She heard herself say, "I need . . ."

"I know."

He lifted her up, and she clung to him, burying her face against his broad chest as he carried her a few strides across the clearing. She felt him lower her to a bed of leaves, then come down on top of her, more real to her than he had ever been before. Or was *she* changing him?

Welcoming the weight of his body over hers, she clasped her arms around his shoulders, hugging him to her.

He gathered her close, then rolled to his side, his hand stroking her breasts, then drifting tantalizingly down her body toward the juncture of her legs.

As her pleasure built, she reached for the fly of his jeans. But he stopped her hand when she tried to open his zipper.

He pulled her hands to his shoulders, then went back to her clothing. First he worked the snap at the waistband, then he lowered the zipper, inch by tantalizing inch.

He was a man who obviously knew how to undress a woman—and how to tease and tantalize her.

Spreading the fabric aside, he reached inside, his fingers tangling in her crinkly hair, playing with her there before sliding lower, pressing his finger over the hood of her clit to bring her up to a higher plateau.

She cried out again, lifting her hips, silently begging for more of what he offered so freely.

She was close to climax when a jolt of static in her brain pulled her rudely from the heated encounter.

CHAPTER
FIVE

QUINN, WHERE ARE you? What are you doing?

The question rang in her head like someone clanging a gong, and she felt her heart clunk inside her chest.

"Great Mother!"

Her eyes flew open, and she looked up, expecting to stare into the face of the man whose weight pressed her down into a bed of leaves.

He felt so solid, but with her eyes open she could only vaguely see his features. Mostly, she saw right through him. He was a gray shape hovering over her in the dawn light. Not a man at all. A ghost who had stopped her as she'd hurried toward the portal.

As he'd turned her blood molten, she had forgotten what he was. Worse, she had forgotten what she was supposed to be doing.

Draden had summoned her, and she must hurry back to Sun Acres. But when she tried to push Caleb off of her, he wrapped his arms around her and brought his mouth close to her ear. She could feel his warm breath on her flesh. And she knew that if she closed her eyes, she would be right back where she had been moments earlier.

"Everything's all right. I only want to give you pleasure," he murmured.

"No, I can't." Desperately, she pushed against his shoulders. They felt so solid, but she understood that was only an illusion. Still, she might as well have been pushing against a giant boulder.

"What's wrong?" he asked, his voice gritty.

"I told you, I came here to help Zarah. She's pregnant and in danger from attack by the enemies of her husband, Griffin. He's calling me. And I have to go there."

Caleb didn't stir. "Called you—how?"

"A psychic message. From one of his adepts. Something bad must have happened. I have to bring her through the portal."

"I called you."

"You did?"

"Yes."

So that was why she had been confused about the message. Draden had called her—and so had Caleb.

"Why did you contact me *now*?" she whispered.

"I knew . . ." He stopped. "I'm not sure. I just knew I had to."

She thought his ghostly senses had picked up Draden's message, and he'd tried to stop her from leaving, even if he hadn't understood what he was doing. But there wasn't time to discuss that at the moment.

"I don't want to go," she answered honestly. "But I promised to protect Zarah."

She waited with her heart pounding. He had the power to hold her here if that's what he wanted to do.

"All right," he said as he heaved himself off of her.

"Thank you," she whispered, relieved and at the same time sorry their encounter had to end.

"I'll go with you—as far as I can."

She hadn't counted on that.

"Why?"

"Because you will be in danger. And I can't let anything happen to you."

"What am I to you?" she asked in a shaky voice.

"You are the first human being who has spoken to me—touched me—in seventy-five years."

The way he said it sent a shiver over her skin. Seventy-five years of being alone. She couldn't imagine how horrible that would be. And she knew that if she'd finally connected with someone after all that time, she wouldn't want to give up that contact.

"How far can you go from this place?"

"A few miles. The farther I go, the harder it is to hold on to myself."

She didn't ask what that meant. It sounded unpleasant. Wondering how long he could stay with her, she scrambled to her feet, put her clothing back in order, then started through the woods again, running to make up for the time she'd lost.

Shifting her gaze to the side, she saw a man to her right, his long strides easily keeping pace with her. She could still see through him. But as he moved, she had a better idea of what he must have been like in life.

He was tall and strong looking. And she knew he would have had a formidable presence when he had been alive. He was still formidable.

She slowed her pace when she came to the outcropping of rock where the portal was located. It wasn't a perfect hiding place, but it was the best that Griffin's adept could manage.

"You came through there," Caleb remarked.

She stared into the dark opening. It looked like the mouth of a cave, and for the first few yards, that was true. At the back was what appeared to be a rock wall. When you pressed your hand in the right place, the rock lost its substance, and you could step through—into another universe.

She started to hurry into the darkness, then remembered something else.

"My clothing."

"What about it?"

"I can't travel through my world dressed like this."

She glanced toward Caleb. "I have to change."

"Go ahead."

"Don't look at me."

He laughed. "You trust me to not look?"

"I have to."

This was another distraction she didn't need. Turning her back, she marched to the clump of brambles where she had hidden the clothing from her own universe.

After pulling out the plastic box, she kept her back turned, hoping Caleb was still where she'd left him. Quickly, she took off the fanny pack and put it into the box. Then she pulled her shirt over her head and unhooked the bra.

Trying to ignore the prickly sensation at the back of her neck, she quickly changed her outfit, then shoved the box back where she had found it.

"You have a nice body," Caleb whispered, his mouth so close to her ear that she jumped.

"You're not supposed to look."

"That was your rule, not mine."

Probably, he was expecting she'd stay and berate him. But she didn't have time for that.

Instead, she hurried into the darkness of the cave, with Caleb right behind her, then stepped up to the rock wall, palm flattened to access the secret pressure point.

"Stay here where I can keep you safe," he whispered, his hand gripping her shoulder.

"I can't. I could never live with myself if I let something happen to Zarah."

He didn't speak again, but the pressure of his hand eased.

She saw the rock thin and stepped into what had been a solid barrier. As she walked forward, she felt the familiar resistance as the membrane between the worlds tried to hold her back. It was like the sensation of walking through water—with your whole body submerged. You could move forward, but the water dragged at your limbs.

She fought her way through and came out on the other side, into another cave that was similar to the one she had entered in Logan's world.

But the barrier had stopped Caleb. She knew it immediately, because she didn't think for a minute that he would have hung back if he could have come with her to the other side.

He had committed himself to her in a way she couldn't understand. With the portal between them, she felt his loss.

She thought she heard him calling her. But the sound was faint. Was there some way to bring him through?

"Stop thinking like that," she muttered to herself. "He can't cross over because he died in his own world."

She didn't know if that was true, but it made as much sense as anything else.

"QUINN!" Desperation driving him, Caleb shouted her name, raising his voice to the highest level he could manage. It was very loud. It seemed to boom inside the rock walls of the cave like a clap of thunder.

He could make noise. But what good did that do him? He was only scaring the little animals who lived in the underbrush outside the cave. And he was sorry for that.

He closed his mouth, and the forest was silent again. He knew that shouting Quinn's name was an exercise in futility. Like his whole existence since that fight with Aden.

He looked toward the rock wall. Quinn had been there, standing right in front of him. Then she had pushed forward—and she was simply gone.

Teeth clenched, he walked up to the solid barrier and pressed his hand to the exact spot that she had touched. But nothing happened.

Because her palm was solid. His was something else. Energy, he supposed. For years he had been nothing more than a transparent being of pure thought floating somewhere above the forest floor.

Then he had started to change, little by little. And the change had come stronger and faster when Quinn had stepped into the forest. He had sensed her and knew she sensed him. And as her awareness of him grew, so did his awareness of himself.

In some way he didn't understand, she brought him back to himself. He didn't have a physical body. But he was feeling things he had forgotten about years ago.

The wind in his hair. The ground under his feet. The feel

of her body under his hands and lips. That was the best part, the erotic contact with her that had become as important to him as . . .

He might have said breathing. But he didn't breathe, although he could imitate the sound.

Balling his hands into fists, he felt the pressure.

He had been like a radio program. Waves of energy went out from a tower and arrived at the receiver in a person's home. But you couldn't see the waves or feel them—or hear them until the radio captured them. He had been the energy waves, and she had been the radio.

"I need you," he cried out.

But she was gone to a world where he could never follow. She had said she had a mission—to bring another woman back to his world. She could be lying, but he didn't think so.

That meant she would return.

He should wait for her here. He could wait a long time. Her entire lifetime. But what good would that do him if she never came back?

Despair threatened to swamp him.

He wanted to howl. He wanted to tear the tops off the trees and scatter them around the forest.

He had caused a landslide—working slowly and patiently over many days, using his mind to dig away at the soil below a large boulder. Now he wanted to call a fork of lightning from the sky and strike the rock that hid the portal.

That was beyond his abilities. But from the depths of his desperation, something else emerged. For the first time in three quarters of a century he felt a hidden stirring inside himself. As frustration roiled through him, a line from the Celtic language stole into his head.

Taranis, Epona, Cerridwen.

At first he didn't even know what it was.

Taranis, Epona, Cerridwen?

As he focused on the strange syllables, memory flooded into him, like a weakened dam finally bursting.

The words were a Celtic chant. The chant his ancestors had said down through the ages that turned the Marshall clan from man to wolf.

Caught in the wonder of it, he remembered the first time he had said the whole thing. He had been sixteen. A boy facing a terrible rite of passage. His father had taken him to the forest, and they had both known that he might die a painful death in the next few minutes.

But he had taken off his clothes and stood shivering in the wind, his body rigid as he said the ancient words.

He remembered the pain. The twisting of muscles and tendons. The blinding agony that felt like the blood vessels in his head were bursting.

Somehow he had come through it. And when he came down on all fours, he knew that he had survived the change from boy to wolf. No—man to wolf. Because now he was a man, one of the Marshall men who stalked the earth as no human could.

He couldn't tear the tops off trees or bring down lightning from the sky. But he could say those words—loud and clear—surprised at the way the syllables flowed off his tongue.

Taranis, Epona, Cerridwen.

It was like that first time, only different.

A rebirth.

He repeated the same phrase and went on to another.

Ga. Feart. Cleas. Duais. Aithriocht. Go gcumhdai is dtreorai na deithe thu.

And as the last syllable tumbled from his lips, something amazing happened. His energy body began to change. His jaw elongated. Fur sprouted on his ghost form.

He braced for pain. But in his phantom form, he didn't have to make that payment. He only had to shift from man to wolf. His true self.

As a man, he would have taken off his clothing first. As a ghost, that wasn't necessary.

Moments ago, he had felt nothing but despair. Suddenly, a kind of joy leaped inside him—a joy long denied him. He bent over and came down on all fours, a wolf standing in the forest.

His head swam. For a moment, he was unsteady on his legs and he scrabbled to hang on to consciousness. Then he gained his footing—and his equilibrium.

Suddenly, everything was different. He would have said that the blood pumped with new purpose through his veins. But he had no blood. No veins. He only knew that he had been made for this.

The wolf. The form he had not taken since that long ago fight with his cousin.

How could he have forgotten this? How could he have gone without this pleasure for so long?

Because he had been dead inside. And Quinn had changed everything.

She was gone now. Gone to that other place where he could never reach her. But he had this. And if she came back, he would show her the gift she had given him.

Because the pain of his longing for her had brought back the missing part of himself.

He raised his head and howled—the cry of the wolf set free after so many years. He forgot that he was a ghost. Forgot that his life had been cut off just before his prime.

The spirit of the wolf seized him as no other power on earth could capture him. He sat up and raised his head for another joyful howl, letting the forest creatures know that he had returned to rule his territory. Then he bounded away from the place that Quinn called the portal. A ghost wolf claiming his heritage.

QUINN brought herself up short. She shouldn't be thinking about Caleb. She should be focused on getting to Sun Acres as quickly as she could. Well, quickly and safely, she amended. She could travel fast, but she must be constantly on guard for Baron's soldiers.

She wished she could ask Draden a question. Was the trail between here and Sun Acres clear? Or maybe there was no point in asking. He might think it was clear, and the situation could have changed. She could walk right into a trap.

The land on Caleb's side of the portal was wooded.

Caleb's side. That was an interesting way to put it. She'd known him only a few days, and already she was thinking of it as *his* world, when she could just as easily have referenced Logan.

She didn't like the implications. But she couldn't focus on that now. She had to tune her mind and her senses to the dangers of her own world, if she wanted to get to Sun Acres in one piece.

She faced a vast plain of ruined houses and larger buildings. It was a depressing landscape, but at least it gave her some cover. And Griffin had showed her the best way to get from the portal to the city.

She moved quickly, stopping to sniff the air and listen for movement. As she approached the city from the south, she couldn't help remembering the first time she had come here. She and Zarah had both been slaves, chained together and forced to walk all the way from White Flint. That had been Zarah's home city. Quinn had been born free in the Preserve at Eden Brook. But it had been raided by soldiers from Hammond Town who had captured Quinn and carried her off. Her life would have been one of drudgery, but the elders of Hammond Town discovered her psychic talents and sent her to school to develop her abilities. Then Hammond Town had been raided by White Flint, and her fortunes had changed again.

That was how this world worked. City-states vying against each other for power and material possessions, including slaves. It was different on Caleb's—no, on Logan's side of the portal. The political units were much bigger. And although she knew that there were some parts of Logan's world that were at war, society in the United States was stable. Not like this place where you could start your life in one city as a freeborn citizen and end up a slave in another and another.

She made good time as she ran across the badlands, stopping to hide once when she spotted a contingent of soldiers hurrying on some mission. She couldn't tell if they were Griffin's troops, or Baron's, but she knew it was better to stay out of their way.

She stopped at the last bit of shelter before the city, the half-standing side of a ruined house. The hundred yards between herself and the city wall had been swept of debris, giving the lookouts on the parapet a clear view of anyone crossing the open space. That made the approach dangerous. But she had the safe passage that Griffin had given her, a bronze disk with a wolf's image hanging on a chain around her neck. It was his symbol, because he was a werewolf— like Caleb. Well, not exactly like Caleb. There were more werewolves here than on the other side of the portal.

She shaded her eyes from the sun. Usually there was a lot of traffic in and out of the city. But this morning the gate was closed, and she was the only person approaching from the badlands.

Other travelers and merchants must know about the turmoil inside, and they were keeping their distance until order was restored.

She watched the gate for several minutes. No one came out either, and she didn't know how to interpret that. Had the guards from one faction or the other forbidden anyone to pass?

Looking up to the open spaces in the crenellation at the top of the wall, she caught flashes of body armor.

Soldiers were up there, ready to fire on anyone who approached the gate. She hoped they were Griffin's men, but she had no way of knowing which side controlled the outer circle of the city.

Her hand went to her throat, and she clutched the charm, holding it up so that the light glinted off it.

She was sorry now that she hadn't brought the fanny pack with the gun. Nobody here would be expecting to get shot with a bullet. But on the other hand, they wouldn't know that it was a deadly weapon until she used it.

With a feeling of resignation, she started toward the gate. She had taken only a few steps when movement caught the corner of her eye. She tried to duck back behind the wall. But it was already too late. Men had been hiding in the shadows of another wrecked building, waiting to see who approached the city.

CHAPTER
SIX

"WHO ARE YOU?" a gruff voice demanded.

She looked at the man who had spoken and his two companions. They were roughly dressed and holding knives.

Not military knives. The knives of thugs who took their chances out in the badlands.

Great Mother, she was trapped by men who had no rules and no code of honor. And they could do anything with her that they wanted.

Her eyes flicked to the city wall; it might as well be a million miles away. The soldiers up there could see her, but why should they risk themselves to help her?

One of the thugs was barrel-chested, with a greasy blond hair. The other two were shorter, but with well-muscled bodies. One wore a cap. The other had dark hair.

"Who are you?" the blond demanded.

She considered her answer, trying to determine the safest course.

Raising her chin, she said, "I am on an important mission for Griffin—one of the chief council members of the city. If you hurt me, you will answer to him."

Both of them stared at her with narrowed eyes. "Prove it," the speaker said.

"Draden sent for me." She saw the man recognized the name. "And I have a talisman from Griffin. Under my shirt."

"Let's see it," the blond demanded.

She considered it a good sign that he didn't reach between her breasts to feel it but let her pull it out.

She turned the charm so that the wolf winked in the sun.

"That's his safe passage," the one with the cap said.

"Maybe she stole it."

"They told us to expect a woman," the blond answered.

She tried to follow the conversation and felt her head spinning. Who had told them to expect a woman?

"Who are you?" she whispered.

"Griffin's soldiers. We were sent to meet you, but we couldn't reveal ourselves too soon."

"I could have attacked you," she snapped.

The blond laughed. "And done what?"

She heard the confidence in his voice. He was a trained fighter, and she would have been seriously injured if she'd tried to defend herself.

Too bad Griffin hadn't warned her about this reception committee. But there had been no way to get the message to her.

"Why are you dressed like slavers?"

"It's safer out here if you blend in. This is a dangerous stretch of ground. We have to be careful about who passes. They could have sent a woman spy," the one in the cap said.

"Have things gotten that bad?"

"Worse." He raised his hand and signaled toward the wall. "I am called Dorber," he said. He gestured toward the man with the cap. "This is Gred."

"And I am Tolan," the dark-haired one added.

"I'm glad to meet you," she managed. They might not be outlaws, but they were still rough and dangerous.

Gred kept his eyes on the gate. Dorber looked toward his right and his left. And Tolan kept turning to make sure no dangers were behind them.

It was the longest walk of Quinn's life. Relief flooded through her as they reached the shadow of the wall.

The guards apparently knew the trio because the door opened immediately, but only wide enough for them to enter single file.

Inside, three horses were waiting. Tolan stayed at the gate. Gred helped Quinn into the saddle, then mounted. He and Dorber rode on either side of her as they headed toward Griffin's house.

Quinn looked around. It was strange to be back in the city after living in Caleb's world and visiting a place like Washington, D.C. The roughly paved streets felt hemmed in by the wood and stone houses and shops, which all looked small and primitive.

This was a weekday, and she expected to see citizens going about their business. But the streets were almost empty. Apparently, people thought it was safer to stay inside.

She wanted to ask questions, but her escort rode in silence, and she realized that they weren't going to give anything away where the wrong ears might hear.

Griffin's great house was outside the commercial district. As the iron gate came into view, she thought of the first time she had come here in a cart as a slave being brought to work in the kitchen.

Her status was much different now. But she felt almost as uncertain as she had that first time. She didn't know what had happened, but she knew it had to be something bad.

They stopped and waited while the guards inside inspected them. Then the gate opened and a short, balding man stepped forward.

It was Philip, who ran Griffin's household. He had escorted her here that first time. Then he had been all business. Now he held out his arms in greeting as she dismounted.

They had become friends, and she gave him a hug, glad to see someone familiar. But this wasn't what she had expected.

"Where are Griffin and Zarah?"

"I'll take you to them."

She bit back her questions as she followed him into the

building and over to the family wing. Griffin's quarters were on the first floor, but Philip led her to a narrow staircase, where a guard stood at attention. They climbed to the second-floor landing, which was guarded by another soldier.

When he saw them, he stepped aside.

Philip knocked on the door, and someone looked through a peephole before the hinges creaked.

Then Griffin was standing before her, his dark hair tousled and his hard features etched with tension.

"What's wrong?" Quinn asked. "What happened?"

He stepped onto the landing. "There was an assassination attempt last night."

"On you?"

"No, they tried to kill Zarah."

Quinn gasped. "But she's all right?

The door opened again, and Zarah stepped out.

Griffin whirled around. "I told you to stay inside."

"I was looking out the window. I saw Quinn cross the courtyard."

"I also told you to stay away from the window!" Griffin snapped.

"I'm safe here."

"We thought you were safe in our quarters," he answered, fear making his voice rough.

"I'm sorry. I know you're worried," she murmured.

"If anything happens to you . . ."

Before he could finish the sentence, she reached for his hand, clasping her fingers tightly around his, and he turned to her. The look that passed between them melted Quinn's heart.

Once again she felt her envy flair. Then she silently reminded herself that someone had tried to kill her friend the night before.

After squeezing her husband's hand, Zarah let go and stepped forward, holding out her arms to Quinn. They embraced, two women who were closer than sisters. Once Zarah's wavy blond hair cascading halfway down her back had been her most noticeable feature. Now the small bulge of her abdomen pressed against Quinn's middle, capturing her attention.

"Are you all right?"

"Yes."

"What happened?"

Griffin looked around as though he expected spies to poke their heads above the stair risers. "Come inside."

They stepped into a small apartment, and he closed and barred the door. He also walked to the window and closed the shutters.

"This room is shielded from psychic probing." Turning to face Quinn, he said, "We were in bed last night, and I heard a scuffle in the hall. I ran out to find one of the guards down. Then a man screamed in the bedchamber, and I knew the part with the guard had been to draw me away. Zarah had a knife under the pillow. The man Baron sent to kill her wasn't expecting that. She stabbed him in the eye."

Quinn winced, her gaze shooting to her friend. "You did that?"

"I've changed from that soft girl who was a pampered noble in White Flint."

"You were never soft. You were always brave. When that soldier tried to rape you on the way here, you hit him with the chain on your wrist."

Zarah nodded. They had been slaves together then. Tied up for the night and helpless to escape. That was one of the first memories that the two of them had shared.

Griffin interrupted the conversation. "They are trying to strike at me through her. I want her out of danger. If this house isn't safe, nowhere in Sun Acres is safe."

Zarah's eyes turned watery. "I don't want to go."

"I know," Griffin answered, his voice gritty. Then he softened his tone and said it again. "I know."

"I want to stay with my husband."

"And would you endanger our baby?" he asked, his tone like a knife blade.

Quinn watched them, aware that Griffin had played his trump card. Zarah would have to put the baby first.

She gave her husband a fierce look. "That's not fair, and you know it."

"Unfortunately. But I have to make you understand that you're still in jeopardy, and so is our child."

"Then come with me."

"You know I have to settle things down here. If I leave, the city will descend into chaos."

The exchange grew rapid, and Quinn gathered that the two people involved were rehashing an old argument.

"Let it fall into a heap of stones! What do you owe them?"

"I want this city to be a better place."

"Baron doesn't have your vision. He wants Sun Acres to stay the same. That's why he attacked me."

"That doesn't make him right and me wrong. Murder and assassination are the only tactics he understands."

She sighed. "I know. So don't stay here and risk your life."

"It won't come to that."

"And you won't leave."

"No. You know I can't."

She bowed her head in defeat.

He crossed to her and wrapped her in his arms. "But we'll be together soon."

"How long?"

His face turned grave. "I can't say for sure. It depends on how quickly I can deal with Baron."

She laid her head against his shoulder, and he held her tenderly. Her arms tightened around him, and the embrace became more potent. If they'd been in their bedroom, she was sure that they would have started undressing each other.

Quinn looked away. It was a very private moment, and she knew she was intruding. These two people loved each other with a passion that was so real it was impossible to hide. What was it like to find a man who cared that much for you? And you for him?

Zarah had that. No matter what happened, she would always have the knowledge of that love.

Quinn savagely cut off the thought. She wasn't going to send her mind down that path. Everything was going to work out. Zarah would be safe and Griffin would get the city back under control. And then the two of them would be together again.

Griffin walked to the door and stepped onto the landing, where he issued terse orders before he returned.

"Will you stay here with me?" Zarah asked.

"I have to make arrangements. I'll keep guards outside at all times. You try to get some rest."

Zarah nodded. But when Griffin had left, she made a dismissive sound. "Rest!"

"Try. You have a long trip ahead of you."

There were two couches in the room and both women lay down, although neither of them could sleep. They talked in low voices, Zarah telling Quinn about the state of things in the city and Quinn talking about the world Zarah was going to visit.

As they spoke, Quinn watched the window. Through the wooden shutters, she could see the light of the sun moving across the sky.

When it was far to the west, Griffin came back with a tray of fruit and meat.

"You should eat," he said to both women. "We'll be ready to leave soon."

Quinn managed to get down a little of the meal. Zarah took only a few bites of melon.

Then they changed clothes.

Quinn hadn't wanted to travel through the badlands or in the city alone wearing what would look like a strange outfit. But surrounded by Griffin's soldiers, the situation would be different—both for her and Zarah. So she'd brought supplies from Logan's world on a previous trip.

Now she showed Zarah how to put on clothing that a pregnant woman would wear in that universe. Not one of the voluminous gowns designed to hide a woman's condition here, but clothes that were tighter fitting.

Zarah inspected herself in the mirror. "This outfit looks indecent."

"But you will fit in."

"Can we ever blend in over there?"

"I feel comfortable there. I just spent a few days visiting one of their cities. You'll like it," Quinn answered as she pulled off her Sun Acres shirt and changed into jeans and a T-shirt with a leather jacket over it. Both women put on socks and running shoes.

A few moments later, a guard knocked at the door. "Draden is ready for you."

When she descended the stairs, a slender, balding man with dark glittery eyes was waiting for Quinn.

"What took you so long to get here from the other universe?" he asked as he led her to a small room off the court-yard.

"A ghost stopped me."

"A ghost? Over there?"

"Yes."

"I'd like to hear about it."

"When we have time." She sighed. "I wish we could hold a conversation when I'm away from you and you summon me."

"So do I. But your psychic talents won't allow it over such a long distance."

She looked down. "I'm sorry for that."

"Still, you have the best combination of skills for the job," he conceded. "Now let me give you an additional treatment—in case I need to call you."

She had done this before, and she stood staring straight ahead as he pressed his hands to her temples. Energy flowed from his mind into hers. Enough energy so that he could send her a message to summon her again.

When he was finished, he led her back to the doorway of the house, where a contingent of ten soldiers waited with Griffin and Zarah.

He escorted them to a sturdy, horse-drawn wagon. It was low and flat, with sacks of grain piled across the top surface. But when Griffin opened a panel at the back, Quinn saw that there was a compartment inside about three feet high and as wide as the wagon base.

"I'm sorry. This isn't going to be very comfortable, but it's the safest way to get you out of here. You'll look like you're a grain shipment. And the soldiers are just protecting the goods."

Zarah fixed her gaze on him. "Do we say good-bye here?"

"No. I'll go another way and meet you outside the city."

"Thank the Great Mother."

"Don't open the door unless you hear me say, 'The moon is up.'"

Zarah gulped. "All right."

"I can only go as far as the portal with you," Griffin warned.

"I understand."

The women climbed inside and arranged themselves as comfortably as they could on the thin mattresses that covered the wagon bed. Then Griffin handed them each a long knife. "In case you need to defend yourselves."

"Are you expecting trouble?" Quinn asked.

"No. But it's best to be prepared."

He closed the door, and they bolted it from the inside. The interior of the space was hot, stuffy, and dark, but some light and air seeped in from several cracks.

Quinn tensed when the wagon lurched and started toward the gate. She couldn't let go of her tension as she felt the vehicle move through the streets. It was impossible not to imagine Baron's soldiers stopping them at any moment.

Zarah reached for her hand, and Quinn knew she was probably thinking the same thing.

"Are you all right?" Quinn whispered.

"As good as can be expected," Zarah answered. "I'm trying not to cry and give us away."

"I know this is hard for you."

"And you. You came back to help me."

"You're my best friend."

Zarah's hand tightened on hers. "And you are mine."

"We shouldn't talk," Quinn whispered.

"I know."

They rode in silence after that. Quinn closed her eyes and lay back, trying to conserve her energy.

When the wagon stopped abruptly, she tensed and grabbed

the knife with her free hand, ready for trouble—until she heard the soldiers conferring with the guards at the gate. Long, tense moments passed before she heard the hinges creak. Finally, they rolled through and out into the badlands.

Zarah made a low sound.

"Are you all right?" Quinn asked quickly.

"Yes. But I'm wondering if Griffin lied to me. Maybe he's not coming."

In the darkness, Quinn touched her friend's arm. "Has he ever lied to you?"

"No."

"He won't start now," Quinn answered, hoping she spoke the truth. "If he can meet us, he will."

They rolled along, the ride considerably bumpier now that they had left the city streets for a rutted lane that led across open country and threaded through the ruined buildings.

Quinn tried to count the minutes, but it was impossible to keep track of time.

Then they stopped again, and Quinn grasped the knife more tightly.

"The moon is up. Open the door," a voice called out.

"Griffin. Thank the gods," Zarah answered as she slid down toward the end of the cart.

In the darkness, Quinn fumbled with the latch. When it clicked, Griffin opened the door, then helped his wife out. She stood swaying on unsteady legs. The ride had been cramped and uncomfortable, and both women moved their arms and legs, trying to get their circulation back.

"Are you all right?" Griffin asked as he led his wife around the side of a ruined building where they would have some protection if anyone had tracked them from the city.

"Yes."

Quinn followed more slowly, still shaking her legs and moving her arms, trying to prepare herself to walk or run the last few hundred feet to the portal.

She saw Zarah fling her arms around her husband's neck and hold on tightly. Then she pulled his mouth down to hers for a frantic kiss.

The passion between them sizzled. And once again, Quinn looked away. She shouldn't be here. None of them should have to be here. They should be back at Griffin's grand house, going on with their lives. But she knew that it would be a while before life would get back to normal here. When Zarah and Quinn had arrived in Sun Acres, Griffin had been content to work behind the scenes. But still, Baron had seen Griffin was gathering power, and he'd wanted to eliminate a rival.

Maybe *that* was really the norm in Sun Acres, endless fighting for position among the nobles. Zarah had told her it was much the same in White Flint, where her father had been accused of robbing the treasury, convicted, and executed—all in a matter of weeks.

Quinn stared at the wagon, then beyond. They had traveled for hours, and the light was almost gone. She could see they were far across the badlands, very close to the portal. It was only a few hundred feet to safety.

She moved a little way from the couple who held each other tightly, trying to give Zarah and Griffin some privacy. Then she heard a noise in the distance and looked up to see a cloud of dust sweeping toward them.

Horsemen, coming at them fast and furious.

CHAPTER
SEVEN

GRIFFIN HAD HEARD the horses, too.

Quinn watched him lurch away from his wife. Snapping into command mode, he turned toward the soldiers who had escorted the party away from the city and began giving clipped orders to his men.

"Vaun, Camber, Robee, Franks, Shuman come with me. I'm taking the wagon and making it look like the women are inside. Marks and Paker, stay here and defend this position. Willis and Jordan, go with the women. Get them to the portal—at all cost."

The well-trained force sprang into action.

Zarah tried to run back to Griffin, but he shook his head, his eyes blazing. "We have no time to spare. And they must not see you now. Wait here until the main party goes after me. Then make a run for the portal."

"But . . ."

"I'll be fine," he said, and Quinn knew the words were automatic. He was taking a terrible risk to lead the soldiers away from his wife.

It was yet more proof of how important Zarah had become to him.

Griffin jumped in the wagon, whipping at the horses as he started off, raising his own cloud of dust from the dry ground.

As he took off across the plain, she saw the large dust cloud that had come toward them veer off on an interception course toward the wagon.

But not all of the troops followed the fleeing vehicle. Some of the soldiers were still headed in the direction of the ruined building that hid Zarah from view.

Quinn calculated their chances of getting away. Griffin had said to stay here and let the soldiers defend them, but more of the enemy were coming this way than he'd thought. She counted six. What if Griffin's troops couldn't fight them off?

She turned to Zarah. "Can you run?"

"Yes."

Quinn hoped it was true. She looked at the four remaining guards. "Do your best to keep them here," she told them.

"Yes, miss."

Zarah's eyes were wide. "Which way?"

"Toward those rocks," she pointed, then heard an arrow hit the ground right in back of her.

"Run," she shouted.

Zarah started off strong, but her pregnant body quickly flagged. They had only twenty-five more yards to go, but that might as well have been miles.

Quinn stayed behind Zarah, guarding her back, praying that Griffin's men could hold off the attackers.

When she looked behind her, she saw Paker go down. Marks, Willis, and Jordan were fighting four of the enemy.

Zarah was breathing hard and holding her belly when she reached the rocks.

Quinn took her hand and pulled her the last few yards into the cave, then toward the back, where she pressed her palm against the wall. As she focused on the psi mechanism, she could see the barrier between the worlds thinning, but she could also hear running feet pounding behind them outside the cave.

She clutched Zarah's hand and urged her forward.

"I'm afraid."

Wishing she had explained what it was like when they'd

had time to talk, she said, "It feels strange, but it won't hurt you. Just follow me."

She plunged into the space between the worlds, feeling the familiar resistance. At the strange sensation, Zarah tried to pull back.

Quinn yanked at her hand, forcing her through, and they almost lost their footing as they tumbled onto the other side of the portal.

"Thank the Great Mother," she whispered as she led Zarah out of the cave and into the moonlit forest.

"We made it," Zarah said in a hushed voice.

"Yes." But when Quinn looked behind her, her blood froze. Before the portal had closed, two of Baron's soldiers had also come through.

She could see them standing at the cave entrance, looking around in wonder at the unexpected surroundings.

"Two of them are here," Quinn whispered. She took Zarah's hand and led her behind a tree, then another, moving farther and farther from the cave, praying they wouldn't be spotted.

Her friend's breath was coming in great gasps. "I can't. You go on."

"No! I came to save you. I'm not going to leave you here." She gripped the knife with one hand.

"You go on. I'll hold them off."

"No."

"Over there," a voice shouted, and she knew the soldiers had spotted them.

All she could do was drag Zarah toward a tangle of underbrush, hoping they could hide in the dimming light.

But the men were closing on them fast. "Don't kill the slim one. She knows how to get out of here."

Oh, great. But maybe that gave her an advantage. She could fight them, and they wouldn't strike a killing blow.

She thrust Zarah behind her, then rounded on the men, the knife held along her leg where it couldn't be seen. She'd let one of them get in close, then bring her arm up and get him.

The first one came toward her with confidence, thinking that a small woman was no match for his masculine might.

She brought the knife up, chopping into his shoulder. As she did, Zarah lunged forward, catching him in the back of the neck and plunging her knife in.

Quinn heard bone crack. He screamed and went down in a limp heap, leaving them facing one man. She liked those odds better.

The other soldier dropped back, regarding them with caution now—and glancing nervously toward the trees behind them before his gaze flicked back to Quinn.

What was he looking at?

He reached into the pack he carried and pulled out a rounded blue stone, with carvings on the surface, which he held up, facing the woods. And she knew what it was. A talisman from her world. A talisman designed to banish spirits.

CALEB knew Quinn was in trouble. He was rushing to help her when the thing in the man's hand stopped him cold. Literally.

He felt an icy, numbing wave plowing toward him like a nor'easter sweeping up the coastline to wrack the land.

As the freezing wind hit him, he understood that whatever the man held could turn him to vapor.

But Quinn was fighting for her life. She needed his help now, and he would do what it took to save her, even if he winked out of existence.

His commitment to her startled him. And that was a good feeling, too.

In the short time he had known her, she had changed him. He had been in a kind of stupor, sometimes awake but more often drifting through the days like a leaf floating in a stream, swept along by the current.

But she had brought him back to life. Well, not life, but to a keen awareness of the world around him.

He had to help her. At any cost.

THERE was only one spirit Quinn had met around here. Caleb.

Fear leaped inside her. Fear for him. Had the man seen the ghost? Could he wipe him off the face of the earth with that thing?

She couldn't risk a glance in back of her, not when the soldier was facing her and could attack at any minute. And for all she knew, he was using the stone as a distraction.

"Stay back." He held up the talisman like a warning, then to Quinn's shock, he threw it at her. It hit her in the stomach, knocking the wind out of her. As she doubled over, she dropped her knife and went down. The soldier sprinted toward Zarah.

Gasping, Quinn rolled to her side, seeing her friend back up, then stumble over a tree root and drop to the ground.

The man looked from Zarah to Quinn and back again.

"If you kill her, Griffin will hunt you down and cut you in pieces—slowly," Quinn gasped out.

She had the man's attention. While he looked at her, she picked up a handful of dirt and flung it into his face.

Coughing and spitting dirt, he lunged at Quinn again, grabbing her by the hair and pulling her down. When she fought him, they rolled across the ground, each struggling to get the advantage.

AS Caleb strained to reach Quinn and the man, he fought the coldness snuffing out his senses. He felt like his chest was being crushed by some invisible force. And his vision was so dim that he was close to blindness.

Just as he was about to stumble to his knees, the other woman—the one who had fallen—crawled forward. She must be Zarah, the friend Quinn had brought to safety here. Only they were hardly safe.

The woman snatched up the blue stone from the ground, then backed quickly away, out of the field of battle.

Some of the pressure lifted from Caleb's energy body, and he dragged himself a few paces forward. His attention was on Quinn, but from the corner of his eye he saw Zarah fumble with the pack she wore and pull out something that looked to him like the gravy boat his mother had used at Thanksgiving.

Then she turned away, and he couldn't see what she was doing—until a flame flared up, blue and startling, shooting toward the sky like the shaft of a sword.

As the flame surged, the cold and crushing sensation evaporated from his energy body, and he charged toward Quinn and the man, howling his rage.

A ghost wolf hunting his prey.

He clamped his teeth on an exposed shoulder, and the man screamed, then turned and stared at him, terror in his eyes. Scrambling to his feet, he ran.

Caleb came after him, growling as he steered his quarry toward a steep cliff above a fast-running river.

They kept going, Caleb nipping at the fellow's ankles. He must have felt the ghost teeth because he moaned in terror as he tried to escape from the phantom wolf who drove him farther and farther from the women.

The man crashed through the underbrush, then went headlong over the cliff edge, screaming as he plunged into water a hundred feet below.

QUINN stared at the spot where the soldier and the ghost wolf had disappeared.

"He's gone."

"Yes." Zarah sat up and pushed her blond hair back. "I felt something. I couldn't see it, but I knew the man was trying to ward off a ghost. He must have some talent to see specters."

"And you used *your* talent with the flame to destroy his talisman," Quinn finished for her.

"Yes. I have more power now that I'm pregnant."

"Still, you could have gotten hurt. Or killed."

"It was a calculated risk. We needed help. And a ghost seemed willing to aid us. But he couldn't do it with the talisman sapping the strength out of him."

Quinn nodded in acknowledgment.

Zarah stared at her. "I couldn't see him, but I felt . . . a ghost . . . werewolf."

Quinn swallowed. "Yes."

"Isn't that something rare in this world?"

"Yes."

Zarah kept her gaze on her friend. "One thing I sensed very strongly. He came to help *you*. How do you know him?"

"I met him the last time I came through the portal to this world."

The ghost in question trotted into the clearing and stopped a few feet from where they stood

Quinn squinted in the moonlight, trying to see him clearly. "He's back," she said to Zarah.

"I . . . can't see him. Only sense him."

Speaking to Caleb she said, "Thank you." Then she felt compelled to say the same thing she had said to Zarah. "You could have gotten hurt. Or killed."

He laughed. "I can't be killed. I'm already dead."

"But that talisman could have . . . hurt you . . . or . . ."

He cut her sentence off. "You were in trouble. I couldn't let him do something bad to you." He looked toward Zarah. "Or the friend you brought here."

"Yes, thank you so much," she repeated. "So you changed to wolf form—and came to help us."

"I was already in wolf form. I . . . changed after you went through . . . the portal."

She stared at the wolf. She could see him better now. He was a handsome animal, as compelling as in his human shape. "I haven't seen you like this before."

"It was . . . new for me."

"What do you mean?"

"I hadn't done it since . . ." His voice hitched. "Since I died. I think I forgot how—until you reminded me."

"How did I do that?"

"I don't know. But it happened after you left." His voice was gritty with emotion.

"Oh." From the corner of her eye, she could see Zarah staring at her.

"Can you hear him?" Quinn asked.

"No. Only you can hear what he says."

"She is brave," Caleb said. "Tell her that. And thank her for destroying that blue thing."

After Quinn repeated the words, Zarah's brow wrinkled. "Wait a minute. When Griffin is a wolf, he can't talk to me or anybody else. How can this one do it?"

Quinn hadn't even thought of that. She tipped her head toward Caleb.

It was strange to see a wolf shrug. "I guess a ghost wolf can do it."

"He says—because he's a ghost."

"And because you're close to him," Zarah murmured. "What's his name?"

"Caleb."

Step by step, the wolf closed the distance between himself and Quinn. She went stock-still, feeling his power as he approached her. Because she was still sitting on the ground, his face was about at her eye level.

"She can't see me either," he said as he rubbed his face against her neck, his fur making her skin prickle.

Then he raised his head. Slowly and delicately, his tongue stroked against her cheek, sending shivers of awareness over her body. When he stroked downward to her neck, she lifted her chin.

"Don't," she whispered.

"You like that. . . . I wanted to be alone with you."

She knew that. But they weren't alone, and she couldn't ignore Zarah. Involuntarily, she glanced toward her friend, but the other woman gave no sign of being aware of the intimacy. Thank the Great Mother.

"We can't talk about it now," she said, hoping the tone of her voice would stop him. She wanted to say, *We can't do this now. We can't do it at all.* But the words stayed locked in her throat because they would give too much away.

She turned her head, and her gaze fell on the man that she and Zarah had both stabbed. It wasn't a pretty sight, but she was glad to have something else to focus on. Getting up, she walked to him, then squatted and touched his neck. His body was cooling, and she felt no pulse. "He's dead. We can't leave him here."

"The other one . . . ?" Zarah asked.

"He went over a cliff, into a river, so nobody will find him around here," Caleb answered. "And if they do, his death will look like an accident."

Quinn relayed the information.

Zarah made a strangled sound. "But it *wasn't* an accident." She hitched in a breath. "I've been responsible for the death of three people in less than twenty-four hours."

"Because *they* tried to kill *you—us*. And if you're talking about the man who went over the cliff, we didn't do that. He ran from the werewolf, and he killed himself."

"It doesn't make me feel better."

Quinn crossed to her and draped an arm around her shoulder. "The important point is, you're safe."

Zarah lifted her head, her eyes brimming with unshed tears. "Is Griffin?"

The question made Quinn's throat go tight. But she managed to murmur, "He's smart. And he had a head start. He got away."

"You're just saying that."

"Let's assume the best."

Zarah swallowed. "I guess I have to."

Quinn stroked her arm. "We need to get rid of this body."

"How?"

"I'd like to take him back through the portal, but that's too dangerous. More soldiers could be over there."

Zarah nodded.

"You can bury him later." The advice came from Caleb. "There's not much risk. Not many people come here. And if they do I can keep most of them away."

"How?"

"I make this seem like a bad place—for the people who sense me."

"Yes. Okay." She looked back toward the portal, then stood and helped Zarah to her feet. She was remembering Rinna's account of closing another portal. When she'd told Draden about it, he'd said there was an easier way, if you were closer. And he'd given her some instruction.

"We should close the portal," she said to Zarah now.

"No!"

"But others might try to come through."

Zarah's features took on a look of panic. "If we close it, how will Griffin get to us?"

"We have to do something . . ."

"Can't we hide it?"

"I don't know."

She ran a shaky hand through her hair. When she'd agreed to come through to the other universe, Draden had given her long lectures on the properties of the portal. She'd listened to his explanations, but she hadn't understood everything. And she'd never thought she'd be in quite this position. Now she had to strike a balance between her friend's fear for the future and their present danger.

"Can you use your flame to create an illusion?" she asked Zarah.

"I don't know. Maybe if you lend me your energy." She fumbled with the small pack she carried and brought out her oil lamp again.

Quinn knew the ghost was watching and listening avidly. Looking in his direction, she asked, "Can you keep guard and tell us if anyone starts to come through?"

"Yes."

He hurried toward the doorway between the worlds, and the two women followed.

Zarah's hands were shaking as she pulled out the cork that blocked the neck of the lamp. Then she set the small vessel on the forest floor. When she stared at the wick, nothing happened.

"I lit it before," she whispered. "Very quickly."

"But you're exhausted now. Take some time to relax."

"We need to do it now." Zarah stared at the mouth of the lamp.

Long seconds passed, and still nothing happened.

Zarah made a small sound.

"I wish I could help you," Quinn murmured.

"Like this?" The question came from Caleb. The flame flared, and Zarah looked toward where Caleb stood. "Thank you. How did you do that?"

"I don't know," he answered, and Quinn told Zarah.

"What will you do to the portal?" Quinn asked.

"Make it so the rock is harder to open when you press the lock spot—I hope."

"Harder?"

"Well, I'll make it so only someone as powerful as Draden can do it. Or two people with lesser powers, like us."

"Okay."

Quinn was nervous about getting close to the doorway when soldiers might be right on the other side, but she looked at Zarah's drawn face and saw that her friend hardly had the energy to drag herself to Logan's house—let alone hide a portal. And getting as close as possible would help.

She took Zarah's hand, and they moved into the cave. Caleb stepped to the side, giving them better access, his teeth bared as he faced the doorway between the worlds.

Moving to the wall of rock, Zarah grasped the lamp in one hand, and took a deep breath.

"Hold one of my hands, and put your other hand against the wall."

Quinn did as her friend asked.

"Send energy to me," Zarah whispered.

Quinn closed her eyes, willing herself to do it. But she was so drained from the earlier fight that she was sure her contribution wasn't going to make a difference.

"I'm hardly getting anything," Zarah murmured.

"I'm doing my best," Quinn said, although her attention was divided. She was watching the portal, ready to react if another soldier found his way through. And she was also watching the wolf.

And as she pressed her hand to the cold stone wall, she couldn't stop herself from wondering if she and Zarah were both too worn out to use their psychic abilities.

Neither of them spoke. For long seconds, Zarah focused on the flame, her face tense, and her fingers digging into Quinn's.

Finally, Zarah made a frustrated sound.

"You're dividing your attention between me and the wolf and the soldiers you think are going to come charging through. I need your total focus."

"I'm sorry. It's hard to stay tuned to only the flame."

"But you have to, or I can't do this."

CHAPTER
EIGHT

QUINN'S CHEST TIGHTENED. Maybe they were both so emotionally drained that this whole exercise was impossible.

Then, from beside her, she felt a hot wind blow. The flame flickered, and she thought it was going to go out. But it steadied, and she knew that Caleb was doing more than guard duty. Again, he was pumping energy to the two of them.

She still didn't know how he was accomplishing it. She only felt the effect and felt the portal in front of them change. It had been a doorway from one universe to the next.

Now it seemed like a solid barrier, although she knew that was just an illusion.

Zarah sensed the change, too. "Thank you," she murmured, "I mean both of you."

"I had the energy to do it. My being is mostly energy," Caleb answered.

Zarah was still staring at the flame with deep concentration.

"What?" Quinn asked. "Can the soldiers get through?"

"I don't think so," Zarah whispered. "But something else is going to happen here. Something to do with you and the wolf."

"How . . . how do you know?" Quinn asked.

"I told you, carrying my child gives me more power. And I caught a flash of something from the future."

Quinn looked around. "Something bad?" she asked.

"Something bad—and something good, I think." Zarah leaned her head back against the rock. "I don't know any more."

After a moment, she blew out the flame and replugged the spout of the lamp so that the oil wouldn't leak out.

Quinn wanted to press her friend for answers. But she knew that if Zarah had any more to tell, she would have revealed it. So she stood and stretched, then reached down to help Zarah up.

Turning to Caleb, she said, "We have to go to my friend's house and rest."

"I will go with you."

"No!" she said, much too sharply. Lowering her voice, she tried again. "No."

"Why not?"

"We must do this part alone," she said, hoping he would accept that answer.

Quinn stared at the wolf, waiting. When she had first talked to him, he had seemed like a man who had just awakened from a long sleep. Now he was more aware—and more assertive. Did that mean he would insist on going with her?

His gaze flicked to Zarah, who was looking at the spot where he was standing. Even if she couldn't see him, she knew where he was. He seemed to stare out at the darkened forest. Then he turned his gaze back to Quinn.

TWENTY miles away, outside Frederick, Maryland, Colonel Jim Bowie stood and leaned his hands against his desk.

He wanted to pound his fist against the wooden surface. But he kept the outward appearance of calm.

He was days away from setting in motion the most devastating military operation the continental United States had ever seen.

And he had identified a traitor in his midst. Because he

had been vigilant. And he had found the bastard with a cell phone down near the firing range. When he'd checked the log of numbers called, he'd gotten a nasty shock. The guy could have blown up the whole mission. But he wouldn't get a chance. Bowie had stopped the bastard in his tracks before he could do any real damage.

He'd interrogated the man, then locked him in the underground cell that served as the stockade on Flagstaff Farm. With the rats and the spiders. He hoped they were giving the guy something to think about.

And the rest of the men as well. All his troops knew about the prisoner. All of them were walking around as if on crushed glass, waiting to find out how the man would die.

Which was one reason he was drawing out the decision.

To his way of thinking, punishment had always been a big part of discipline. And he wanted the lesson to sink in—not just for one individual. For everyone on the compound.

He had studied history. And there were so many ancient and modern models he could choose from. He could go all the way back to the Bible. An eye for an eye. A tooth for a tooth. And he liked the lesson from Machiavelli, who had cut out the tongue of an informant and blinded him, then sent him back to his loving family.

Branding was also an interesting option. Maybe he should burn a mark into the guy's chest before killing him. Or cut off his balls. No, that had sexual connotations that certainly didn't fit the case.

But one thing he knew. The man would die slowly and painfully, knowing full well that his life was ebbing away. The question was, what method would send the most telling message to the other men?

He clenched and unclenched his fists. He could feel his blood pressure rising as he thought about the traitor.

Months ago the bastard had seemed committed to the cause, as he understood it. Now he'd shown what a snake he was.

"Don't let him get to you," Bowie muttered to himself. To regain his equilibrium, he turned his thoughts to something a lot more constructive. Like the bombs waiting in the locked building five hundred yards beyond the barracks.

Albert Einstein had warned President Roosevelt that the United States must have an operational nuclear weapon before Nazi Germany. So the government had set up a secret program—the Manhattan Project—to produce one. In Chicago and at Los Alamos, the best nuclear physicists the United States could assemble, led by Robert Oppenheimer, had spent years figuring out how to make the bomb work. And they'd ended the war by dropping two of them on Japan.

But you didn't need a true atomic bomb to cause havoc. All you needed was a conventional explosive—and enough radioactive material to spread over a wide area when the payload went off.

And he was ready to prove it. In a little more than a week.

Getting the explosives had been easy. The radioactive waste was a little more of a problem. There had been no U.S. source he could get to. So he'd investigated obtaining the stuff from one of the former Soviet Socialist Republics.

Now he had that, too. And he would proceed with Operation Eagle's Flight, as soon as he took care of the traitor.

QUINN waited to find out what Caleb would do.

After a moment, he said, "I will let you go."

She breathed out a little sigh and turned to Zarah. "We should hurry. I left Rinna and Logan a note, but they'll be worried about us."

They started off in the direction of the house, but it soon became clear that the past few hours had been too much for Zarah.

Stopping beside a fallen log, she sat down heavily. "I have to rest."

Quinn looked at the slump of her friend's shoulders. "I'm sorry. I was pushing you."

"That's okay. I know you want to keep me safe. But I think no more soldiers are coming after us with the doorway hidden." Then, to Quinn's horror, Zarah burst into tears.

"Oh, sweetheart." Quinn sat down awkwardly on the log. Her friend had fought so bravely, but now reaction must be setting in.

"Great Mother, it's too much. Too much," Zarah sobbed.

"I know. I understand." Quinn moved over and gathered her close, rocking her in her arms. "Just cry. Let it out and cry."

"I love him. So much. He changed everything for me. Everything. What we have together is . . . fantastic. And I may never see him again," Zarah managed to say between sobs.

"You will!"

"You said that before. But how can you know?" Zarah gasped and began to cry harder.

Quinn tried to imagine it. She'd envied Zarah and Griffin. They were so close. And now that bond might be broken.

"You said your powers had increased. You can't see your future?"

"No! Not about me and Griffin."

Quinn held her friend, giving as much comfort as she could. The flood of tears lasted for minutes, but finally Zarah cried herself out.

Quinn fumbled in her pack for a tissue—something from this world that she had brought along in case she needed it. She handed it to Zarah. "You can wipe your eyes and blow your nose with this."

"Thank you."

The other woman blew, then held up the crumpled tissue. "What do I do with it?"

Quinn scraped aside some leaves, pressed the sodden mass into the ground, and covered it again. "It will fall apart with the rain."

"Okay." Zarah heaved a sigh. "I'm sorry I did that to you."

"You're holding up better than most women would. You've been through so much over the past year. Your parents' death. Slavery. Griffin's wrath when he found out you'd been spying on him. And now this."

"You had a lot to deal with, too."

"Not compared to you."

Zarah tipped her head to the side, studying her. And Quinn fought the impulse to look away. "You're . . . different. The ghost has changed you."

She closed her eyes and opened them again. "What you can have with a ghost is . . . limited."

"He saved us. And he could turn out to be very good for you."

"How could he be?"

Zarah shrugged. "In school, when they brought ghosts to class, I could never see them. Or sense them. Could you?"

"Yes."

"Well, my psychic powers were never great."

"They were good enough to cure Griffin. And to hide the portal just now. And to tell me something would happen in the forest."

Zarah's eyes welled up, and Quinn was instantly sorry she had mentioned her friend's husband.

Zarah dragged in a breath and let it out. "I won't go to pieces on you again. Tell me about the ghost."

Quinn considered the question. "I wish I knew how to direct his interest away from me."

"Do you really mean that?"

She turned her hand palm up. "I don't know."

"I think the two of you are good together. And you will mean more to each other than you can imagine."

Quinn nodded. She had some ability to sense the future, too. And she knew that she hadn't seen the last of Caleb Marshall. She cleared her throat.

"Unfortunately, there's a problem."

"What?"

Quinn pressed her hands against her thighs. "In our world, there are many people who are werewolves. Griffin is. So is Rinna. And she had the bird form, too."

"But there aren't so many here. I realize that," Zarah answered.

"As far as I know, there is only one family of men. The women can't carry the trait. They are all in the Marshall family—Logan's family." She paused, wishing she could just drop the subject. But it had to be said.

"And?"

"They are all aggressive men. They fight among themselves. Or—they used to until Logan's cousin, Ross Marshall, started getting them to work together. The ghost, Caleb Marshall, was killed by one of his cousins seventy-five years ago. Caleb stayed here to avenge his death. The man who killed him is long gone, but he has to be related to Logan."

Zarah winced.

"I don't want to tell Logan and Rinna about him."

"Maybe you have to warn them. What if he acquired the power to come after them?"

It was Quinn's turn to draw in a sharp breath. "I was hoping he wouldn't. But I see he's getting stronger. That's why I told him he couldn't come with us."

"So his need to avenge his death complicates your relationship."

"Yes."

"Like with me and Griffin. I was sent to spy on him. Then I wanted to confess, but I knew he'd be furious." She heaved a sigh. "Why can't anything be simple?"

Quinn shook her head. "Because life is never easy. I thought that when Griffin freed me, everything would be better."

"And now you're saddled with me," Zarah said softly.

"That's not what I meant."

"I know it's not. But I feel like a burden."

"You're not. You're my best friend!"

"And what if Rinna and Logan hate having me in their house?"

"Stop!"

"I can't help it."

"I know. So maybe we should get the meeting over with as soon as we can. You'll like them. And they'll like you."

Zarah stood and looked down at her tummy. "You're sure I don't look like a pregnant whore in this outfit?"

"Not here."

Zarah reached to pluck some dried leaves off of Quinn's shirt. "Let's get it over with."

"You're still nervous."

"Of course. But I have to keep myself safe—until Griffin and I can live together again."

Quinn nodded. Neither of them said the obvious, that it might never happen.

FORTY minutes later, they approached the Marshall house. Zarah stopped and stared. "You told me that they live out in the woods. And it's safe. I had trouble believing it was true."

"I did, too. But things here are very different."

"I studied the books and . . . magazines . . . you brought me. But I have so much to learn."

"That will keep you busy."

"Yes."

When Quinn knocked on the door, Rinna opened it almost at once. "Thank the Great Mother," she said. "We were so worried about you." She gave Quinn a questioning look. "You left in the middle of the night. We knew you'd gone to get Zarah, and we were worried."

Zarah was hanging back, but Rinna stepped forward and held out her arms.

"Welcome to our house."

After a little hesitation, the other woman stepped forward, and they embraced.

"I'm so glad to have someone from home come stay with us," Rinna said.

"But I think you don't have servants. I'll make extra work for you," Zarah answered.

"Over here, we don't need servants. There are ways to get things done quickly. You'll see."

Logan came striding to the door and saw the two women. Looking at them carefully, he asked, "What happened?"

Quinn heaved in a breath and let it out. "Maybe we shouldn't talk outside."

"Right."

They filed into the front hall.

"To give you a summary of the past twenty-four hours, Baron's men tried to kill Zarah in her bedchamber," Quinn explained. "She stabbed one of them instead. Griffin got us to the portal in a wagon, disguised as a shipment of grain.

But soldiers caught up with us. He led them away, and we got through the portal."

Rinna peered at Zarah. "You look worn out. Come sit down."

"Thank you." It was obvious that Zarah was overwhelmed by the situation.

Quinn leaned toward her. "Relax," she said in a low voice. "You're safe now. Everything's okay."

Rinna led the way down the hall to what they called the great room, where large windows looked out over a wooded area.

"Make yourselves comfortable. This is your house now," Rinna said. "Let me get you something to eat and drink. I'd been thinking you'd come back soon. So the refrigerator's full. I have fruit. And cheese. And meat. And we have juices or tea or spring water, if you prefer."

"Water," Zarah whispered.

"Try the orange juice," Quinn said. "You'll like it."

Zarah gave her a doubtful look. "But I hate for Rinna to use up her supply. Or go to any trouble squeezing it."

Rinna laughed. "No trouble. I don't have to pick the fruit and make the juice. I bought it at the grocery store. I just have to pour it out of a carton."

"Oh."

"We have a lot of conveniences here." She smiled. "Let me play hostess. I don't get to do it a lot."

Quinn went with Rinna to help bring the food, but all the time she was feeling the weight of her secret pressing against her chest. Because her nerves were jumping, she almost dropped the carton of juice.

"Are you all right?" Rinna asked.

"A little shaky."

"You look pale." Rinna gave her a closer look. "You had an ordeal escaping from Baron's men. I think you haven't told us all of it yet."

"That's right."

"You should sit down, too."

"I'll sit when we bring the food in."

Back in the great room, Logan was talking to Zarah.

"So you think you weren't followed," he said as Rinna and Quinn set down plates of food.

"We were," she answered. After cutting a piece of melon with the side of her fork, she said, "Two soldiers followed us. We killed one." She stopped and swallowed. "A ghost drove the other one off a cliff and into the river."

Logan's gaze shot to her. "A ghost? Are you sure it was something supernatural?"

"Yes."

Quinn scuffed her foot against the rug under the coffee table. She caught Zarah's eye, then looked away. Before she could stop herself, she turned her gaze back to Logan and said, "I think I have to tell you about him."

Now that Quinn had spoken, she hovered between relief that she was about to be honest with Rinna and Logan and dread at the consequences.

"The ghost found me . . . the last time I came through the portal."

Logan was staring at her with an intensity that made her want to squirm in her seat. Obviously he'd picked up on the import of what she'd said. But she managed to keep her gaze level and her body still.

"And you didn't mention him?" he asked.

She swallowed, wishing she had prepared herself better. She'd known all along that this moment was coming, but she'd kept hoping it would stay in the future. "I wasn't sure what to say. He was a werewolf killed in a fight with his cousin. The other werewolf buried him in the woods."

"Werewolf! How do you know?"

"I talked to him. His name is Caleb Marshall. He said he was still on earth because he wanted to avenge his death. And I think one of your relatives killed him."

CHAPTER
NINE

FOR SEVERAL SECONDS, there was dead silence in the room.

Finally, Logan spoke. "Do you happen to know how long he's been dead?"

"Seventy-five years."

His gaze turned inward, and she saw his lips thin. "That fits."

"What?" Rinna asked.

"The time period. I think my grandfather might have killed him."

Everyone had been looking at Quinn. Now their gazes shifted to Logan.

"What makes you think so?" Rinna murmured.

"I've told you all the men in my family want to be top wolf. So they fight for territory. Or that was the Marshall tradition, until my cousin Ross started changing things. First he contacted his brothers. Then he got together with me and his other cousins. He showed us how to work together and got us together socially—with our life mates." He laughed. "Once that happened, the women played a big part in socializing us.

They want the contact with each other, so they arrange family events."

He shook his head regretfully. "But it wasn't like that years ago. Not hardly. The Marshalls rarely saw each other. And when they did, there was likely to be a fight. There was talk in the family—of something happening. I never could get a straight story out of my parents. But I know there was a cousin named Caleb Marshall. He was my grandfather's age. I know people used to whisper about bad blood between him and my father's father. Some said that he went out west, like Ross's brother Johnny, who changed his name to Sam Morgan. But I always wondered if that was just a cover story for something more sinister. Like in the *Sopranos*, when they whacked a guy and said he'd disappeared into the witness protection program."

Quinn put her hand to her forehead. "The *Sopranos*? Singers? And what does it mean to *whack* someone?" She'd thought she was doing so well in this world, but she wasn't following very much of what he'd been saying.

Logan laughed again. This time it was a grating sound that did little to break the tension. "The *Sopranos* aren't singers. They're a family in a television show—where the dad is in organized crime. And sometimes they kill their rivals."

Quinn nodded. "But it's just on television?"

"Well, it has some basis in reality."

Before she could ask about that, Logan tipped his head toward her. "Do you know where Caleb Marshall is buried?"

"Not exactly. It's in the general direction of the portal, but not on a direct line from your house. I told you there was a landslide, and I had to detour. That's when I ran into him."

She saw Logan shudder. "I roam all over the woods around here. But there's a place I never like to go. Maybe it's around his grave. It could be that I sensed him, and I didn't want to run into him."

Rinna had reached out and grabbed his hand. "He could have hurt you."

Quinn answered quickly. "When I first met him, he seemed . . . dim," she whispered. "I don't mean stupid. I mean . . . not all there. In a ghostly sense."

The others nodded.

"But he's getting . . ." She stopped and shrugged. "I don't know what to call it. Stronger? More aware of himself."

"You said he drove one of Baron's soldiers off a cliff. Did he push him?" Rinna asked.

"I didn't see it. But I don't think so. I think he just scared the man into diving off into space."

She looked down at her hands and back at Logan. "I'm sorry. I think I stirred him up. He said I was the first person he had talked to in all this time. He said he was lonely."

"Then how did he talk to you?" Rinna asked.

"You remember the lessons we had in school? Did they ever bring a ghost to visit your class?"

"Yes, but I was never good at seeing them. Maybe I sensed something, but it was . . . vague." She paused for a minute, then added, "But other students could do it."

"I think it's hard for most people—even adepts. But, for some reason, I was good at it." She stopped and swallowed. "Unfortunately, he was able to reach out to me."

"And he's formed a connection with you," Zarah said. "So if you asked him to stay away from Logan, he would."

Quinn wanted that to be true, but she had to be honest about her fears. "I can't count on that." She swiped a hand through her hair. "I'm going back there tomorrow. I can talk to him."

"Don't go back!" Rinna said.

"I have to. I have to bury the soldier we killed. I can't just leave him there."

Across the room, Zarah moved in her chair. "I stabbed him, too. I should go with you."

"No. The rest of you should stay away from the ghost—until I find out what he intends." Quinn turned her eyes toward Logan. "I'm sorry I didn't tell you as soon as I met him. At first I thought it would just stir up trouble. And it seemed he was too weak to do anything . . . bad."

Logan sat up straighter on the sofa. "I'm not afraid of him, so he's not going to drive me off a cliff."

"Stay away from him," his wife begged.

He moved closer to her and draped his arm around her shoulder. "A ghost can't hurt me."

Quinn looked down at her hands, then up again. "He hurt the soldier. I hope he can't do anything to you. I feel responsible. What if he follows me here?"

"Isn't he tied to his grave or something? How far is his range?" Logan asked.

"I don't know," Quinn answered. She didn't realize she was twisting her hands together until Zarah said, "You can't help it that you can sense a phantom—and that he responded to you."

Quinn nodded. There was more she could say, but she wanted to end the conversation.

They hadn't really resolved anything. But she knew she didn't have the energy for it tonight.

Apparently, Rinna wanted to change the subject, too, because she looked over at Zarah. "You're worn out. And you must find this world very strange. I know I did."

"Yes," Zarah murmured.

Quinn stood. "I should go to bed, too."

"Yes, you had a long trip," Rinna murmured. "And then the fight with the soldiers."

"We're taking up so much of your household," Quinn answered.

"We have the space," Logan said.

"And I'm so glad to have company from home," Rinna added.

The house was built into a hill, with the master bedroom and adjoining office on the main level and the guest bedrooms on the floor below. Rinna went down with them to show Zarah some basic things like how to avoid electric shocks, how to flush the toilet, and how to adjust the water in the shower.

Quinn went to her own room and closed the door. She had left some clothing here, so she took off the shirt and pants she'd worn and pulled on a clean T-shirt. But when she lay down on the bed, she couldn't sleep.

She kept imagining Logan tangling with Caleb. She didn't want anything to happen to Logan. Or Caleb either. He had risked the talisman to save her life. That meant a lot.

No man had risked so much for her. Ever. Caleb might have stayed on earth for the wrong reasons. But that was a long time ago. He was still here, and he had saved her life and Zarah's. Even before that, she had felt a bond with him.

Now that she had time to think, she couldn't stop worrying about him. Could the Marshall men hurt him—the way the soldier had tried to do?

She knew they had some psychics in this world, a few people with talents like the adepts in her own universe. Were they able to call Caleb's ghost to them, then banish him?

A shiver traveled over her skin. Much as she wanted to deny it, she knew she was becoming emotionally involved with a man who was dead. And the idea was unnerving.

Lying rigid on her bed, she watched the numbers change on the clock on the bedside table. Maybe she slept for a few hours, but she woke again before the sun was up. Too restless to sleep, she got up and dressed again, then ate a little of the food that Rinna had gotten out the night before.

She wrote a note, saying that she was going back to bury the body, and she would return as soon as she had finished.

Logan was a landscape architect, and she knew he kept many of his gardening tools in a shed outside.

Quietly, she exited the house, then found a shovel and hoisted it over her shoulder, before starting off toward the spot where they'd left the soldier.

It was still before dawn, and she heard rustling in the underbrush all around her as the forest creatures went about their early morning business.

Little animals were watching her. Maybe some larger ones, too. She might have turned back, but she knew she had to see this task through. She had a good sense of direction, and she moved quickly through the woods.

The air was cool, but gray light had penetrated the canopy of leaves by the time she approached the little clearing where the soldier had caught up with her and Zarah.

They had to kill him or be killed themselves, and as she stepped into the clearing, the scene flashed back to her. She remembered her terror. And the soldier's confidence. He'd been sure that two women couldn't beat two men.

Then Caleb had arrived and changed the odds.

She walked carefully over the ground, keeping her gaze

down, looking at where the leaves were scuffed. When she
reached the place where she thought the man had fallen, she
was hardly able to believe what she was seeing.

The body was missing.

CHAPTER
TEN

"I TOOK CARE of him."

The voice came from behind Quinn. And she knew who it was.

Turning, she saw a dark-haired man with intense eyes and a strong jaw. Well, she mostly saw him. He still wasn't entirely solid, but he was definitely more visible than before.

He looked very masculine and very aggressive, and she wondered if his werewolf traits were rising to the surface now that he had changed from wolf to man and back again last night.

She took an involuntary step back.

"I won't hurt you." He took a step forward, keeping the distance even between them.

"What did you do? Carry him away?"

He made a frustrated sound. "No. I can barely touch the world."

"You can touch me."

"It's strongest with you."

She felt his words as a gift—and a responsibility.

Looking away, she gestured toward the empty place on the forest floor. "Then what happened—to the man?"

"A bear dragged him away from here."

"A bear! I didn't know they had bears here."

"Not many. You do not have to fear him. I led him here. And he is gone now, after a good meal."

Quinn shuddered, struggling to get the image out of her mind.

"And then coyotes fought over the rest. So if anyone finds the . . . remains, they will think that the bear killed him."

"Yes."

She had come here prepared for an unpleasant task, and now she was relieved of the duty.

Caleb didn't speak, and the silence between them stretched.

Really, she wanted to talk to him about Logan, but she wasn't sure how to introduce the subject. She could make things worse by saying the wrong thing.

Caleb finally broke the silence, his voice husky. "I'm glad you came back."

"For business."

"But the business is finished."

"I should . . . go."

"Is your friend all right? The journey must have been hard on her."

"Yes, thank you." She moved away from the clearing.

"Don't leave yet."

His voice tingled along her nerve endings. She took another quick step back and found that her shoulders were pressed to the trunk of a tree.

Caleb stepped forward again, and this time there was nowhere for her to go. She was trapped between the tree and the man standing in front of her.

Yes, a man, because he seemed more like a living, breathing human than he ever had before.

"What do you want?" she whispered.

His voice was warm and intimate. "We mean something to each other."

"Yes," she breathed. "You risked your . . . existence to save me."

"I had to."

"Why did you do it?"

"You know why. You change the colors of the world for me. You make the sounds and the textures richer. Only you can give that to me."

She had felt something similar, but she couldn't say it out loud.

"Doesn't changing to wolf form make you feel ... alive?"

"Yes, but what we have is different."

"I shouldn't stay here."

"You don't want to be with me?"

She'd be lying if she said no.

Before she could form an answer, he bent to brush his lips against hers. She might have gotten away in the moment before his mouth came down firmly on hers. When it did, she was lost.

She wanted to fight her response to him, but that seemed to be impossible.

She sighed out his name as his mouth settled on hers, and it was the most natural thing in the world for her arms to slide around his shoulders and clasp him tightly.

It felt as if she had finally come home to her long lost lover. But it couldn't be. She had met him only days earlier. And he wasn't even a man.

Still, she was swamped by so many sensations that coherent thought fled. His shoulders felt so solid. His mouth was warm and wet over hers. And once again she could detect his scent—he smelled like the woods.

Incredibly, his body felt hot, a heat that transferred itself to her.

His lips on hers were exquisitely erotic. She knew that she wanted everything from him that a man could give a woman. And she wanted to give it back to him as well.

Could she?

"Caleb." His name tumbled out of her, and he sighed in response.

"Quinn."

His fingers tangled in her hair, tipping her head first one way and then the other. He was good at kissing. She had already found that out. He slid his lips over hers, then took her bottom lip between his teeth, nibbling at her in a way that sent the blood surging hotly through her veins.

She knew he loved her response, knew he was intent on giving more than he took.

He drew back, holding her gaze for a long, potent moment. She had time to think that looking into his eyes was so strange.

Then he dipped his head again, his arms tightening around her as he took the sensuality to another level. His tongue swirled inside her mouth, stroking the sensitive inner tissue of her lips, then probing more deeply, claiming possession as though she were his mate.

Before she could let that thought disturb her, he eased her far enough away so that his hand could cup her breast, his fingers playing over her beaded nipple, sending hot currents through her body.

His other hand cupped her bottom, pulling her center against his erection.

"Oh!"

The position was so elemental. Male to female. And when he swayed her hips against his, she cried out again.

She should tell him to stop.

No. Why should she? This wasn't real. Maybe it was only a dream that the Great Mother had given her as a gift. Her most heartfelt wish. A man of her own, but only for a little moment in time.

He was more real and solid than he had ever been before. Although she knew he could have touched her through her clothing if he wanted, she felt his hand open the snap at the top of her jeans and slip inside to flatten against her abdomen. It was a very sexy gesture. With his hand wedged against her body, he moved his fingers, playing them over her heated flesh, making her cry out. Making her want to feel his hand travel lower.

Finally, when she thought she might go mad if he didn't do more, he opened the zipper all the way. Slipping two hands into the sides of the jeans, he dragged them down, along with her panties.

The pants tangled around her legs, and she kicked them away, feeling the cool morning air on her heated flesh. With one hand holding her in place, he reached under the back of her T-shirt and pulled it up, stripping it off as easily as he had dispatched the jeans. She hadn't worn a bra. She'd told herself it would be uncomfortable when she used the shovel. Now she wondered if she had been thinking about something like this.

He held her a little away, his hot gaze traveling over her body.

"You are amazingly beautiful," he said in a husky voice.

She didn't question him. Or question herself. She was caught up in the spell he was weaving around her.

But she was completely naked, out here in the woods. And he was still dressed. When her hands went to the belt buckle at his waist, he stopped her.

"Don't."

"You're so different from when I first met you. I want you naked, too. So I can touch you. Touch all of you. Feel your body. See you."

His words were rough and jerky. "You can't."

"Why not?"

He didn't answer the question. "Just let me do all the things I've longed to do. Let me give you pleasure."

Before she could protest, he captured her mouth again, using his lips, his tongue, his teeth to feast on her.

At the same time, his hands moved over her body. He cupped her bottom, caressing her as he slid his fingers over her exposed flesh, then slipping lower, reaching from behind to dip into the folds of her sex.

"I love the way you feel. You're so alive, so warm and wet for me. Like thick, warm cream," he murmured into her mouth.

He continued to kiss her as he brought both hands to her breasts, holding their weight in his palms while he played his fingers over her aching nipples, then caught them between his thumbs and fingers, pulling and twisting.

His touch was so real. So masculine. So intense.

Nothing in her life had ever felt so good, yet she wanted

more, wanted it with a desperation that made her senses spin.

"I need you inside me," she gasped out.

"We have to do it this way. But it will be good for you. I promise I'll make it good."

One hand traveled down her body. He stopped at her clit, circling that throbbing place, bringing her to a higher level of need.

"Please."

"I know. Soon." His lips were against her ear now. His teeth worried her lobe, then he pointed his tongue and probed her ear canal, sending tingles through her.

"That's good," she gasped in surprise that such a place could be so erotically sensitive.

"For me, too."

His lips traveled to her jawline, then her neck while he stiffened two fingers and slipped them into her vagina, going in at an angle so that the edge of his hand could stroke back and forth across her clit as his fingers made love to her.

Great Mother, he knew how to pleasure a woman. Exactly how.

She hung on to his shoulder with one hand. The other slid down his body, pressing over his erection, seeking more intimate contact as her hips worked frantically against his hand.

"You are so sexy. So alive. So beautiful," he whispered as he brought her up and up, so that her body tightened as she felt climax approaching.

Then she was spinning out of control, her whole being vibrating as a wave of pleasure crashed over her. It was followed by another and another so that she had to cling to him to stay upright.

She heard her own breath racing in and out of her lungs. Again her hands went to his waistband, but when she pulled at the button that closed his jeans, she couldn't open it.

"I want to touch you there."

"I want that, too, but we can't."

Her eyes flew open, and she stared into his dark eyes. They were resigned—and sad.

"Why not?"

"Because my clothes are part of me. They don't come off."

She blinked, trying to take that in. And then the truth slammed into her like an iron ball from a siege cannon. He had changed so much that she would have sworn he was a flesh and blood man. But he was a ghost, not a man.

"This isn't real."

"Yes, it is! As real as we both want it to be."

"No. You gave me pleasure, and there's nothing I can do for you."

"That's not true! You did something for me. You let me bring you to climax. I loved doing it. I loved *knowing* I could do it."

"But . . . it's not . . . normal."

"Don't use that word!"

"Why not?"

"Don't make rules for the two of us. Sex between two people is whatever they agree on."

She struggled to speak around the lump that had formed in her throat. "Where can this possibly end up? You're in one reality and I'm in another."

He waited a beat before answering. "We can be together— here in the forest."

She stared at him, seeing the solid man's body and yet still seeing the shafts of morning light cutting right through him. He felt so alive. But when she really looked at him, she knew the truth.

"For how long?" she asked with a catch in her voice.

"As long as you want."

"And then what? I have to go back to my own world. In the end, I'll be left with nothing. And so will you."

"You can stay here. Don't you like it here?"

"I do. But it's not where I belong. I only came to help Zarah. Then I have to go back."

"Why?"

She felt like she was talking in circles. "This place isn't my home."

Sadness tore at her. They had made a very intimate connection—a connection they both craved. He was a wonderful lover. He knew the secrets of a woman's body, and he had given her more pleasure than she would have imagined possible. But there could be nothing beyond that. She couldn't even offer him the same satisfaction he had given her. And that was the worst part of all.

She couldn't risk another look into his eyes. She didn't want to see his sadness—or her own mirrored there.

Stepping away from him, she looked down and saw her clothing scattered across the ground. Quickly, she bent and scooped up the discarded articles, then began pulling on her panties and jeans.

She didn't look at him, and he didn't speak, didn't try to persuade her that she was making a mistake by leaving.

When she was dressed, she picked up the shovel, then turned and started walking back toward Logan's house. She must not come here again. No matter what Caleb said, there was nothing real for her in this forest. If she came back, she would just slip farther into a fantasy that would consume her.

She walked slowly, dragging her feet. She didn't want to talk to anyone. Maybe she could hide what had happened from Logan and Rinna. But Zarah would know right away that she'd had sex.

She made a strangled sound.

Had sex!

Caleb had been incredibly generous. He had brought her to a blinding climax. She could go back, and they could do it all over again.

It was so tempting. She had been alone for a long time. And she was envious of Zarah and Griffin. And Logan and Rinna, too.

She thought she might have had that same kind of relationship with Caleb Marshall. If he had been alive. If they could have made a life together.

But that was impossible, no matter how much she wanted to be with him.

She trudged on, wondering what she was going to do when she got back to the house. She could see it through the trees now, and she stopped, feeling so alone and isolated.

She sat down on a fallen log and cradled her head in her

hands, struggling not to cry. There was no use crying. It wasn't going to help anything.

Resignation settled over her as she got up and started off again, her legs stiff and wooden.

When she walked in, she found Logan, Rinna, and Zarah sitting at the table in the breakfast room.

"Did you bury him?" Rinna asked.

"I didn't get a chance. Animals took him away and scattered his bones."

"Did you see them?"

"No. The ghost told me." She gave Logan a guilty look. "I took a shovel from your toolshed. I hope that's okay. I put it back," she added quickly.

"That's fine."

Zarah was watching her with assessing eyes. She could almost hear her friend's thought. Zarah knew something had happened between Quinn and Caleb.

"You talked to the ghost?" Zarah murmured.

"Yes."

"How did he look?"

"More like a man."

"He's getting stronger," Rinna said. "You have to . . ."

"What? Kill him?" Quinn challenged, hearing the sharpness in her voice. "He's already dead," she said more softly.

"Make sure he can't hurt Logan."

Quinn winced. "In our world, there would be books that would explain how to put a . . . prohibition on him."

"But you can't go back and get them now," Zarah said.

Quinn nodded.

"There's information on ghosts and psychic phenomena here," Logan said. "Maybe there's a clue in my library. Or on the Web."

"A spiderweb?" Zarah asked.

Logan grinned and launched into an explanation of computer search engines.

When he finished, Quinn said, "I'll start with your library." That would give her something to do. And maybe it would keep Zarah from asking questions about what had happened in the woods a little while ago.

To Quinn's relief, Rinna changed the subject. "Zarah and I are going to some shops where we can find some more maternity clothes for her."

"I don't have money from here," Zarah said softly. "But I can pay you in gold coins."

"You're our guest," both Rinna and Logan said.

"But I don't want to be a burden. Let me pay you."

"Yes. Thank you," Rinna answered, then turned back to Quinn. "So, do you want to go on a shopping trip?"

"No. I'll stay here and read," she said, glad that she had a reason to be separated from her friend.

Zarah gave her a long look, a look that said, "We'll get back to this later."

CHAPTER
ELEVEN

LATER TURNED OUT to be that afternoon, when the women had come home, and Logan and Rinna went out to buy groceries. *And probably to be alone,* Quinn thought. She could imagine that having two strangers in the house all the time was hard on them, but they weren't going to say so. Maybe they were stopping somewhere in the woods to have some quality time together.

As she thought of quality time in the woods, she took her lower lip between her teeth.

"What?" Zarah asked.

"Nothing."

"Did things go badly with Caleb this morning?"

"I don't want to talk about it."

"I gather that," her friend answered immediately.

"It's personal. And I have to work it out by myself."

Zarah was silent for several moments, then she cleared her throat and began to speak very quickly. "You remember when we were both slaves. I was humiliated in that auction and sold to Griffin, and I knew I was going to end up in his bed—and I had no experience with men. You told me things that helped me get through it. More than that. You told me it would be so much better for me if I let myself respond to him. You gave me the courage to help myself. So can I do the same for you?"

"How do you know this has to do with sex?"

"I don't. But you're obviously emotionally involved with him."

"Griffin is a powerful member of the Sun Acres council. Caleb is a ghost."

"And?"

Quinn wanted to keep her encounter with him to herself. But at the same time, she wanted to tell someone what had happened. And she and Zarah *had* shared intimate secrets before. She turned toward her friend and struggled to speak in a calm, flat voice, even though her insides were clenching. "I went back to bury the soldier's body. But Caleb said the animals had already taken him. He held me and kissed me and touched me. He took off my clothes and made love to me. Just with his hands and mouth. He made me come. But when I tried to take off his pants, he told me that was impossible."

"Because he didn't want you?"

"No. While he was arousing me, I could feel his cock— big and hard—pressing against me through his jeans. He wanted me. But afterward he told me that his clothing is part of his ghost image. He can't undress."

Zarah made a small, gasping sound.

"So, it's an impossible relationship. We can go so far, and no farther."

"And what you can do together isn't enough for you."

"It was wonderful. But how could it be enough—for him?"

"If he wants it to be. And . . . uh . . . you said you could feel his erection. Maybe you can bring him to climax without taking off his pants."

Quinn folded her arms across her chest. "It's not just about sexual satisfaction. He's a ghost. We can't marry. Can't have children, like you." She stopped short when she realized what she'd said.

"And that's what you want?" Zarah said.

"I see how happy you and Griffin are, and I envy you."

"Even though I may never see him again."

"You will!"

Zarah hitched in a breath. "I wish I could be sure of that, but I'm here and he's in another universe. And maybe Baron's soldiers caught him when he drove the wagon away from us."

"He got away."

"I hope so. I pray that's true." Zarah's eyes brimmed with moisture.

Quinn reached for her hand and squeezed it. "I don't think this discussion is doing either one of us any good."

"Don't you think it helps to talk?"

"Can you use your flame magic to bring Caleb back to life—or even to take off his clothing so I can lie down beside him like normal men and women?"

"I wish I could." Zarah firmed her expression. "Did you find anything in Logan's books that might help?"

"Not really. What they have here is far less correct information than you and I learned when we were ten-year-olds in school. Their society just isn't oriented toward the psychic. They have wild guesses and . . . and outlandish assumptions about things that we've studied in detail."

"Like what?"

"They don't know what lessons to use to enhance psychic power. They don't know that childhood is the best time to foster those skills. They don't know how many forms a 'ghost' can take."

She might have said more, but she heard the front door open and closed her mouth. Logan and Rinna were home. End of discussion. Which was a relief.

There was no more talk of the ghost that evening. Or the next day, and Quinn wondered if Logan was trying to decide what to do about him. She prayed he wasn't planning to confront Caleb because she didn't want either one of them to get hurt.

Quinn spent most of her time with Rinna and Zarah,

helping Zarah study the lessons that would allow her to fit into this society. Logan also made Zarah an appointment with a doctor called an OB-GYN who took care of pregnant women.

Quinn found she was learning more about this world, too. And despite her feeling of sadness about Caleb, she was fascinated by such things as ATMs, grocery store scanners, credit cards, and food processors—which Rinna warned her to keep her fingers out of.

Then, four days after they'd arrived on this side of the portal, Logan's cousin Ross came over.

He looked a lot like Logan. And a lot like Caleb—from what she'd seen of him. And when she thought of Caleb, her heart squeezed. He hadn't contacted her since she'd told him it couldn't work between them. She should be relieved, but she couldn't help feeling depressed.

Ross had brought a driver's license and credit cards for Zarah, like the fake documents he'd gotten for her.

She knew that they had to be expensive. But nobody talked about any kind of payment.

Well, she would find some way to pay Logan back for the documents he'd gotten for her. Maybe he could give her a job in his landscape business. Even if that was a low-paying job, at least she'd be contributing something.

Ross stayed for several hours, asking questions about the universe where Zarah and Quinn had come from. She expected Logan to tell him about the ghost. But he said nothing, at least as far as she could tell.

Was that part of the werewolf code? Where they took care of their own problems? She wanted to ask, but she thought that was much too personal a question.

After Ross left, she and Zarah helped Rinna prepare dinner: spaghetti and meat sauce for the women and barely cooked steak for Logan, in the tradition of the Marshall men.

Then they watched one of the DVDs Logan had brought home from the video store. It was the program Logan had mentioned, the *Sopranos*. The first season. And Quinn was surprised by all the violence and by the cursing.

She went to bed tired. Which was good. Because that kept her from thinking about Caleb.

COLONEL Bowie had come to a decision about the execution. He called his twenty troops to attention on the parade grounds and made the announcement, watching their faces

He could see they were each thinking about how it would feel to die in that horrible manner, and each thinking that they wouldn't risk putting themselves in the prisoner's position.

Then he called Portland and Spencer forward and gave them the job of carrying out the sentence. They were both tough guys who wouldn't hesitate to kill. And they were both as loyal as anyone in the squad.

After he dismissed the troops, he went back to his quarters. He thought for a while about the procedure, making sure he'd considered all the details.

Then he turned his mind to a more gratifying subject—the bomb.

He needed to set it off on a day with no rain. And ideally, a time with moderate wind, so the fallout would spread over a wide area. Would the government tell people if they were downwind and have them scurrying around sealing their windows with duct tape?

Or would the Department of Homeland Security downplay the threat? Either way, he could picture the roads clogged with people trying to get out of town, like when a hurricane was going to hit the gulf coast or Florida. Only in this case, they'd be sitting in their cars, soaking up radiation. Some of them would die from it. And some of them would increase their lifetime risk of getting cancer to 30 percent. Too bad most of them would be dumb enough not to know it—unless the authorities clued them in.

He thought of the chance of the government doing the right thing. Then thought about covering the U.S. Congress with radioactive dust.

The senators and representatives who hadn't been contaminated could crawl down to that fallout shelter that had been built for them under the Greenbrier Hotel in West Virginia. It had been a big secret in the fifties when President Eisenhower had suggested constructing a new wing of the hotel and salting away an underground bunker beneath it.

And the U.S. government had maintained it for forty years—waiting for the Soviet attack that never materialized. It was out of service now. But still there.

The Ruskies hadn't managed to land a nuclear bomb on U.S. soil. But Colonel Jim Bowie was going to show them how to do it. The homegrown, all-American way.

While the men were setting it off, he'd get the hell out of town—and take on a new identity—ready for his next big attack. If he needed to do it.

Or maybe this mission would do the trick.

QUINN lay in bed, wishing she could keep Caleb out of her dreams. But whenever she fell asleep, he was there.

Sometimes he made passionate love to her. It wasn't like reality. As she slept, he started off kissing and touching her the way he had done. But then she would take off his clothes, and play with his wonderful cock, making him hard and big. They would be naked together in a wide bed, hugging and rocking and kissing as they aroused each other. Then he would spread her legs and plunge inside of her, and she would wake knowing that she had had a shattering orgasm in her sleep.

Other times, he would be in the woods, calling her. And she would press her hands over her ears so she couldn't hear him.

Tonight was one of those nights. He kept reaching out to her in the dream, and she kept resisting. But finally she awoke with a start to realize that someone really was calling her, like the night when she'd gone to get Zarah.

Then it had been both Caleb calling her and Draden sending a message from the other universe. Now it was only Caleb.

Come back.

Confused, she sat up in bed, wondering if he was in the room—if he'd come here as she'd feared all along, to hurt

Logan and his family. And there was no way she could stop him.

Finally! I've been trying to wake you.

Her whole body rigid, she stared into the darkened room. "Where are you?"

His answer helped steady her.

I'm in the woods. Come back to the place where you met me. Hurry.

She was alone in bed, and the words came from inside her head, but she answered aloud. "No."

Something's happened. Come back. You have to help me.

"Is this a trick?" she asked in a shaky voice.

No. I need your help. Before it's too late. Hurry.

CHAPTER
TWELVE

QUINN TURNED HER head. Out the window she could see dim light.

She should stay here and break all contact with Caleb, but the voice ringing inside her head sounded on the edge of panic.

A ghost in a panic?

Something had happened. Something bad from the sound of Caleb's voice. And she couldn't leave him to deal with it on his own—not when he had reached out to her.

She had warned herself to stay away from him. And for days, she had kept her resolve.

But everything had changed in an instant. She climbed out of bed and ran to the chair in the corner where she'd laid the jeans she'd taken off. Her shoes and socks were on the floor in front of the chair.

She had been sleeping in her T-shirt. But because she knew the early morning might be chilly, she added a man's shirt over it before pulling on her socks and running shoes.

She was glad there was an exterior door on the lower level, so she wouldn't have to go upstairs. But as she tiptoed down the hall, a shaft of light knifed into the hall, and Zarah stepped out of her room, pulling a robe across her rounded belly as she came.

"Quinn?"

She stopped short, feeling like a schoolkid caught sneaking down to the kitchen at night. "What are you doing up?"

Zarah turned her palm up. "One of the curses of being with child is that you have to keep getting up at night to go to the bathroom."

"I was trying to get out of the house without disturbing anybody."

Zarah's expression said, *I'll bet*.

"Where are you going?"

Quinn hesitated a split second—long enough for Zarah to answer for her.

"To Caleb?"

She kept her gaze steady, when she wanted to look away. "How do you know?"

"Where else would you be going so early in the morning?"

Quinn shrugged.

"Sometimes when Logan or Rinna is talking to us, I'll see you staring into space, and I'll know you're thinking about Caleb, wondering what he's doing and what it would be like to be with him. And that's all right. You don't have to feel guilty about it."

"I do if he brings trouble to Logan."

"I don't think he will."

"Is that a psychic prediction? Or wishful thinking?"

"I don't know," Zarah admitted.

The confession didn't soothe Quinn's nerves.

"Well, this is different," she said. "Something's happened."

"The thing I told you was coming?"

"I don't know." Quinn swallowed. "Don't tell Logan I've gone—unless I don't come back."

Zarah stared at her. "I can't lie."

"Then I hope he doesn't ask you if we spoke."

Zarah answered with a quick nod and stepped forward to embrace Quinn. Quinn's own arms came up, and they held

on to each other for a long moment. Then Quinn eased away
and continued toward the back door.

"I'll lock it behind you," Zarah said.

"Thanks," Quinn answered.

She stepped out into the cool morning air and heard the
lock click behind her. Which meant she wasn't getting back
inside without knocking. So, was she burning her bridges?
What?

She had been seriously off balance since she had met
Caleb. Too bad she wanted something from him that he
couldn't give her.

With a grimace, she wrapped her arms around her shoulders as she hurried through the woods, heading for the place
where she'd last met him.

The birds had awakened, and they chirped in the trees
above her head. By now, she knew the way, and her feet flew
across the forest floor.

"Caleb?" she called softly when she neared the spot.
"Caleb?"

"Quiet." He spoke aloud. It seemed like his voice was
right beside her ear, and she almost jumped out of her skin.

"Sorry," he said. "I didn't mean to startle you. This way."

He was beside her, pointing toward his right, and she
changed her course to match his.

He kept pace beside her as she ran, and she watched him
out of the corner of her eye. He looked exactly the way he
had before. A man wearing clothing that wasn't quite right
in the modern world.

He moved in front of her, then stopped and held out his
arm. Her chest came up against his sleeve, and she felt
him—the way she had when he'd made love to her.

At her quickly indrawn breath, she saw his hand clench.

"Over there," he whispered, pointing to a place on the
forest floor where dirt had been mounded.

"What is it?"

"A fresh grave."

She sucked in a startled breath.

"Two tough-looking men came here. They were carrying

another man. They wrapped him in . . . a tarp and buried him."

"Great Mother! Another body." Involuntarily, she looked in the direction of the portal. "A soldier from my world?"

"No, they were all from this place."

"Why did they do it?"

"I do not know. But they were carrying out orders."

"Whose orders?"

"Someone they called 'the colonel.' And I know the man wasn't dead when they left him under the ground."

"They buried him alive?"

"Yes. There was a little air inside the tarp under the dirt. But he used it up, and I could feel him struggling to drag air into his lungs. Then I could feel the life in him ebbing away. It may be too late."

Quinn went stock-still. This had nothing to do with her, yet she felt a wave of panic. Buried alive! Trying to drag air into your lungs and finding only dirt. That must be horrible.

"I knew you wouldn't want another death here," Caleb whispered.

"Yes. What should I do?"

"Dig him up. Uncover his face. Turn him over and press on his back—the way they do with a person who drowned."

"There's something different now. Mouth to mouth . . . something," she whispered. She'd seen it on a TV movie where they did it to a woman who'd had a heart attack. She didn't think she could do it properly. But what if she had no option?

"They left their shovel." He pointed. "It's on the ground, over there."

She ran forward, aware of the ghost hovering behind her.

"I'll keep guard."

The earth was newly turned, which made digging a lot easier than if she'd been breaking solid ground.

Caleb was still behind her. He could keep watch. But that was probably all he could do.

A man's life was in her hands. And that knowledge made her heart pound as she began to scoop away the loose soil.

The work was agonizingly slow because she was afraid to dig too deeply, lest the sharp edge of the shovel bite into the man's body. Yet at the same time, she could feel the seconds ticking away. His life ticking away.

She kept working at a steady pace, lifting away the soil and throwing it to the side. And maybe Caleb was helping because a little wind seemed to blow the dirt away.

When she hit something solid, she worked more carefully and came to a heavy tarp. It was part fabric, part waterproof material. Plastic, Logan would call it. Or maybe rubber. She knew he used it in his work to keep dirt out of the back of his SUV when he was hauling plants.

Kneeling, she began to scoop away the dirt with her hands.

"Pull him out."

She didn't think she could do it by herself. But as she started pulling, she was able to jerk the body upward. And she realized Caleb must have been helping her get him out of the grave and onto the ground.

The seam of the tarp had come partly open. When she pulled the edge, she saw a man's beige shirt covering a broad chest. It should be rising and falling. Instead, it was absolutely still.

Tugging upward, she uncovered the man's head. She saw dark blond hair. Pale lips. Skin that had turned from pink to gray. One eye had a black smudge underneath. His cheek and jaw were bruised. He looked like someone had beaten him up.

But worse than the beating, when she lowered her cheek to his nose, she felt no breath.

She jerked the tarp farther aside and leaned over him, trying to remember what the paramedic had done in the movie when he'd saved the woman with the heart attack.

He'd held her nose and put his mouth over hers so he could blow into her lungs. Then he'd pressed on her chest.

He'd done it in a regular rhythm, and Quinn had no idea what the interval should be. But she silently said a prayer to the Great Mother as she blew into the man's mouth, then pressed on his chest.

When she did it several times and nothing happened, she wanted to blast air into his lungs. But she was sure that was the wrong way to do it. So she kept silently praying and kept up the steady, even breaths and the alternating pressure on his chest.

It felt like centuries were dragging by as she prayed and continued to give the man the treatment she'd seen in the television program.

She pressed against his hard muscles, but the damp earth had given his skin a clammy chill.

He was already dead, and there was nothing she could do about it. She wanted to scream at Caleb for putting her in this impossible situation. Yet she couldn't scream and administer the treatment.

Then, when she had just about given up, he sucked in a breath on his own.

Startled, she jerked her head away in time to see his eyes open. They were icy blue and fringed with dark lashes. But they were also unfocused with no intelligence behind them.

As she stared into those flat, dead surfaces, she felt her heart sink. She was too late. All her work had been for nothing.

What if she hadn't stopped to talk to Zarah? Would she have been in time to save this man?

CHAPTER
THIRTEEN

QUINN MADE A high keening sound as she hovered over the man.

She'd worked so hard to save him, and she might as well have stayed back at Logan's house. He was breathing, but his mind was gone.

Then, from one second to the next, the world turned upside down.

The man's body jerked, and the blue eyes changed. They had been dead. Now they were infused with a spark of life.

He started coughing, and her hand went to his shoulder as the spasms made him rear up off the ground.

He kept it up, his face turning red with the effort. Each time he coughed, his eyes squeezed closed. Then they immediately blinked open and focused on her with an unnerving intensity.

He tried to speak, but the terrible coughing kept him from getting any words past his throat.

When he couldn't talk, he raised his hand, pressing his palm over the hand that rested on his shoulder, his fingers stroking against hers.

From the way he was touching her, staring at her, it seemed like he knew her. Intimately.

He knew her? But she had never seen him before she'd shoveled the dirt off his body.

Panic made her try to jerk away. In response, he tightened his hand on her shoulder. Then he wheezed her name.

"Quinn."

A shock wave went through her. "How do you know me?"

He took several breaths, dragging air into his lungs and expelling it before he was able to dredge enough breath to answer.

His voice was barely above a whisper when he said, "I know you because I am Caleb."

She tried to wrap her head around his words. "Caleb is a ghost."

"I was. This man died, and he passed me as he went upward into the afterlife. He told me to take this body before it was too late."

"He told you? Why? Why didn't he come back?"

"He did not want to stay here."

She couldn't take in the words. Not really. Rearing away, she scrambled to her feet, backing up as he peeled away the tarp from his body. Dirt fell away from the sides of the tarp as he slowly heaved himself to a sitting position. Then, like something out of a horror movie she'd seen on late-night TV, he clambered to his feet. He was wearing a beige shirt, beige pants, and leather boots.

This was Caleb? A man with blond hair and blue eyes?

Was he telling her the truth?

Her mind scrambled for an explanation and came up with something concrete. How else could he have known her name?

She couldn't move. She could only watch him.

He groaned, and the sound tore at her. What other bruises did he have on his body in places she couldn't see?

She braced for him to step toward her. But to her vast relief he staggered in the other direction, his movements jerky, as though it was difficult for him to work his muscles.

His muscles! No. He was in the body of another man. No wonder he was having trouble walking.

Did she believe what he'd told her—what she'd just seen? Or was she going mad?

He propped his shoulder against the tree trunk. "You wanted me to be alive." It wasn't a question but a statement.

"So you stole a body!" she gasped out.

"No." The syllable rang in the morning air. "Two men buried him alive. He was dead when you uncovered his face. He left his body, and he told me I could have it."

She struggled to find the truth in his words. "What did you do, stand there and watch them bury him?"

"No! That would not be honorable. I called you when I figured out what they were going to do."

She was still having trouble believing any of this.

"Who were they?"

He raised one hand in a jerky motion and raked stiff fingers through his hair. "I don't know more than what I said before. They came here because they thought this was a safe place for . . . murder."

She brought the conversation back to the most important point. "When Zarah and I came through the portal, you scared the soldier away. You said you keep hunters away from this part of the forest. Why didn't you scare the men away—before they killed him?"

His gaze turned fierce. "I couldn't!"

"Why not?"

"The soldier from your world had belief in me. He had that blue stone to ward off spirits. He was tuned to the invisible world, so a ghost could scare him. The men who came here were frightened of someone else. Someone they called the colonel. They were too focused on him and on their task to pay any attention to me."

Truth or lies?

"You wanted a body," she accused.

"No. I didn't think about a body—until you tried to bring this man back to life. You couldn't do it because he didn't want to live. Then I realized he had offered me an opportunity."

"Do you expect me to believe that?"

"It is the truth," he said in a hard voice. Pushing away from the tree, he moved his arms and legs and winced. Then he looked down at his right forearm.

"They beat him."

"Who is he?"

His brow wrinkled, and his gaze turned inward.

He didn't speak for several seconds, and she waited with her breath frozen in her lungs.

"I don't know."

"Why? You have his body."

"But I do not have his memories."

"Why not?"

"Because he is dead! So I do not know." He raised his head and looked directly at her. "I called you—to save him. But you didn't get here in time."

He had succeeded in turning the tables and putting her on the defensive. And she couldn't help crying out, "I tried!"

"You got him out in time for me."

"Yes."

She was still having trouble coping with truth and reality. "Tell me something you wouldn't know unless you really are Caleb."

He kept his gaze firmly on her. "You came here to bury the soldier who followed you from the other . . . universe. But a bear took him away and tore him apart." His voice turned husky. "You and I were alone in the clearing. I took your clothes off and started kissing you and touching you . . ."

"Stop."

"You believe me?"

"Yes!"

She stood there, staring at him, thinking he looked so different from the man who had undressed her in the woods. Caleb had dark hair and dark eyes. This man was blond. With blue eyes. And he was a couple of inches shorter than Caleb.

"What's your name?" she threw at him.

"This man's name? I told you, I don't know."

She kept up a rapid series of questions.

"What's the name of my pregnant friend?"

"Zarah."

"What happened to the other soldier from my universe?"

"The wolf chased him over a cliff."

She was about to ask another question when the sound of voices made her go rigid.

Who was that? She strained her ears and heard men arguing.

One of them said, "Was that someone talking?"

"You're hearing things." He made an angry sound. "Listen, Spencer, let's get the fucking shovel and get out of here. This place gives me the creeps."

"You left the damn thing."

"Me—it was you. You drug it from the car."

"You were in such a goddamn hurry to get out of here."

On wavering legs, Caleb shambled toward her and grabbed her arm. "It must be the men who buried the body. They are . . . bad. They will hurt you—or kill you. You have to hide."

She glanced over her shoulder as he tugged on her arm but let him lead her behind the trunk of a large oak tree about twenty feet away. He kept his arm protectively around her, and she felt the tension in his muscles.

Neither of them spoke.

Moments later, two men walked onto the scene. One was about six feet tall with a barrel chest, coarse features, and thinning hair. He looked like he was in his late thirties. The other was younger, maybe midtwenties, with wiry dark hair, deep-set eyes, a nose that looked like it had been broken more than once. Both of them were dressed like the man beside her, in heavy leather boots, beige pants and shirts, giving the impression that they were all in uniform.

They walked into the clearing and stopped short when they saw the empty hole where the grave had been.

"Holy shit!" the bigger one shouted as they both ran toward the open grave.

"We just left him here. Where the fuck is he?"

"Gone, you moron."

"Yeah. But it's impossible."

"I told you we should shoot him, Portland."

"Don't blame this on me. It was the colonel's call. He told the troops he wanted him alive when he went in the ground, so he could think about why he was getting the ultimate punishment."

As though he could change reality, the smaller one picked up the shovel and began poking in the hole. "He's gone, all right."

The bigger one balled his hands into fists, and for a moment it looked like he was going to hit his partner. "You jerk. Stop digging. You can see he's gone."

"I told you I heard voices. Somebody was here."

"Who?"

"That's what we gotta find out. And make sure they don't live to talk about it."

Caleb gripped Quinn's shoulder and brought his mouth close to her ear. "Stay here."

She turned her head to whisper back. "You can't fight both of them—not in your condition."

"I won't. I'll haunt them."

"You said they couldn't sense the ghost."

"They couldn't. But I'll give them something to see. Like Frankenstein."

"What?"

"A monster I saw in a movie."

She held on to his arm. "You just . . . woke up . . ."

"Don't worry."

Her pulse was pounding in her ears as she watched him step away from her, out from behind the tree. "Spencer. Portland. Over here," he called in a high, wailing voice that hardly sounded human.

The two men's heads jerked toward him, and they stared at him in frozen silence.

He kept his gaze fixed on them, his voice booming out. "Spencer. Portland. You killed me and gave me power over this place. Now I will drag you to hell."

"What the shit?" the bigger one wheezed.

Caleb stiffened his legs and stretched his arms in front of

him as he began walking toward them with wide, jerky steps.
"You cannot escape me."

"Get away."

Both men backed up as Caleb kept walking toward them
like some kind of unstoppable supernatural creature.

As he came closer, the men turned and ran flat out across
the clearing to the trail where they'd come from. Caleb followed them, disappearing from sight.

Quinn's heart blocked her windpipe. She had never hidden behind a tree while someone else was in danger. She
wanted to help Caleb now. And she had to grab onto the tree
bark to keep herself from stepping into the open. But she
knew that if she did, she could mess up Caleb's act. He was
playing a ghost, but what if the men realized there was a live
person here? They might be able to figure out that she had
dug him up and saved his life.

Only she hadn't done that. The man they'd brought here
was dead. Or that was what Caleb said. She didn't know if it
was really true. They'd have to sort this out later—if they
both lived.

Long seconds passed. Then bursts of noise rang in her
ears. When she realized they were from a gun, she gasped,
then took off toward the trail at a dead run.

CHAPTER
FOURTEEN

AS QUINN CHARGED through the woods, a figure clad in a beige uniform stepped into her path, blocking her. She would have screamed, but a large hand clamped over her mouth. It took her several seconds to realize it was the new Caleb, not one of the men.

"Come on." He knit his hand with hers and pulled her into the woods, heading away from the trail and from the clearing.

"What the hell were you doing down here?" he asked, his voice grating against her nerve endings.

"I heard shooting. Are you all right?"

"The jerks finally got out their guns, but they were too scared to shoot straight and run at the same time."

"Thank the Great Mother."

"Don't waste your breath. We've got to disappear in case they work up the courage to come back."

"Where are we going?"

"Away." He led her into the woods, in a direction she'd never been. He made her keep going until she was gasping for breath. And so was he—worse than she was herself.

* * *

TED Spencer pulled the SUV to the side of the road and cut the engine.

Al Portland gave him a questioning look. "What are you doing?"

"We gotta go back to the grave."

"Not me."

"You wanna explain to the colonel what happened?" Spencer asked.

"We don't have to explain nothin'. We did the job we were supposed to do."

"Yeah, but Reynolds didn't exactly stay put, did he?" Spencer muttered. "He turned into a ghost. Or somebody dug him up, and he wasn't really dead."

"You believe in ghosts?" Portland asked.

"I did when I saw him comin' down the trail. Now I'm not so sure."

The sky had turned the color of a fresh bruise, and thunder rumbled in the distance.

Spencer looked back the way they'd come. "The colonel could blame this on us."

Portland followed his gaze, then faced forward again. "Not if we go back to Flagstaff Farm and say we took care of our business. How would he find out?"

"If Reynolds comes after the colonel?"

"He said he had power over *this place*. He can't come out to the farm."

"If he's really a ghost."

"We shot at him."

"Maybe we didn't hit him. And maybe somebody saved him. And if we go back there, they could kill us," Portland argued. "I say we just tell the colonel we completed the mission. Then, we come back later and look around."

"Later when?"

"The next time we have a job to do off the farm. Like when we pick up supplies."

Spencer thought about the alternatives. "It could be bad

either way. But if we believe in the cause, then we should go back to the colonel and give him a choice."

"He wanted the bastard dead. What do you think he's gonna do to *us*? Think about what he does when you don't have your shoes shined to his specs."

"Yeah," Spencer admitted. He started the engine again and continued in the direction they'd been going—back to the compound.

QUINN watched Caleb lean over, resting his hands on his knees, sucking in great drafts of air.

She turned to him in concern. "You . . . shouldn't be . . . running like this."

"We have to get away. They could come back—with reinforcements."

She nodded, gasping in air.

"You . . . took a . . . big chance, playing ghost."

"I . . ."

"You weren't thinking!" she answered for him. "You're used to being . . . untouchable. But everything's changed. They could have shot you and killed you."

"Yeah. You're right. The rules have changed—and I haven't caught up with them yet." He gave a harsh laugh. "But it wasn't as much of a risk as you think. I scared the piss out of them." He laughed, enjoying his victory. "Come on." He started off again, but now she saw that he was walking more slowly and pressing his hand against his ribs. Once or twice, he almost tripped.

"You're not used to this. You have to stop."

"I don't want you out in the open!"

He kept going, and she slung her arm around him, helping him stay on his feet, hearing the breath wheezing in and out of his lungs.

"This body's in good shape—physically fit. Except for the bruises."

"But you're not used to having a body."

"Yeah. And my stomach feels . . . empty."

"Probably they didn't feed him before they brought him here."

He nodded, then clamped his teeth together and kept going.

As she held on to him, she was aware of his solid form pressed to hers. Despite her use of the name, it was still difficult to convince herself that this was Caleb. She cut him a sidewise glance, taking in his blond hair again. She couldn't see the blue eyes, but she remembered the moment when they had blinked open—and then focused on her with frightening intensity.

She wanted to ask him where they were going, but she didn't want to make him talk. He was having enough trouble dragging himself through the woods—and she thought that only dogged determination kept him going. But he was aiming for some destination that he knew.

As they trudged on, she felt him weakening.

"You have to stop."

"Soon. It's dangerous to be outside."

"You think they're coming back?"

"Someone will come back with them. Someone who thinks they were on drugs when they talk about the ghost."

"People were on drugs seventy-five years ago?"

"Of course. Native Americans smoked dried mushrooms before Columbus discovered America. And reefers were big in my time."

"What are reefers?"

"Marijuana."

She didn't know what that was, and she didn't have the breath to ask.

They trudged on, and finally they came to a narrow gravel road. It led uphill, which made walking more difficult for Caleb, but he kept doggedly putting one foot in front of the other. Then, through the trees, she saw a long, low building, different from anything she'd seen in this world—or her own.

"What's that?"

"A . . . hunting lodge. Men come here to stay for a week and shoot deer."

"For food?"

He made a disgusted sound. "For fun."

"Why?"

"Some men enjoy it."

She peered at the house. "They could be here now."

"This is not hunting season."

"How do you know?"

He managed a bark of a laugh. "I've been in the woods for a long time."

In the distance, thunder rumbled. It was raining somewhere, and maybe the storm was moving this way.

"They don't come here often?"

Caleb struggled to the front steps and sat down heavily, then leaned his head against the stair railing and closed his eyes. It took several seconds before he answered, "They may come around holiday times."

His face was flushed and covered with a fine sheen. She hated to keep asking questions, but it wouldn't be good if the owners came back and found someone in the house. She knew from Logan that they might call the police. Or they might use guns to defend their property. "Which holidays?" she asked.

Again, the answers came slowly. And now his speech was slurred. "Thanksgiving. Christmas."

She knew about Christmas. In her world, it was a big winter celebration, although it seemed to have lost the original religious meaning.

Logan had explained Thanksgiving to her. Maybe when there had been a United States of America, people in her world had kept the holiday. But not now.

"It's a long time till Thanksgiving and Christimas," she answered.

"Good."

She watched Caleb sitting with his eyes closed and his head thrown back. He couldn't have gone much farther. But they were still outside the house.

Lightning flashed in the clouds. This time the storm was much closer. And the branches of the trees around them began to sway in the wind.

Quinn glanced at the sky, then the hunting lodge.

"How do we get in?"

"They leave the key under there." He pointed to a rock beside the steps.

"Nobody in my world would do that."

"This is not your world," he said, his voice heavy. "When I was alive people didn't lock the front door."

He had said it automatically. But now he *was* alive. That was sinking in. Still, she kept arguing. "We don't have the right to use this place."

"We won't stay long. And we will clean up after ourselves."

"We'd better take off our shoes, then."

"And bring them in. So nobody will see them." He fumbled for the laces on the boots, but he seemed to have reached the end of his strength.

When a few fat drops of rain hit the steps, she knelt beside Caleb and untied the boots for him. Then she hurried to the rock and found the key.

The sky had turned as dark as the inside of a storage room. Quickly, she unlocked the front door, kicked off her shoes, and went back to Caleb.

He was holding his hand in front of his face, turning it one way and then the other.

"What are you doing?"

"It's not my hand," he said in a strangled voice.

"You just figured that out?"

He didn't answer.

More drops began to fall, along with leaves the wind had blown off the trees, and she knew they were moments from a downpour. "We're going to get wet. We have to get inside."

He dropped his hand and pressed against the stairs, trying to heave himself up but didn't quite make it. Quinn leaned over him. On his next try, she pulled upward under his arms and got him to his feet.

Wavering as he walked, he staggered through the front door just as rain pounded the porch.

Inside, he leaned against the wall, breathing hard.

"Got to lie down."

Wind shook the house as he started down the hall. She followed close behind to make sure he didn't fall. When he came to a bedroom, he threw himself on the bed, not bothering to take off his clothing.

"Don't leave the shoes outside. And don't go out," he muttered.

A bolt of sound crashed nearby, but he seemed to not notice.

She went back for the shoes and set them on the little rug in the front hall. Then she locked the door. When she returned to Caleb, he looked like he was dead, lying facedown on the bed.

Fear stabbed through her, and she crossed quickly to the bed. Easing onto the edge, she pressed her hand to the back of his neck and was reassured by the warmth of his skin. And as she looked at his back she could see that he was breathing steadily and evenly.

"Caleb?"

He made a muffled sound, but he didn't wake.

A crack of thunder made Zarah shiver.

"Are you afraid of storms?" Rinna asked.

"Not usually." She licked her lips. "But Quinn must be out there."

"She was gone again when I got up," Rinna said. "I wish I knew what she's up to."

Zarah turned her spoon over and over in her hand as she and Rinna sat at the kitchen table. Since Logan was out working on a landscaping job, they had made themselves a cauliflower and cheese soup for lunch, but she was only able to get down a few swallows before she started feeling sick.

"You're worried about Quinn," Rinna said softly.

"Yes." She stopped turning the spoon and raised her head. "I saw her this morning. I knew why she was going out."

Rinna tipped her head to the side. "And you didn't say anything?"

"She said not to."

"What happened?"

"The ghost called her. He said something had happened, and he needed her." Once she had started speaking, the words tumbled out in a rush. "She said not to tell anyone—unless she didn't come back."

"And she's not back," Rinna finished.

"I should have told you sooner."

Rinna stood. "I'm going to call Logan."

"No!"

"Why not?"

"What if the ghost wants to hurt him?"

Rinna knit her fingers together. "What if he already hurt Quinn?"

"He wouldn't do that," Zarah answered quickly.

"How do you know?"

"He loves her."

Rinna stared at her. "Where do you get that from?"

"He risked his life, well, not his life—his existence—to save us. He didn't have to do that. He did it because she meant something to him."

Rinna kept her gaze on Zarah. "What are you not saying?" she asked.

Zarah dragged in a breath and let it out. She had gone this far, and she knew she had to go a bit further, if she was going to be honest about the situation. "I think she loves him, too."

Rinna absorbed the words. "She loves a ghost? What good is that going to do her?"

"I wish I knew."

CHAPTER
FIFTEEN

OUTSIDE, THE STORM raged, but Caleb slept on. Quinn stroked his broad shoulder, still struggling to absorb what had happened in the past few hours. She'd gotten into a relationship with a ghost. Now he was alive, and he looked completely different. But it was still Caleb. At least, he knew what she and Caleb had talked about—and what they'd done together. Or was this some horrible trick that she didn't understand?

She wanted to wake him and ask him questions. But he was obviously so tired that he didn't even know she was there.

And she couldn't leave him—in case he needed her. Then there was his caution about going outside. It could be dangerous, although maybe not for her because the two men hadn't seen her.

Or they could have seen her rushing down the trail. She couldn't even be sure of that.

Still trying to figure out what to do, she took a tour of the house. In her world, rich people would have lived in a dwelling this big. And she suspected it was the same here—at least for someone who could afford to keep a large house empty most of the time.

It had a living room, six bedrooms, and three bathrooms. And a spacious kitchen. She stepped inside, opening cabinets and the refrigerator. There were cartons of beer and other drinks inside. The freezer compartment at the bottom was large and stocked with a lot of carefully labeled packages that contained meat. There were also many vegetable combinations. She'd seen Rinna thaw meat and cook frozen vegetables, so she knew how to do it.

In the pantry were boxes of cereal and other grain products as well as boxes of milk and cans of soup, pork and beans, and stew.

A phone hung on the wall. Hurrying across the tile floor, she picked up the receiver. But she heard no dial tone. Apparently, it was turned off.

Sorry that she couldn't communicate with the Marshall house, she went back to check on Caleb again. He hadn't moved. And he didn't stir when she leaned over and put her hand on the back of his neck.

She gnawed on her knuckle, fighting the impulse to wake him. She had so many questions. About the two of them. And about the two men who had buried him alive.

They'd beaten him. Or somebody had. They had been talking about a military man—a colonel—who had sent them. Or could the title be just a courtesy term? Like the Colonel Sanders who sold fried chicken?

She was too exhausted to think about it. Maybe rest would give her some perspective on things. And maybe when Caleb woke up, he'd remember something about the blond-haired man. It was strange to call him that, but it was the best she could do.

The storm eased away as she began opening drawers and closets. After finding a man's T-shirt she could wear, she went into one of the bathrooms, took a shower, and washed her hair, then dried it with a towel.

She thought about lying down next to Caleb. But that seemed like a bad idea. So she investigated the other rooms. Most were furnished only with a wide bed and a chest, and nobody had made much attempt at decorations, which reinforced

Caleb's assertion that men came here to hunt. Women would have added some homey touches.

The sun had come out again, and she pulled down the window shades to darken the room before crawling under the covers. The bed was comfortable, like the ones in Logan's house.

For a few minutes, unanswered questions swirled around in her head. But she was bone-tired, and she quickly dropped off into a troubled sleep.

SOME time after he had fallen onto the bed, Caleb's eyes blinked open. He pushed himself up, grimacing as pain shot through his arm. Rolling to his back he looked to his left and right. When he realized he was alone, a chill skittered over his skin.

He had come here with Quinn. He remembered stumbling into the house in the middle of a thunderstorm with her.

Where was she now?

Quickly he levered himself out of bed, then had to stand still for a moment because his head was spinning.

Staggering across the room, he leaned against the doorjamb and saw a hallway that he barely remembered. When he found Quinn two doors down the hall, he breathed out a sigh of relief.

She was here. He stood gripping the door frame for long minutes, just staring at her.

He could see her face and her beautiful hair, but her body was covered by a blanket and sheet. He wanted to wake her.

But he felt an unfamiliar pressure in his abdomen and struggled to identify the sensation. Then it came to him. He had to pee.

Exiting into the hall, he found the bathroom between his room and Quinn's.

After using the toilet, he stood with his hands clenched for long moments. He wanted to avoid the inevitable. But he knew he had to deal with reality. So he walked the few steps to the mirror and stared at his face.

He suppressed a gasp as he regarded his image. Not the face he remembered. Not at all. He saw blond hair. Icy blue eyes. Thin lips. A wide chin. He rubbed the blond stubble on his cheeks. It was thinner than the facial hair he remembered.

With a feeling of unreality, he raised his hand, looking at his broad palm, seeing a row of calluses. How old was he? Who was he?

To hang on to sanity, he said his name, "Caleb Marshall!"

Then said it again. It sounded wrong in his mouth. This man's teeth were bigger, and his tongue hit them differently.

He closed his eyes, trying to call up some memory from the man's past. He could only remember Caleb Marshall.

He had been dead. A ghost. And now he was alive. The reality made his throat close and his vision swim. His heart started to pound wildly. His heart?

He gripped the cold edge of the sink, waiting for the physical sensations to settle down.

He wasn't even sure how he had gotten into this body. He'd sensed the man die. Heard him call out. Not aloud, but in Caleb's mind.

He shuddered as he remembered the feeling of the man's spirit passing his—shooting upward toward the place he'd never been able to go himself.

He couldn't go to the other side. But somehow he'd been able to change from ghost to man.

He came back to the question of what—exactly—had happened. There was still no answer.

He only knew that he had been dead. And now he was alive—in another man's body. Apparently, because the man had wanted it.

He felt his chest tighten and his body begin to shake. Struggling for calm, he held more tightly to the cold porcelain of the sink.

He felt his heart pounding again. Another man's heart beating inside another man's chest. If he thought too much about it, his head started to spin.

He looked at a smudge of earth on his neck, and another

truth came slamming back at him. He'd been in a grave, and the clammy feel of the dirt made him shudder. He looked toward the shower and pictured water cascading over his body.

Not his body. Another man's.

"Stop it," he muttered. "He's dead. It's your reality now."

He reached to turn on the water and stopped. Instead of knobs there was one sleek-looking lever sticking out from a circle of shiny metal.

He'd never seen anything like it, so he twisted the lever. Still nothing. Finally he figured out that he needed to turn it like the hand of a clock. He yanked it all the way to the opposite position. At first it ran cold, but soon the water turned warm, then hot.

Moving it back, he got the right balance between hot and cold and stepped under the spray that came down from above like rain falling on his head.

The sensation of the water hitting his body was amazing.

After a few minutes of simply enjoying the falling water, he washed his body with the cake of soap in a wall niche, captivated by the way the soap slicked over his skin and made him feel new-minted.

The sensuality of it made him think about Quinn, and he found himself instantly hard. He looked down at his cock. He had no foreskin, and he blinked as he took that in. Circumcision. He had heard of it. It was supposed to make you less sensitive during sex.

He circled the girth with his fist and slid his hand up and down. Big mistake. He was plenty sensitive. Yeah, with just a few strokes he had made himself so hot that he thought he might go off like a Roman candle.

He pressed his hands to his sides, willing himself to calm down. When he had a measure of control, he stepped out of the shower and toweled himself dry, avoiding looking at his face in the mirror.

The towel slid over crisp blond chest hair. Hair that should be dark. The look was all wrong. And when he glanced farther down, he saw that the hair above his cock was blond, too.

Wrong again. The guys in the Marshall family were all similar in appearance. No matter who they married, they bred true to type.

He made a low sound.

He didn't want to think about his physical self and what it meant now. He only wanted to use the vessel he'd been given.

Quinn had accused him of stealing another man's body. He supposed you could call it that. But the man had left it for him. Invited him to take it.

Did that make a moral difference?

He hoped so.

He opened the medicine cabinet and found a can of something that read "shaving cream." It was like nothing he had ever seen before. He shook it and tried to turn the nozzle, like the shower control, but nothing happened. By accident, he pressed on the top, and white foam came shooting out.

Next to where the can had been was a plastic thing that might have been a razor. But again, it was totally unfamiliar.

It suddenly struck him that he had a man's body. Thank God. Would he have taken a chance at life if the dead person had been a woman?

He could hardly imagine that scenario. And he realized all over again how lucky he had been. He was a man. And the woman he wanted to make love to was just down the hall.

But before he went to her, he should brush his teeth. The medicine cabinet also held a new toothbrush in a see-through container. He pried it out, then used something called "toothpaste" that promised to whiten his teeth, sweep away plaque, and give him healthy gums. He squeezed too much out of the tube and had to rinse the foam out of his mouth several times.

But the clean taste felt good.

The dirty clothes he'd been wearing were scattered around the floor. Burial clothing. With a grimace, he stuffed them in the trash can, then returned to his room where he rummaged in the dresser drawers until he found soft, loose pants made out of some knitted material. They had a stretchy band and a drawstring at the waist.

He didn't bother with a shirt. Just the pants, and he hoped he wouldn't be wearing them for long.

Then he went back to the room where Quinn was sleeping and stood looking at her. She was under the covers, but they had slipped to her waist, revealing the T-shirt she wore. Had she put on panties? Or was she naked below the waist?

As he contemplated that possibility, he grew instantly hard again. Instantly wanting.

She had known him when he was a ghost. And she could have run away from him after he'd gotten into his new body. But she'd come here with him to the hunting lodge. And she'd stayed, even when she could have slipped away while he was unconscious.

Days ago, he had settled for a pale imitation of lovemaking with her. Because that was all he could have.

And what could he have now?

He took a step closer, watching the rise and fall of her chest, seeing her breasts through the thin fabric of the T-shirt, with the darker circles of her nipples in the centers.

Raising his eyes, he focused on each one of her features in turn, loving the way her dark lashes lay against her cheek.

Then he looked at her sun-streaked hair.

It suited a woman like Quinn.

Everything about her pleased him. He had felt connected to her. He thought she had felt it, too. Would it be the same—now that everything had changed?

THE two wolves with light packs on their backs trotted through the woods toward the spot where neither one of them had ever ventured.

Logan had been out on a job, supervising the construction of a waterfall at an estate in Montgomery County. When he'd gotten a call from Rinna, he'd hurried home.

He was in the lead. His cousin Ross followed a few paces behind. Since this was Logan's territory, Ross was letting the other werewolf take charge.

Ross was good at that. And he kept a cool head. Not like Logan who was likely to go into confrontational mode when he was under stress.

And he was under stress now. He'd agreed to take in Quinn and Zarah, the pregnant wife of a council member in Sun Acres, Rinna's home city.

He'd been glad to help. Partly because he knew his wife appreciated the company of women from her own world.

But things hadn't worked out exactly the way he'd expected. Quinn had met a ghost who held a grudge against the family. And she'd run off this morning to meet up with him again.

Was she helping the ghost plan an attack? Or what?

A sense of unease gathered in his chest as he trotted toward the patch of ground that had always made him nervous.

It was probably the place where the ghost's body was buried. But he didn't even know that for sure. He had never seen the spirit. Or really sensed him. Yet some deeply buried instinct had warned him away from this place.

Now he felt a kind of electricity tingling over his skin as he ventured into the clearing. It looked like an ordinary patch of Maryland hardwood forest. And it smelled like that, too.

He dragged in a deep draft of the humid air, trying to catch Quinn's familiar scent. But the rain had washed it away with casual efficiency.

He took another step forward, then stopped short when he spotted a gaping hole in the soil. It was long and thin. About the size of a man, and it went down several feet, below the layer of forest loam to the familiar red clay that blanketed this part of the country.

Had the ghost somehow risen up out of his grave?

Ross came up beside him, and Logan gave him a questioning look. Ross was a private detective, and he had more experience than Logan in investigating burial grounds in the woods. A couple of times, he'd unearthed private cemeteries that had helped the cops take down serial killers.

He gave a signal with his head, and Ross trotted forward, sniffing the hole and poking with his right forepaw at a large piece of black plastic, not unlike what Logan used in his landscape business.

A shovel was discarded nearby on the ground. Not the shovel that Quinn had taken from the toolshed earlier. This one had a rounded blade and a red-painted handle.

Someone else had brought it. And the plastic. That wasn't seventy-five years old. He knew the details of his trade, and he knew that such plastic hadn't existed in the 1930s.

A wide trail led downhill. Ross started down that way, and Logan followed, keeping alert for danger—or for some clue to what had happened here.

He stopped short and made a woofing sound when he spotted something interesting, a place where the bark of a tree was newly grazed by a horizontal line.

Ross came back and eyed it.

It looked to Logan like a bullet had made the mark. Ross must be thinking the same thing because he turned and followed the trajectory of the horizontal line until he came to a round hole in a nearby elm tree.

A bullet hole. So someone had been shooting recently.

Jesus! Was that why Quinn hadn't come home? She was dead—or wounded?

Slipping from tree to tree, they followed the trail downhill to a spot where tire tracks dug into the mud. Tracks from an SUV or a pickup truck, judging from the size of the treads and the space between them. The vehicle was gone, but someone had left a crumpled wrapper from a sandwich shop on the ground. Also a beer can.

Ross wiggled out of the pack he carried. His eyes took on an inward focus, and Logan knew what he was doing.

He did the same thing, discarding the pack before he began to silently say the ancient chant that would turn him from wolf to man.

Ross was already pulling on sweatpants and running shoes from his pack by the time Logan stood erect and worked his shoulders—then began to dress.

"That wasn't where the ghost was buried. That was a new grave. Someone came in an SUV and planted a body," Ross said.

"Why not a truck?"

"Would you drive around with a dead guy in the back of a truck?"

"If it had a cover."

"Okay. It could have been a pickup," Ross conceded. "And there were probably two guys. One dropped a beer can on his side of the car. The other threw out a sandwich wrapper on the other side."

"And they shot at someone."

"Quinn? Did they get her?"

"I hope not." Logan ran a hand through his dark hair. "What do you think happened?"

"I wish I knew," Ross answered. "Either Quinn got away, or not."

Logan winced.

"What about the ghost?"

"I didn't feel him," Logan said.

"Can you show me his grave?"

Logan walked back up the hill and strode into the patch of ground he had always avoided. He walked in a circle, keeping his gaze down, looking for a spot where a man might have been buried seventy-five years earlier. But there was no indication of where that might be.

Ross did the same, tramping carefully around the area. "You sensed him, sensed something around here prior to this?"

"Yes. But it's like he's gone."

"We can search in a wider circle and see if we can pick up Quinn's trail," Ross suggested.

Logan could tell from the tone of his cousin's voice that he wasn't hopeful about finding anything after the rainstorm. But he wasn't sure what else to do. Really, he didn't want to go back and tell the women that they'd uncovered a nasty mystery in the woods.

"Maybe Quinn will call you," Ross said.

"Maybe," Logan answered, wondering if he was ever going to hear from her again—or if she was going to show up making a surprise attack on the house.

CHAPTER
SIXTEEN

CALEB TOOK ANOTHER step toward the bed. Then another, feeling like invisible ropes were drawing him toward the woman sleeping there. Whatever happened, he had to wake her, because he couldn't stand not knowing where he stood with her.

As he drew closer, he could tell that she had showered, too. He caught the scent of the same soap he had used—but on her it was different, with an underlying feminine quality that teased his senses.

"Quinn."

He wasn't even aware that her name had escaped his lips until her eyes snapped open. For a moment she looked confused and panicked, and his chest contracted.

Then she focused on him, and her expression changed.

"Caleb?"

"Yes."

"Are you all right?"

"Yes."

Quickly, he crossed the last few feet of space between them, wondering if she was going to leap off the bed and back away from him.

But she stayed where she was, and he felt as though he had won a major victory. He eased onto the side of the bed, his hands clenched at his sides.

She was looking at him with those beautiful dark eyes of hers.

"You fell asleep so fast. Are you feeling better?" she asked.

"Yes." He raised one shoulder. "I guess I needed to recharge." His hand trembled as he raised it to her face, stroking his finger against her cheek, marveling at the sensation of skin against skin.

"It was different before. I can really feel you now," he murmured.

"You couldn't feel me?"

He cast his thoughts back, trying to explain how it was. "I could. Sort of. But it was different. Not solid. "

It had been a disconnected feeling, he realized. Although it had been all he could hope for, he didn't really want to talk about it now.

He was sure she could sense the difference in him. And he knew damn well that she was reacting to him—as he was to her.

Or, he hoped he wasn't reading what he wanted into the way her body quivered under his touch.

She opened her mouth to say something, but he didn't want any more talking. He wanted her. Fiercely. Completely.

Gathering her close, he brought his mouth down to hers, his lips moving urgently, the contact threatening to swamp his senses.

He had felt alive under the shower. But the sensation was nothing compared to what he was feeling at this moment. He was aroused to a fever pitch of need, and the woman he wanted was in his arms. On a real bed with him. Not on a bed of leaves out in the forest.

The covers had become an intolerable barrier. Standing again, he stripped them away, looking up and down the length of her body—from her small feet, to her long, beautifully shaped legs, to the hem of her T-shirt. It had hiked up, and he could see the dark triangle of hair at the top of her legs. He wanted to touch her there. But not yet.

From some unwanted place, a wayward image flashed into his mind—the stranger's face he had seen in the mirror. He clenched his jaw.

Quinn's expresson changed. "Caleb, what's wrong?"

"Nothing."

He pushed the image away. It didn't matter what he looked like. What mattered was making Quinn his own.

He came down beside her on the bed again and lowered his head, kissing her softly as his fingers stroked over her face, then her neck and collarbone. Her shirt was in the way of further progress, so he dragged it up, then stripped it over her head so that she lay naked before him.

Her eyes were large and luminous in the dim light, and when she reached to touch his lips, he murmured, "You want this as much as I do."

"Yes."

"Thank God."

He heard a sound roaring in his ears and understood that it was his own blood rushing in his veins.

His own blood!

Lord, he could hardly believe this was happening. Hardly believe that everything had changed in a split second. Fate had given him his life back, and he could make love to Quinn as he had longed to do.

He reached for her hand, knitting his fingers with hers, and his heart squeezed when she returned the pressure.

He could barely breathe. Barely keep his body from trembling.

He lifted his other hand, so that he could stroke her hair back from her face, then tangle his fingers in the thick strands before angling his head so he could bring his lips to hers again.

His reality had contracted to this bed. This woman. And he sought contact with her everywhere he could.

His mouth on hers, his hands moving over her body. His cock pressed against her thigh.

He thought he might explode with need. But he knew he had to hold himself back long enough to give her the same firestorm of pleasure that gathered inside him.

It had been so long since he had been a flesh and blood man holding a woman in his arms. And now Quinn was here. With him. The right woman.

His life mate.

That startling thought almost swamped him.

His life mate.

He had thought that joy would be impossible for him. Yet here she was. And it felt so real. So right.

If you counted the years of his life, he was too young to have bonded. But he thought maybe the time of being a ghost had made a difference.

Thrusting the ghost out of his mind, he rubbed his lips against hers. "Quinn, I love your sweet mouth and your sexy body. I love the way you smell. I love your silky skin."

He punctuated each phrase with little kisses, starting with her face then moving downward over the tops of her breasts and the valley between them, burying his face in her softness and breathing in her intoxicating scent.

Her hands cupped the back of his head, holding him to her as she combed her fingers through his hair.

"Oh, Lord," he gasped. "I want to drown in you."

He turned his head one way and then the other, glorying in the feel of each breast and the beautiful sight of her erect nipples. Then he moved a few inches so that he could circle one tight bud with his tongue. The taste was glorious. And when he sucked it into his mouth, she surged against him, wordless vibrations coming off her like waves of pleasure.

He rolled her to her side, keeping her hip against his cock, clasping her against his heat and hardness as he devoured her mouth.

He was almost dizzy with the sensations zinging through him. Touching her. Tasting her was almost too much for him. Yet he couldn't stop.

"Lord, I can't believe you are here with me. After all this time," he said, his voice husky, his hand tracing the curve of her hip, then drifting lower to tangle in the wonderful crinkly hair at the top of her legs.

"Oh!"

Touching her there sent darts of sensation to his nerve

endings. Craving more, he slid his hand lower, into the slick, moist heat of her pussy.

She was plump and swollen. Ready for sex. Ready for him.

Wordlessly, she told him how much she wanted him as her hips rose against his fingers.

He stroked through her sensitive folds, dipping two fingers inside her and withdrawing. Her breath was coming broken and fast as he built her pleasure.

He wanted everything. All at once. He wanted to run his tongue through the wonderful moisture of that most intimate part of her. But they would have time for that later. All the time in the world. For now, he was afraid that if he didn't finish this soon, he would embarrass himself.

When he ripped off the loose pants, his cock sprang free. He was so hard that he wavered between pleasure and pain.

"Now. I need you now," he gasped.

"Yes!"

His blood had turned to a molten river, but his physical response was only part of what he felt. He sensed she was with him—body and soul.

He rolled her to her back, parting her legs with his knee.

"Now!" he said again, claiming her with one powerful thrust.

He heard her catch her breath.

"Are you all right?"

"Yes."

For a long moment he held himself still, staring down at her in wonder. He was inside her. It was real. And physical.

He wanted it to last forever. This gut-wrenching moment of claiming his mate.

But the urgency was too great. He began to move inside her, with measured strokes at first, until it was impossible to keep the pace slow and deliberate.

She clung to his shoulders and his hand moved between them, stroking and pressing as he urged her toward completion.

"Caleb!"

The sound of his name on her lips made his breath catch.

It caught again as he felt her tighten around him, heard her cry out in ecstasy. And as she came, waves of pleasure took him, carrying him to some far place where he had never expected to travel again.

He felt her clinging to him. When he tried to look down into her face, moisture blurred his vision. He didn't want her to see that weakness, so he clasped the back of her head and pressed her face against his chest.

He felt her lips moving over him. "Caleb," she said again, her voice a soft caress.

He kissed the top of her head as he folded her close and rolled to his side. Climax had left his body limp. But the emotions he felt were even more intense than when he'd first taken her into his arms.

There was so much that he wanted to say to her about what the two of them would mean to each other. But he sensed that it was too soon. At least for her.

And maybe for him.

He held her, sliding his fingers over her damp shoulder, kissing her cheek.

"Thank you," he murmured.

She reached to stroke her fingers against his lips. "I thought we could never have this," she whispered. "And I was so sad."

"Yes."

"I'm glad you're here. Like this." She slid her hand down his arm, over his hip, tracing the length of his body. The body that didn't match his mental image of himself. But he would learn to deal with that. He had to.

"There's a lot you don't know—about this world." She laughed. "A lot I don't know, either. But I can show you some of it."

She cleared her throat. Her head was tipped down, away from his face, and he wondered what she was going to say.

"Did you remember anything?"

"About what?"

"The . . . man . . . they buried."

He had been avoiding that subject. Deliberately, he turned his thoughts inward. When he tried to recapture any

of the memories from the man, he drew a big fat blank.
"No."

"We have to find out who he was. And why they wanted
to kill him."

"Yeah. But not now."

She looked like she was going to protest, but she ended
up closing her mouth.

He reached for the covers he'd tossed to the end of the
bed and pulled them up, snuggling down beside Quinn. It
was such an ordinary thing to do. Yet it hardly felt ordinary
to him.

It was a moment he had never expected to experience
ever again. And he ached to go on with his life. If he could.
With Quinn at his side. Yet he knew there were issues he had
thrust aside. He had been focused on himself. Then focused
on the magic of being with Quinn.

But he had stayed on earth, hovering around the place
where he was buried, because he had a job to do. And now
he had the opportunity to do it.

CHAPTER
SEVENTEEN

CALEB WOKE AND turned his head toward the window. Light drifted in from around the edges of the shade, and from its quality he judged that it was late afternoon.

When he reached for Quinn and found the bed empty, he felt a spurt of panic—until he heard sounds that were vaguely familiar. She must be in the kitchen fixing food.

The full bladder feeling assaulted him again, and he got up and used the facilities. When he caught a glance of his face in the mirror, he clenched his teeth. How long would it take for him not to feel a little shock every time he looked at himself?

Back in the bedroom, he pulled on the pants he'd worn and padded barefoot down the hall toward the kitchen.

She was standing beside the sink, also barefoot, wearing jeans and a T-shirt, running water on a flat white package. She looked up, her expression uncertain as she saw him standing in the doorway.

"Quinn."

He walked quickly across the tile floor and took her in his arms, clasping her to him, and she melted against him.

He absorbed that miracle as he bent to stroke his lips against her hair, her cheek.

When she tipped her head up, their mouths met in a hungry kiss. He was still having trouble coping with reality, but the kiss grounded him.

He knew he wanted her right then. He also sensed that his body needed food.

She eased away. "Let me fix you . . . dinner."

He stared at the white package in the sink. "It's in there?"

"Yes. They had steak in the freezer. I'm thawing some."

He was back trying to cope with the totally unfamiliar. "They freeze meat?"

"Yes."

"Deliberately?"

"That keeps it fresh for a long time. You can buy some frozen foods at the supermarket. But people freeze some things at home, too."

"Supermarket?"

"A big grocery store. They have everything from canned and frozen food to fresh vegetables and fruit that might be shipped in from California or Florida or even South America, if it's not the right season here."

He tried to square that with what he remembered. "I used to walk down to a little store in the next block."

"What could you buy there?"

"All the foods. When I was a kid, we also had a garden out back of our house. Mom and the kids worked it."

"Not your dad?"

"He didn't eat many vegetables, so he wouldn't do that kind of work."

"What was his job?"

"He was a scrap metal dealer." He cleared his throat. "So the corner store is gone."

"They have something like them—convenience stores—now. With milk and bread and junk food."

"Junk food?"

"It tastes good. It has a lot of calories but not a lot of nutrition."

"Like what?"

"Chips."

He wrinkled his nose. "Cow chips?"

She laughed. "Potato chips. Corn chips."

He liked the sound of that laugh. And the way she looked with her hair tousled.

She started to say something, then looked like she'd changed her mind.

"What?"

"I was wondering if you eat meat raw?"

"Yeah."

"But probably not so cold. I'll warm it under the broiler." Her face took on a faraway look.

"What?"

"Back in my world, my old job was running kitchen equipment."

"So you know a lot about this."

She lifted one shoulder. "No. I ran the oven with psychic powers."

He goggled at her. "How?"

"I was trained to do it. In my world lots of people have powers that haven't developed here."

"There's a lot I don't know about you."

"Yes." She swallowed. "Do my psychic abilities turn you off?"

"Of course not!" When she kept staring at him, he added, "Maybe they will come in handy."

She seemed to relax a little. "Well, cooking is easier this way."

He watched her turn a dial on the stove before getting out a flat pan with ridges in the bottom. She set the meat in the pan. By the time she was finished, a narrow tube at the top of the oven was starting to glow red.

He pointed to it. "What's that?"

"The heating element. It's very hot. Don't touch it."

She sprinkled some salt and pepper on the meat, then slid the pan underneath the red glowing tube. She waited for a couple of minutes, then pulled the pan out again and cut the steak, leaving some of it in the pan and putting it back under the red glow.

She lay the bigger portion on a plate and handed it to him.

He stared down at the red and white surface with anticipation. His first meal in seventy-five years.

As he brought it to the table, where she'd already laid out a knife and fork, his stomach growled. But when he cut a piece of the meat and started to chew, it tasted all wrong in his mouth.

She caught his expression. "What?"

He snatched up a paper napkin and spit the meat into it, then wadded it into a ball. A kernel of alarm had wedged in his gut. "I would have eaten it like this. But it doesn't taste right . . . now."

While he took a gulp from one of the water glasses on the table, she picked up the plate. "I can cook it some more."

"Yeah."

She put the meat back with the other piece and shoved the pan under the heating element again. He watched it sizzle.

He took a deep breath of the aroma filling the kitchen. "It smells wonderful."

"Yes. Most people eat it cooked."

She turned back to the counter and slathered something from a jar onto two pieces of bread, then handed him one.

"Fresh bread? You didn't have time to make it, did you?"

"From the freezer, too."

When he took a bite, the wonderful taste of fruit and sugar filled his mouth.

"What is this?"

"Blackberry jam."

"I didn't used to like anything sweet."

"I guess . . ." She let the sentence trail off.

"You guess what?" he asked sharply.

She raised her head and gave him a direct look. "I guess the man they buried had different tastes from you."

"Yeah," he muttered. He didn't like that surprise. He'd expected to reclaim his life as he remembered it. But things weren't working out exactly the way he'd figured they would.

"They had boxes of cereal."

"Puffed wheat? I remember that."

"Cocoa Puffs."

"Puffed wheat with . . . chocolate?"

"I think so."

He grimaced, then swept his hand toward his lower body. "What are these kind of pants I'm wearing?"

"Sweatpants."

"They're comfortable."

"Yes."

THE conversation died away again, and Quinn turned back to the stove. She hadn't known what to expect. She suspected it was the same for Caleb. Or, he'd had expectations and they weren't panning out.

Glad of the cooking lessons Rinna had given her, Quinn grabbed the pan with two pot holders and set it on the stovetop. Then she used a big fork to transfer the meat to the plates, which she brought to the table.

She watched Caleb cut a piece and lift it to his mouth with the fork. And this time she could tell from his expression that it tasted good.

When he caught her watching him, she bent to her own plate and cut some steak.

"It's wonderful," he said.

"I'm glad."

They ate in silence for several moments.

"Tell me the things that surprised you the most about this . . . universe," he said.

She pondered the answer. "I could say . . . airplanes."

"We had them."

She remembered the small craft she'd seen at the Air and Space Museum. "These are big. Some of them hold five hundred people."

"You're kidding, right? How do they get off the ground?"

"They have jet engines. And don't ask me how those work." She cut a piece of meat, chewed, and swallowed. "In everyday life, I guess electricity is what surprises me the most."

"I know about that. For lights."

"It runs the stove. And the washing machine. And the microwave."

"What's a microwave?"

She laughed and gestured toward a rectangular box with a window that hung between the cabinets over the stove. "I don't have the technical knowledge to tell you how it works, either. But it's another way to cook food. Well, I guess it works best when you're just rewarming stuff from the refrigerator."

"Like an icebox?"

"Yes. But you don't use ice. There are cold coils that work by electricity."

"Oh."

She cleared her throat, wondering what subjects were okay to bring up. "I see you stuffed your clothes in the trash can."

"Yeah."

"We can run them through the washer and dryer. Then they will be completely clean."

"My mother had a washer . . . with a wringer."

Now it was her turn to ask, "What's that?"

"You washed the clothes, then put them through these rollers to get the water out."

"Electricity does it now. Well, it runs a dryer with hot air and a blower," she said.

When they finished eating, he stood and picked up both plates, set the water glasses on top of them and carried them to the sink. That surprised her. But maybe he was showing that he could help a woman in the kitchen.

With his back to her, he said, "I saw the car those guys were driving. It was like nothing I've ever seen before. Sleek."

"You still don't remember who they are?" Quinn asked before she could stop herself.

His shoulders stiffened. "No. And don't keep asking me. I'll tell you if I come up with any insights."

"Okay," she murmured, wishing the memories were accessible to him. Probably he did, too.

His voice softened. "I don't like it any better than you do."

She wanted to tell him she knew where to go for help. But she was pretty sure he didn't want to hear her suggestion. And before she could speak, he strode back to her, lifted her out of her chair and pressed her body against his.

He was aroused. And as he lowered his mouth to hers, she sensed a savage urgency running through him.

It sparked her own need. Still, she wasn't prepared for his direct approach. As they stood beside the kitchen table, he grabbed the hem of her T-shirt and pulled it up and over her head, then worked the snap at the top of her jeans and lowered the zipper. His hands slipped inside—over her hips, dragging the jeans down and leaving them in a pool at her feet.

She helped him by kicking them off. And while she did that, he tore off his sweatpants, then gathered her body to his, naked skin to naked skin.

He bent to ravage her mouth while his hands stroked down her back, cupping her bottom and pulling her against his cock.

She clung to his broad shoulders, then dragged in a breath when he eased away.

The smoldering look in his face was enough to make her legs weak.

Then he turned her in his arms, pulling her back against his front. He had held her in that position out in the forest. That earlier encounter was a pale imitation of this one.

His hands cupped her breasts, taking their weight in his hands as he used his thumbs to play over the erect centers.

"Lord that feels good," he gasped out.

"Yes!"

She reached back to press her palms against his hard thighs as he used his lips and tongue and teeth on her neck and then her ear while his hands played with her body.

He traced the curve of her waist, dipped into her navel.

She caught her breath as he took her nipples between his thumbs and forefingers, tightening and twisting and sending a hot current of arousal downward through her body.

"Please."

"What do you want?"

"You know."

"I want to hear you say it."

"Touch me between my legs," she cried.

"Like this?" One hand traveled downward, into the swollen folds of her sex, drawing a circle around her clit, then sliding lower so that he could ease two fingers into her vagina.

She moved her hips, pressing against his hand, craving firmer pressure, and he gave it to her.

"I want you now," he growled.

She raised her head, looking toward the bedroom.

"No. Now. Like this." He bent her at the waist so that her arms came down on the tabletop and her bottom was sticking into the air.

"What are you doing?" she gasped.

"This." He stroked her ass, gliding down between her cheeks to find her vagina again, this time with his cock.

He opened his mouth against her shoulder as he entered her from that position, burying himself deep inside her and reaching around to cup her breasts in his hands, his fingers playing over her nipples as he thrust into her from behind.

Then one hand pressed over her clit, working his magic there as he pumped in and out of her.

She stiffened her legs and braced herself against the tabletop, caught in the moment. Caught in the grip of the need he had aroused.

She came in a quaking explosion of pleasure, followed seconds later by his shout of satisfaction.

Dazed, Quinn turned her head and stared up at Caleb. She had never experienced anything like that in her life. The urgency. The white-hot need. The swift coupling—with her leaning over the kitchen table.

"You were planning that when you cleared the dishes away," she whispered.

He gave her a knowing look. "Did you want me to sweep them off—and break them?"

"No."

He withdrew from her and turned her around, pulling her to a sitting position, holding her against his sweat-slick chest.

"You belong to me," he said, the words very clear and distinct.

"Yes."

A modern woman from this universe might have bristled at the bold statement. But she was from a different place. She felt the truth of his words, all the way to the marrow of her bones. She had never belonged to anyone in her life— not of her own free will. Well, she had been in love a long time ago. As a teenager. But that had been different. A girl's love for a boy. And she had been a slave, which certainly implied ownership. But that was also different. The feeling of belonging came from within herself—and from within Caleb. When she had met him, anything real between them had been impossible. Now the world had opened up with limitless possibilities.

She wrapped her arms around him, holding on tight, simply craving the contact. She had longed for a man of her own. And now she had forged a link with Caleb. But in her life, she had learned that nothing is easy. And that was so true now.

Questions burned behind her lips. She wanted to understand him, connect with him on every possible level. And she didn't know what to ask him first. He had been a ghost, and that had given him special powers. Had he lost them when he had become a man? She suspected that was probably true, but she also thought he might not want to talk about that.

So she started with something easy. "How old were you when you . . . ?"

"Twenty-six."

"You were young."

He tipped his head to the side. "How old are you?"

"Twenty-six."

He laughed. "An old lady!"

They smiled into each other's eyes, but she knew they had to think about practical problems.

"We have to find out who tried to kill . . . you. I mean the man they buried in the woods."

His voice took on a confidence that surprised her. "It's not me. Not now."

"They won't know the difference." She felt her lower lip tremble, but she managed to say, "You look like him."

"Not for long."

"What do you mean?"

"My hair should be dark. And my eyes. Maybe they will change."

She stared up at him. "How?"

"I don't know! Maybe the real me will show through."

She heard the doubt in his voice. He wanted it to be true. But it might not be possible. Maybe it was just some fantasy he'd conjured up to make himself feel better.

"But we don't have to stay around here waiting for them. We can get away from this part of the country. Move to a place where they won't find us."

She licked her lips. "There's a lot you have to think about, wherever you live."

"Like what?"

"How did you make a living . . . before . . . you died?"

"I drove a truck. And I fixed things for people. Radios. Washing machines. Cars. I was good at understanding how things worked."

"All of that's different now. Trucks are huge. And a lot of machines have computers. Even cars have them."

"What are they?"

She flapped her hand. "I don't know this place so well, either. There are different kinds of computers. But the ones in machines . . . I guess you'd say they . . . know how to carry out complex processes."

"Well, some things have to be the same about driving a truck." His eyes took on a faraway look. "The freedom. The open road. Seeing different parts of the country. Meeting people."

"Meeting women?" she said before she realized she might be getting herself into trouble.

He gave her a direct look. "Yeah. But that was just fooling around." He stroked his hand over her naked shoulder, then down to the top of her breasts. "What we have . . . this is what was meant to be."

She responded immediately to the intimate touch. "Yes."

He started speaking again, a satisfied look on his face. "And I know how to make extra money. A lot more than for repair work. There are places you go, where they have boxing matches; you see if you can beat the town bully."

She winced. "You were a real tough guy."

"I liked it that way."

"None of those boxers were very old, were they?"

"No. But I'm still young enough to do it. You win a big purse, and it can be enough to buy a house."

She doubted it. Not today. And she didn't know if he was young enough for that kind of punishment. Caleb Marshall had died when he was twenty-six, but his present body was older. She wasn't sure how much older, but she'd put him in his early thirties if she had to make a guess.

He was still speaking. "The men in my family get the rough stuff out of their system, then they . . . settle down."

He was saying he wanted to stay with her. She wanted that, too, but she was still thinking of all the problems they faced—and he faced.

"You can get a better job and earn more money if you have an education," she murmured.

"That was never important to me! I didn't want a job that tied me down."

"Okay," she answered, knowing that his values were still those of a young man with no responsibilities. A young man from an age when life wasn't so complicated. He was thinking he could disappear into some distant part of the country. But with the Web or with private detectives, the killers might be able to find him, no matter where he went.

"It's not that easy to hide. You need a new identity. A driver's license. A birth certificate. A Social Security number. You have to have them today. If you don't have the real thing, you have to buy fake ones. And you need help to get them."

She felt him stiffen. He tipped her head up and looked down into her eyes. "What kind of help?"

She had only one answer to give him. "The Marshalls will help us. You're one of them."

She watched his expression turn savage, and a dart of fear zinged through her.

When he spoke, his voice was like ground glass. "I am not *one of them,* as you put it. I am the head of my own pack."

"Things have changed."

"The men in my family do not change. They have been the same for hundreds of years. They are strong and independent. And when they invade each other's territories, they fight. That is the way things work."

"Not now!"

"If you think that, you believe in fairy tales," he ground out.

"But . . ."

He cut her off with a look and words that hit her like a biting lash from a slaver's whip. "Do not argue with me. There is no way in hell that I would ever go to any of those bastards for help."

"You don't understand."

"You are the one who doesn't understand."

CHAPTER
EIGHTEEN

QUINN STRUGGLED NOT to let her emotions show. Not long ago, Caleb had swept her into a whirlwind of sensuality. And afterward he had told her they belonged together. She had felt it, too. Not just because of the fantastic sex. She had known a special connection was growing between the two of them.

Suddenly, she felt like a cold breeze had blown across her skin.

Caleb's eyes were fierce, and she wanted to look away, but she kept her gaze steady. "We should get dressed."

"You understand?" he asked.

"Yes." It wasn't a lie. She understood too well. He was a man from another age, when the rules of life had been different. He was from a time when men were in charge and women fell into line with their plans—the way they did in Sun Acres. And like the men of her universe, he also thought in terms of settling disputes with violence.

Why should she be surprised? He'd been killed in a fight with another werewolf.

But if Caleb wanted to fit into life in twenty-first-century America, he had a lot to learn. The question was, would he let her help him learn it? And could she convince him they needed Logan's help?

She saw him make an effort to relax his features. He turned his head toward the window, and she followed his gaze. It was getting dark, and she was afraid he was going out. She was more afraid she knew where he was headed.

To Logan's house. And not to make a friendly call on his cousins.

She felt torn in two.

She wanted what she and Caleb were building together. Or was that just a false promise? Because she had wanted a man. Was the new reality no better than trying to forge a relationship with a ghost?

She couldn't answer those questions. Not yet. But she knew she had to keep Caleb from hurting Logan. Or Rinna. Or worse.

They were her friends, and she had to protect them. Without making Caleb turn on her.

She bent to pick up her T-shirt and pull it over her head. Then she picked up her jeans and climbed into them. Caleb was also pulling on his pants.

Struggling to keep her voice even, she said, "You need to learn more about the way the world works now—if you want to fit in here."

She could see he was also making an effort to sound reasonable after his angry outburst. "I know. I saw some magazines and newspapers in the living room. I can study those."

"There's a quicker way. You remember movie theaters?"

"Yes."

"They have something like that in people's houses now. The screen is smaller, but you can watch a lot of different programs."

She led him down the hall to the living room and pointed to the flat-screen television on the wall over the fireplace, then to the sofa. "Sit down, and I'll show you how to use it."

The remote was lying on the coffee table. She clicked the power button and waited until the television warmed up, then clicked to the cable channel where Logan got CNN. It was the same here.

Caleb's eyes widened as he watched the picture spring to life. They were talking about New York traffic, and she could see him gaping at the scene behind the reporter standing on the sidewalk.

"It's like *that* now?" he asked, his voice filled with awe.

"Not everywhere. That's a big city. One of the biggest in the world."

"Yeah."

"You can watch other channels. A couple of hundred," she said, pressing the up arrow and watching a soccer game replace the newscast.

Hoping she was concealing her own tension, she sat down beside him and handed him the remote.

"Play around with it," she suggested. "There are stories, like the movies you used to see. Some of them were originally made for the movie theater. Other ones were made for televison. And in between scenes, they have commercials, like ads in magazines where they try to sell you things. You can also see a lot of 'reality' shows where people talk about their problems—or decorate their houses. There are shows that teach you how to cook. Or how to landscape your yard. There's news on all day. They repeat it over and over."

He began changing channels, stopping at each one to take a peek, until a car racetrack caught his attention, and he watched the vehicles whizzing around the course.

"They go damn fast."

"Yes."

She kept her gaze on the screen, but her mind was furiously working. She had always had some talent to influence another person's decisions. She had done it back when she and Zarah had both been slaves.

She called up that power now, focusing all her inner concentration on sending a silent message to Caleb. If she could keep him from going to Logan's house tonight, she could wait until he was asleep, then slip out of the house and warn them. Not just warn them. She could ask for their help. Maybe Logan's cousin, Ross, could reason with Caleb. Or maybe they could show him how they worked together.

You're tired. You don't want to go out tonight. You want to stay here with me. We can go to bed in a while and make love. I can cook you some more food. You've been through an ordeal. You need to relax. You should go to sleep early, and Quinn will go to bed with you.

She repeated some variation of those words over and over, and after a few minutes she felt Caleb relax beside her. When his eyelids drooped, she smiled.

She hadn't been sure it would work. But it looked like the tactic had been successful. And after he was asleep, she could go out and find a telephone.

He gestured toward the television set. "This is interesting, but it's making me tired. Maybe I should go to bed early."

"Do you want something to eat first?"

"Not now."

She clicked the remote, and they stood, their bodies pressed side to side. He slung his arm around her as they made their way down the hall to the bedroom where she'd slept earlier. Beside the bed, he turned her toward him and gave her a long, intimate kiss.

Lifting his mouth a fraction, he murmured, "I can't get enough of you."

"I can't either."

It was true. She might be worried about what he was going to do, but when he began to kiss her and touch her, she couldn't help responding. It was as though the sexual pull between them took over her body and mind.

"Quinn. Quinn."

This time they undressed each other slowly, kissing new territory as they uncovered each other's bodies.

After the wild encounter on the kitchen table, they made a silent agreement that there was no need to hurry.

They stood swaying beside the bed until both of them were too aroused to stay on their feet. Caleb brought her down to the surface of the bed, and they kept up the slow pace until she knew she had to take it to the next level. Circling his cock with her fist, she began to stroke him.

"No fair!" He made a strangled sound and pulled her on

top of him, letting her take charge. She brought him inside her and teased him with slow strokes, until he forced the issue by pressing against her clit.

She exploded in a starburst of pleasure, watching his face as he followed her over the edge. Then she collapsed on top of him, too worn out to move.

He stroked his hand through her damp hair. "That was so good."

She was getting used to the new way he looked. She wanted to know if he was getting used to the body, but she didn't want to ask any disturbing questions.

Instead, she turned her head to sweep her tongue against his salty shoulder. "Yes."

They lay joined for a long time, kissing and stroking each other tenderly until his penis finally slipped out of her. She was sure she had diverted him from doing anything dangerous that evening. And she rolled off of him and made a wobbly trip to the bathroom before turning off the light.

When she snuggled down beside him, he held her close. She tried to stay awake so that she could slip out of the house later. But he had worn her out, and she told herself it would be all right to sleep for a few hours.

COLONEL Jim Bowie stepped into the darkness and drank in the clean country air. His shoulders squared and his arms swinging easily at his sides, he began walking around the militia compound, his eyes roving over his empire with satisfaction. It was the perfect base of operation. Close enough to D.C. so he could get in quickly to carry out his mission. And far enough away so that he was just one of the big landowners out here in the boonies.

The traitor was dead. That potential crisis was behind him. A small blip no longer on his radar screen.

His men were in top fighting form. And everything was back on track for Operation Eagle's Flight.

He could get it rolling tomorrow, if he wanted. But he preferred to wait for a more symbolic date. A new date in the

American consciousness that would become as important in the history books as 9/11.

He passed the recreation hall, where the men were watching a baseball game on a wide-screen television.

He didn't deny them leisure time activities, although he preferred the wrestling matches and boxing tournaments he staged for them, where they could blow off steam.

But he had strict rules about what they could do here. No drinking. No smoking. No gambling. No chewing gum.

Any man caught breaking those rules would be up for public punishment. And any guy caught jerking off would be stripped naked and have his ass flayed with a whip.

SOMETIME later, Quinn woke with a start. Her hand moved to the side of the bed where Caleb had been sleeping. The sheets were still warm, but he wasn't there.

She glanced at the clock. It was early in the morning. Two o'clock. Sitting up, she cursed herself for drifting off. In the darkness, she listened intently, trying to figure out where he was. Had he gotten up to go to the bathroom? Or could he be in the kitchen looking for something to eat?

When she didn't hear sounds from either of those places, she climbed out of bed and hurried down the hall. The light was on, and she saw him. He was naked, standing beside the front door. He stood very tall and straight. His muscles tense.

And she knew in that moment that he'd been doing the same thing to her that she had been doing to him. He'd made tender love to her with a purpose. He'd been trying to make her drop her guard—so he could slip out of the house and change to wolf form.

She had thought she had convinced him to stay here through the night. But he was going out—to hunt. And not for deer. He had been focused on revenge for too long. Now that he had the means, he was going to seek out the werewolf he thought was his enemy. Tonight.

If only she had one of those cell phone things! But she didn't.

It flashed through her mind that she could run back to Logan's and warn him. But even as the thought formed, she knew it would never work. She didn't even know what direction to go—not from here. And once Caleb changed to wolf form, she had no chance of catching him.

Either he didn't know she was there, or he didn't think she could do anything to stop him. Decisively, he stepped out into the darkness and closed the door behind him.

No.

With no time to think, without any real plan, she charged down the hall and threw the door open.

In the light from the doorway, she saw Caleb standing a few yards from the house, his face turned away from her and his hands at his sides.

He was saying something. And the hairs on the back of her neck rose as she recognized the words.

She couldn't understand them. But she knew what they were. Because she had heard Logan outside saying the same thing, and he had explained their purpose. It was the ancient chant the Marshall men used to change from man to wolf.

"*Taranis, Epona, Cerridwen,*" Caleb intoned, then repeated the same phrase and went on to another.

"*Ga. Feart. Cleas. Duais. Aithriocht. Go gcumhdai is dtreorai na deithe thu.*"

"No!" She charged toward him. "No. Don't do it."

He turned toward her, his face suffused with shock, but he didn't stop the chant.

Pushing off from the porch, she threw herself at him. Maybe because he couldn't believe she would attack him, she was able to knock him to the ground. With no thought for her own safety, she followed him down, wrapping her arms and legs around his body.

"Get off me," he growled.

"No. Stop it. You don't know what you're doing," she panted.

"Yes, I do."

"Caleb, stop."

"The woman does not make the rules. The man does."

"Not in this century."

"Let me go."

"Stay here. Please. Come back inside, and we can talk. You can't go after the Marshalls. You don't understand how things are now."

He didn't answer, but he changed tactics. When he stopped struggling, she knew that he had decided she couldn't hang on to a wolf. What was he going to do, bite her with his animal jaws?

He gave her a long burning look. Then he turned his head away, and began to chant again.

"*Taranis, Epona, Cerridwen.*" She heard him say it again, then go on to the second phrase, just the way she had heard Logan do it.

"*Ga. Feart. Cleas. Duais. Aithriocht. Go gcumhdai is dtreorai na deithe thu.*"

"Caleb, I can't let you do this."

Desperate to keep him from his awful purpose, she clamped her grip on him, bracing herself for the worst, prepared to hold on to him as he changed from wolf to man.

CHAPTER
NINETEEN

IT DIDN'T HAPPEN.

His voice became frantic as he said the first phrase again, but still nothing changed.

"Christ!"

With a burst of strength, he fought her off, rolling to his side and rocking back and forth. "Christ," he repeated again, his voice sounding lost and broken.

Alarm shot through her as she took in the horror on his face. "Caleb, what's wrong?"

"What the hell do you think is wrong? It doesn't work! I can't change."

"But you did it when you were a ghost. I saw you running through the woods."

"Yes. I changed when I was a ghost. When I was still me. But this goddamn body won't do it."

She stared at him, comprehension dawning. Thinking aloud, she said, "You can't do it because the man who died wasn't a werewolf."

But Caleb wasn't listening to her now. He was too wrapped up in his private pain. Throwing his head back, he raised his face to the sky and a long low howl escaped from his lips.

A wolf's howl, from a man.

Then he pushed himself to his feet and looked toward the forest.

"Caleb, don't go. Let me help you."

He made a snarling sound. "You can't help me. Nobody can help me."

Without waiting for an answer, he raced away.

"Caleb. Stop. Caleb." She might as well have been calling to the wind to stop rustling the leaves in the trees.

CALEB ran into the night, ignoring the woman calling his name. He needed to outrun the agony and the fear and the sorrow, even when he knew there was no escape.

He wasn't even sure what he'd intended when he'd tried to change. Maybe he'd just been going to have a look at the descendant of the bastard who'd killed him. Or maybe he would have taken care of the guy. He didn't know.

When a rock stabbed into his foot, he winced, but he didn't slacken his pace. He was a werewolf. That was his heritage. His hard-won right.

Since he had fought through the pain of his first change, he had transformed from man to wolf whenever he wanted. He had hunted as a wolf. Eaten his kill as a wolf. Fought as a wolf. Gloried in his secret strength.

In a terrible moment of recognition, all that had been ripped away from him.

He was like a man who had both arms lopped off. A man who couldn't unzip his pants to piss. Or feed himself. Only this was worse, because arms were only part of a man. Taking away the wolf had stripped away everything that he was and everything that he could be.

He thought he had found his life mate. Years before the traditional time of mating, but true nonetheless. Now his feelings for Quinn were only a cruel joke on both of them.

He laughed, the sound echoing through the chill of the early morning.

Quinn couldn't be a werewolf's mate because he was only the dried husk of what he should be.

He had been a ghost, and he had taken the body of a man who had just died. He had felt reborn. And he had started making plans.

He had taken a chance—and lost everything.

He kept running, trying to escape from his utter and complete despair. But as he ran, he began to feel dizzy. Sick. And another suspicion began to creep into his mind. He had tried to make the change and something had happened. Not just his lack of success. Something more.

Nausea clogged his throat. He stopped running and bent over, heaving up the food he had eaten earlier. When he moved on again, he began to shake. He was limping now, his foot throbbing from the place where the rock had dug into his flesh, and he cursed the man who had such tender feet that he couldn't even walk through the woods without shoes.

The shaking grew worse, and finally he could go no farther. He sank to the ground, propping his back against the trunk of a tree, his body alternately too hot and then too cold.

His head began to pound. And when he tried to hold on to any thought, it skittered away from him.

Wrapping his arms around his shoulders, he struggled to cling to consciousness. But it was a losing battle.

QUINN crashed through the underbrush, looking for Caleb. But he had disappeared into the forest, and there was no way she could find him. When she scratched her ribs on a bramble, she realized that she was running naked through the woods at night.

She stopped, panting. She wanted to call his name again, but that would probably drive him farther from her. This was his territory. Not hers. And she was going to get lost in the dark.

Turning around, she was relieved to see light in the distance. Hoping it was from the lodge, she started walking back.

As she plodded along, she knew that she was in over her head. She needed help. And there was only one place where she could go.

To Logan. But she didn't even know where his house was in relationship to this place.

Cautiously, she approached the building and was relieved to see that no cars had pulled up in the meantime. With a little sigh, she climbed the steps and walked inside. Caleb had said they would leave this place the way they had found it. But there was no time to clean it up now.

She ran back to the bedroom where they'd slept, picked up her clothes from the floor and pulled them on. Then she started opening drawers. In another one of the bedrooms, she found a cache of coins, which she stuffed into a fanny pack she also found.

It flashed through her mind that she should wipe all the surfaces they had touched. She remembered from a show she'd seen on television that you could find people through their fingerprints. Hers weren't on file anywhere. But what about the man whose body Caleb had inherited?

She didn't know, but she was going to have to take a chance because she didn't have time to deal with something she couldn't even see.

Instead, she grabbed the T-shirt Caleb had worn and stuffed it into the fanny pack. Then she walked out and closed the door.

Shoulders slumped, she trotted down the narrow road that led to the house. When she came to a wider road, she didn't know which way to go. So she turned right, sticking to the gravel strip at the edge of the blacktop. A car passed her, and honked, making her jump. She remembered that you were supposed to walk facing oncoming traffic, so she crossed the paved surface.

At least she was used to traveling long distances on foot. She had gone two or three miles when she came to a small community. It had a convenience store that wasn't open yet. But a telephone stand was outside. She hurried up to it and put in the right amount of change, then called Logan's number.

Rinna answered.

"Quinn, where are you? What happened? Are you all right?"

"I'm all right. But I don't know where I am."

"Did you get kidnapped? What?"

Logan took the phone away from his wife. "Are you all right?" he repeated.

"Yes." She gulped. "But I need your help."

Cars were starting to pass the store, and she knew that the world was waking up. And every moment she left Caleb alone in the woods was a moment when something terrible could happen to him.

"Tell me where you are."

She ordered herself not to panic, then pulled on the phone cord so that she could look at the store. There was no address number, but she spotted a small sign on the sliding glass door of the store. "I'm at a little store. It says it's operated by James Pendelton in Henderson, Maryland.

"Okay. That's not too far. We'll be there soon."

"Don't bring Zarah or Rinna."

"Why not?" he asked, his voice sharp.

"It could be dangerous."

"I guess you'll explain that when we get there."

"Who is coming with you?"

"My cousin, Ross."

"Okay."

After she hung up, she sat down at the picnic table on a grassy strip beside the store and lowered her head to her hands. Then a car passed, and she decided that would make her too conspicuous. In fact, maybe sitting in the open wasn't a good idea. So she walked to a patch of woods and stood leaning against a tree as she waited for Logan.

When his SUV pulled up in the parking lot, she breathed out a small sigh and ran over.

Logan rolled down his window. "Get in."

She climbed into the backseat, looking neither at Logan nor Ross, and shut the door.

"This is the second time you've had us worried sick," Logan said.

"I'm sorry."

Logan pulled the car to the side of the parking lot and cut the engine. "What happened?"

Both men turned to look at her as she struggled to orga-nize her story. So much had happened that it seemed a long time ago when Caleb had last summoned her.

"The ghost called to me. He told me he needed help. I ran back to the place . . . I guess where his grave is, and he told me two men had come and buried another man alive. They had left their shovel, and I dug the man up. But he died." She hitched in a breath and let it out before telling the next part. "Caleb got into his body."

"What?!"

"His . . . his spirit had departed. I gave him . . ." She stopped and flapped her arm. "I can't remember what it's called. It's when you breathe into someone's mouth."

"Mouth-to-mouth resuscitation."

"Yes, that. He was dead, but then Caleb was able to take over the body. We were still there when the men came back for the shovel, and he scared them off, pretending to be the man's ghost."

"Yeah, I'll bet that scared them," Ross said. "Who were they?"

"We don't know."

"What did they look like?"

Impatiently, Quinn answered, "One was big with a barrel chest and a balding head. The other was smaller with dark hair and a nose that looked like it had been broken."

"You never saw them before?"

"No!" She continued the story of what had happened to her and Caleb. "We ran through the woods to a hunting lodge that Caleb knew about. We stayed there. Then Caleb tried to change to wolf form, but he couldn't do it. He ran out into the night, and I knew I couldn't find him."

She gave Logan a pleading look, feeling compelled to be brutally honest and hoping he would understand. "I think he wanted to hunt you. I tried to plant a suggestion in his mind that he shouldn't hurt you. I was going to try to warn you, but he got up in the middle of the night to change."

"We found the new grave," Ross said.

"You did?"

"Yes. We talked to Zarah, and we were worried about you."

"I'm so sorry."

He laughed. "You're like Rinna when I first met her. I guess you can't stay out of trouble."

"I didn't mean to make trouble."

He waved his arm. "Don't worry about it. That's old news. We went looking for you. But we couldn't follow your trail because the rain washed the scent away."

She unzipped her fanny pack and pulled out the T-shirt. "Caleb was wearing this. Maybe you can follow his scent."

"And what? Let him attack us?" Logan asked.

Ross put a hand on his shoulder. "Imagine what it would be like if you suddenly found you couldn't change to wolf form."

Logan nodded. "Yeah. Maybe I'd go crazy."

"Maybe he did," Quinn whispered.

"Take us back to the lodge, and we'll see if we can follow his trail."

"Thank you."

"We haven't found him yet," Logan said.

"Thank you for trying." She swallowed. "I'd better tell you—he doesn't look anything like he did. The body he took over has blond hair and blue eyes."

"Jesus," Logan muttered.

"It was a shock to him."

Logan made a sound of agreement.

All the way to the lodge, Quinn kept hoping that Caleb had come back. Running inside, she checked the rooms. When she didn't find him, she felt a giant knot twisting in her stomach.

Had he run away because he couldn't stand to face himself? Or was this something worse?

Logan called Rinna on his cell phone to tell her what they were doing. Then Quinn showed them the place where she'd fought with Caleb.

The two men conferred, then disappeared around the side of the house. When they returned, Logan was carrying a backpack, and Ross had changed into a handsome gray wolf.

When she handed him the shirt, he sniffed it, then trotted off into the woods. Quinn and Logan followed.

He kept his eyes straight ahead. "How was he? Other than not being able to change? What else did he do?"

She felt her face turn warm and was glad Logan wasn't looking at her. There was a lot she could say about what Caleb had done, but she didn't want to talk about the intimate details of their relationship.

"He was weak at first. Then he was happy to have a body." She swallowed. "He found out he couldn't eat raw meat."

"Christ!"

She kept her gaze focused on Ross, who was now fifty feet ahead of them, partly hidden by the underbrush. "And he liked bread with jam."

"Yuck!"

They detoured around a patch of what Logan had told her was poison ivy. When she looked up, Ross had stopped in front of a large elm tree.

Quinn's heart leaped into her throat. It looked like the wolf had found something. Would Caleb know who he was? Would he be angry enough to attack?

She ran forward, and fear shot through her as she saw a pair of bare legs and feet motionless on the ground.

Dashing around Ross, she found Caleb sprawled naked and unconscious.

CHAPTER
TWENTY

QUINN KNELT BESIDE the still form, looking for some kind of injury. She ran her hands over his arms and legs, finding no breaks. And when she examined his skin, she found no new bruises or cuts or bites from animals that might have found him while he lay unconscious.

But his skin was gray and his breath was shallow, as though some sickness had taken possession of him.

"Caleb? Caleb?"

She knew that Logan was standing behind her, but he faded into the background of her awareness as she bent down to press her ear against Caleb's chest. She could hear his heart, but it was slow and shallow.

Fumbling for his hand, she squeezed his fingers.

"Caleb. It's Quinn. Caleb."

She raised her free hand and stroked his cold cheek, fear threatening to swamp her.

With no warning, his eyes snapped open, and she gasped.

He focused on her, his gaze sharp but bloodshot. "Quinn. How did you get here?"

"I had help," she murmured, afraid to tell him that his werewolf cousins had come to his rescue.

As he stared at her, his features softened, and he raised his hand to touch her hair. His fingers lingered there for a moment before his arm fell to his side.

"Just rest," she said. "You're going to be all right."

"Am I?" he asked, sounding truly puzzled. Then he gave her a warm smile. "My life mate," he said, his voice barely above a whisper.

Her heart gave a sudden jolt inside her chest. She had heard that phrase before, and she knew what it meant. In this world, werewolves were different from the kind she knew back home. Rinna had told her that the Marshall werewolves found the right woman—then mated for life.

She leaned down, pressing her cheek to his chest, overcome with joy at what he had told her. She had known it in her heart, known her feelings for him ran deeper than anything she had ever experienced.

"Oh, Caleb. I love you so much. I knew that finding you was the most important thing that had ever happened to me."

Her happiness overflowed, until his next words shattered her. "No. That is impossible . . . now."

She raised her head, staring into his eyes. "It's true. We both know it's true."

"But I am no wolf," he said, his voice broken. "I can have no life mate."

A kind of hollow desperation rose inside her. She had dared to think of her own happiness. And he was snatching it away. "You can! You told me it was true."

"Before I remembered."

"If you want it—we can have it."

"No." His body jerked, and he began speaking again, only now she couldn't follow his thoughts. "The cold is coming. It swallows me."

"Caleb, what?"

"The old car needs a new distributor. That's going to cost a lot of money."

She stared into his eyes. They had turned misty, his gaze far away.

He kept talking, on a completely different subject. "He

and I wanted the same woman. He asked me to meet him in the woods, and we would settle it."

He looked past her, his gaze falling on Logan.

"Aden! You bastard. What are you doing here? Have you come back to kill me again?"

Snarling, Caleb lurched up, his hands curled into claws as he lunged at Logan.

Ross was coming around a tree, tucking his shirt into his pants. When he saw what was happening, he leaped forward, catching Caleb by the shoulders and pushing him back to the ground.

"No, get off of me." His eyes widened as his gaze bounced from Logan to Ross. "There are two of you! You never did fight fair."

Ross held him down. Logan pulled Quinn out of the way.

"Don't!"

"You'll get hurt," Logan answered.

She looked down, seeing Ross struggling with Caleb. Ross was breathing hard, and Caleb's breath sounded like the rattling of canvas in the wind.

He couldn't keep up the fight for long. Or, if he did, the exertion might kill him. Yet she knew Ross had to protect himself.

"Don't hurt him," she shouted.

"He's trying to hurt us," Logan answered. He pushed her behind him, then came down beside the naked man, holding him from the other side. Caleb struggled against the Marshall cousins for a few moments, then went limp, his eyes still open.

Though he lay still, disjointed words tumbled from his lips.

"I live in the woods. In the light of the moon. The animals know me. But no man can see me. Only Quinn. Only Quinn. My life mate."

She felt tears sliding down her cheeks.

His life mate. He still thought that, even when honor forced him to deny it to her. Or maybe it was worse than that.

"Leave him alone. He's sick. Please."

"He's dangerous," Logan answered, but both men eased the pressure on Caleb's shoulders.

"He's sick," Quinn said again.

"Sick in the head," Logan growled.

"We have to help him," Quinn said softly. She knew Logan had heard her private conversation with Caleb, knew he had heard the part about being his life mate.

"What can we do for him?" Ross asked.

She gave him a grateful look.

When Caleb's body began to shake, she asked, "Do you have a blanket? Something to keep him warm."

"In the car," Ross said. He turned and ran back the way they'd come.

Quinn was left alone with Logan and Caleb again. She leaned over Caleb, trying to stop his shaking. Then suddenly he went still again, his face pale as death.

She kissed his neck, then closed her eyes, and hung on to him.

It seemed to take forever before Ross returned with a blanket. Quinn draped the covering over Caleb's still form.

"He sure as hell doesn't look like one of us," Logan said. "No Marshall has blond hair and blue eyes."

"Because this is not his original body! I told you what happened."

"Not many people would believe you," Logan muttered.

"It's the truth. Why would I lie?"

"You tell me," Logan challenged.

"Everything I said is the truth," she protested.

"But you snuck out of the house again."

"I told Zarah."

"Okay, let's not argue about what's already happened," Ross broke in.

"Thank you," she whispered.

"Do you know what's wrong with him?"

She looked up at him, then back to Caleb. Her lips trembled when she started to speak. "I have a guess. And it scares me."

"He has some rare sickness. Something from your world, and he's contagious?"

"No! How would he get something from my world?"

"You could be a carrier," Logan muttered.

"No. It's nothing like that. I'm sorry I've made you think the worst of me." She gulped, then forced herself to try and explain. "You have organ transplants here."

"Yes," Ross answered.

"And the person can reject the organ."

"Yes," Ross agreed.

"I think that's happening to him. He didn't have an operation, but he took over this body. And I think it's rejecting his soul." She felt her throat clog, because what she feared was so monstrous that she could hardly imagine it. "And if they separate, I don't know what will happen to him."

"Jesus!" Logan swore.

"Is there anything you can do about it?" Ross asked.

"In my world, there are adepts who may be able to help him. I don't know for sure."

"You're going to take him back there?"

She looked up at the two grim-faced men. "If I can. But I can't do it by myself. Zarah and I hid the portal. I need her to help me . . . uncover it again."

"Zarah's pregnant. You want to bring her out here in the woods?" Logan asked.

She didn't want to, but she saw no alternative. "I can't do it without her. Can I use a cell phone to talk to her?"

He didn't answer, and she imagined what he must be thinking. *You want to cure him so he can kill us.*

Before he could voice that objection, she made a promise. "If we can save his life, I'll make sure he doesn't go after you," she said.

"How?"

"I'll keep him in my world," she answered, because she knew that was the only sure way she could honor her promise. Yet at the same time, she didn't know what that would mean for Caleb. He had been born here, and he wasn't prepared for the dangers of her environment.

She saw Ross weighing the consequences, and she knew that he had the power of life and death over the man she loved.

CHAPTER
TWENTY-ONE

QUINN FELT AS though her own life were hanging in the balance. When Ross finally pulled a phone from his pack and handed it to her, she let out the breath she hadn't known she was holding.

"Thank you."

Trying to keep her hand from shaking, she called Logan's house and asked to speak to Zarah.

"I was worried about you and Caleb," her friend said as soon as she came on the line.

Quickly, Quinn explained what had happened. "I need to take Caleb home to our world where an adept can treat him. If you can help me unblock the portal."

"I think we can do it, but how do I know where to find you?"

Quinn looked at Ross. "Can we take Caleb in the car as close as we can get to the portal?"

"If you tell me where to find it."

"It's not too far from the place with the open grave. The place where big rocks tower over a stream." She swallowed. "I guess that's not very descriptive."

"I think I know where you mean," Logan said.

"Thank you," she breathed, then put the phone to her mouth again and spoke to Zarah. "We can meet at the portal. You remember how to get there?"

"Yes. I'll come as soon as I can. If you're going back, I want to send some things to Griffin. Nothing hard to carry."

"Of course."

She handed the phone back to Ross, and he spoke to Rinna, telling her which roads to take to get close to the portal.

When she turned back to Caleb, she saw his eyelids flutter. They opened, and he stared at her.

"Quinn."

"I'm right here. I'm going to help you. The Marshalls are going to help you, too."

"Why should they?"

Ross answered. "Because it's a family problem."

Caleb turned his head toward the other man. "You look like him."

"We all do."

"I don't!"

Quinn knelt beside him. "What you look like doesn't matter."

He grimaced. "It's more than how I look."

"Caleb, I love you. If you die, something inside me will die."

His expression softened, and he started to speak. But the words came out garbled again, and she knew that he had lapsed back into a state where he couldn't communicate with her.

And now she had another fear. She had said she would try to find a healer who could help Caleb. But what if he didn't want to be healed? What if he simply wanted to die?

How could she give him back the will to live without reminding him why his spirit had stayed on earth in the first place?

She was wondering how they were going to get him into the car when he lost consciousness again. Ross and Logan picked him up and carried him between them, back toward the hunting lodge.

It was a slow trip because Caleb was heavy.

But they managed to get him into the SUV, then drove as close as they could get to the portal.

Rinna and Zarah were already pulled off the road and waiting in Logan's truck.

The men carried Caleb into the woods and toward the rock outcropping.

Zarah and Quinn embraced. "Thank you for helping me," Quinn said.

"I'm helping myself, too. You're planning to go to Griffin's house, right?"

"Yes."

"Then you can tell me if he's all right."

"He is!"

"Then why haven't you heard from Draden?"

"Because all their efforts are going into defending themselves."

"Or Griffin is dead."

"Don't say that! You have to be optimistic."

"I'm trying, but it's difficult," Zarah answered. She took out a small envelope and gave it to Quinn. "Give him my love. And give this to him."

"What is it?"

"A letter. And photographs he'll want to see. There's a picture of you and me together—in case someone stops you, and you need proof that you've been with me." She went on to explain about one of the other pictures, and Quinn felt her heart contract.

"They can do that here?" she asked.

"Yes," Zarah answered. "They can do things we would never have thought of."

Quinn knew they had to cut the conversation short. "Okay," she said. "I'll give all this to him and give him your love." As she spoke, she silently prayed that she could find Griffin—for Zarah and for herself. He was her protector in her own world. And if he was dead, she was in serious trouble.

Quinn went to the plastic storage bin and took out the clothing that had come from her own world. Disappearing into the bushes, she changed quickly. But she kept the fanny pack. And the gun that Logan had given her.

As she stuffed extra magazines into the bag, she thought about Logan. He had been her friend. And her chest tightened when she considered what he thought of her now. She'd put his family in danger. And probably he was hoping that she would disappear into the portal and never return.

She hadn't exactly promised that. She'd said she would leave Caleb there. But when it came time to bring Zarah home, Quinn would be the one to do it. And, by the grace of the Great Mother, maybe Griffin would come with her.

She slipped the envelope Zarah had given her into the fanny pack as well, then she walked toward where the group was waiting.

Caleb was lying on the ground. While she'd been busy, the men had dressed him in a dark T-shirt and sweatpants. And Ross had taken off his running shoes and socks and put them on Caleb's feet. It wasn't much like clothing from Quinn's universe. But it was certainly better than being naked.

"We could barely carry him," Ross said. "How are you going to get him to help?"

"I can't," she admitted. "I'm going to have to find someone who can come to him."

Ross nodded.

Logan and Rinna were standing a little apart, talking. He looked up when he saw her approaching, then walked forward.

"I'm sorry I was rough on you," he said.

"I know you want to protect your family."

"Caleb died because of one of us. The least we can do is try to help him."

"Thank you."

He scuffed his foot against the ground. "Uh, how much time does he have?"

"I don't know for certain. But the longer he stays like this, the worse it's going to get. He should be treated as soon as possible."

"What do you need from us?"

"Energy."

He laughed. "I'm not sure how to provide it."

"Zarah can gather it from you."

"Okay."

Quinn looked around the group. "I'd better say good-bye now. When the portal is uncovered, I'll have to leave quickly."

"The gods protect you," Rinna said, holding out her arms. Quinn went into them and hugged the other woman tightly. Then she hugged Zarah.

The two male werewolves looked like they weren't sure what to say. But before they could shake Quinn's hand or whatever they were going to do, Caleb woke and began flailing around.

Quinn hurried to his side and knelt. "It's all right. Everything's going to be all right."

"Where am I?"

"In a cave. We're going into my world where we can find someone to help you."

He looked wildly around. "Your world?"

"I told you about it."

Zarah came over with her lamp. Holding it in one hand, she placed the fingers of her other hand on Caleb's forehead, stroking his cool flesh. "Everything's fine," she murmured. "You're going to be all right."

He calmed down, and Quinn let out a small sigh. "Thank you."

"I can't cure him, but I can calm him."

They walked toward the back wall of the cave, where the portal was hidden.

"What do we do?" Ross asked.

"When Quinn and I join hands, send us your thoughts." She gestured toward the back of the cave. "Think about a space opening up where that rock wall is. When it does, you'll see straggly trees and a plain beyond . . . with ruined houses."

She sat down on the ground, Quinn sat beside her, and the others gathered around, watching her hunch over the lamp.

Quinn could feel Zarah sending her consciousness into the flickering flame. Probably, Rinna could, too. She had once opened a portal by herself, using the energy from three other adepts and a squad of soldiers.

When Zarah reached for Quinn, she gripped her friend's

hand tightly and clung. Back in the school for adepts, she had learned to share energy with others, and she was able to give Zarah extra power. Rinna did it easily, too.

The others had never joined together in this way, but she felt them doing their best.

For a long moment, nothing happened, and Quinn felt her throat clog. What if it was too hard to undo what they had done earlier?

But she felt Zarah probing at the rock wall, and felt Rinna pouring energy into the process. And finally she saw a place where the stone thinned.

As it disappeared, she felt her heart clunk inside her chest. She was looking into her world. She had lived there all her life until the past few weeks, and it should be a familiar place, but somehow it felt like a foreign country.

A rustling sound made her turn. Caleb had climbed to his feet. He stood swaying on unsteady legs, then he ran toward the opening between the worlds.

"No. Wait," she called, but he ignored her.

She glanced at the other people. "I have to go after him."

"Should we come?" Logan asked.

"You may not be able to get back," Quinn shouted over her shoulder as she dashed through the portal with no idea what she was going to find on the other side.

Caleb had seemed so weak and helpless. But he was already twenty yards ahead of Quinn by the time she charged through the portal.

Had the door closed behind her? She didn't know, and she kept her gaze fixed on Caleb as he ran across the plain toward a wooded area.

Too bad Ross had put those shoes on his feet. Tender feet might have slowed him down.

As she watched him pull away from her, terror seized her. She could lose him among the ruined buildings. Heedless of her own safety, she pushed herself to run faster, the breath sawing in and out of her lungs as she plunged ahead.

CHAPTER
TWENTY-TWO

THE LAST TIME Quinn had been in her universe, Baron's soldiers had been chasing her.

Had they left a contingent to watch for her and Zarah?

As she tried to catch up with Caleb, she looked to her left and right but didn't see any troops. Of course, soldiers weren't the only threat in the badlands. She was just as likely to run into slavers or thieves, or all manner of lawless men who had taken refuge in the open lands between the cities.

To her vast relief, she saw no one.

Praying that nobody was waiting behind the nearest ruin, she closed in on Caleb, thankful that he was slowing his pace.

He never reached the house. As suddenly as he had made his escape attempt, he stumbled and went down, falling head-long in the dirt.

She rushed to his side, and when she rolled him over, he began flailing at her. The only thing she could do to keep from getting hurt was to back up—or throw herself on top of him. She chose the latter, struggling to press his arms to his sides while ducking away from his head when he tried to bash her with it.

Again, everything suddenly changed. He went limp, and

she was left lying unprotected and exposed in the middle of a dusty plain.

She climbed to her feet, looking in a circle as she brushed herself off. Then she grabbed Caleb under the arms and began to pull him toward the closest building. It was hard going, and she was panting by the time she reached the shadow of the wall. But at least she felt a little safer.

The problem now was what she was going to do with Caleb. She had to leave him to get help. But if she did, he was likely to run off, so that when she came back with a healer or a wagon from Sun Acres, he might be anywhere.

LOGAN walked to the rock wall and peered at the portal. It was still open.

"Shouldn't it be closed?" he asked Zarah.

"Yes. But I'm too worn out to do it now." She turned toward Rinna. "Do you think we can do something?"

"Maybe. But let's wait for a few minutes."

Logan gave Ross a sidewise glance. He could tell his cousin was astonished to be looking into another world.

"I hope they're going to be all right," Ross said.

"Yes," Zarah agreed. She sounded exhausted.

Ross got bottles of water from his pack, and they all took a drink. The two male wolves went to scout the area while the women rested.

When they came back, Zarah and Rinna were huddled together over the lamp. Logan could see the wall shimmering in back of them. After a time, it seemed to turn solid, unless you tipped your head to the side.

"That's the best I can do," Zarah said apologetically.

"It's good," Logan said. "But maybe we should keep a guard up here—in case we get unwanted company."

"Not a bad idea," Rinna agreed.

"And we should block the opening of the cave with brush, so no one stumbles in from this side," Logan said.

"Yes."

When Zarah started to get up, Logan shook his head. "You stay here. We'll bring branches."

"I'm not an invalid."

"And I'm not your husband. But he would tell you to wait here."

"Yes."

"You get brush and vines," Logan directed Rinna. "Ross and I will get larger branches."

They all scattered into the woods and came back a few minutes later.

Logan, the landscape architect, set branches upright in front of the portal. Then they piled on brush. When they were finished, the opening was hidden.

They started back down the hill toward the place where they'd left their car.

But the werewolves' senses were sharp. They'd gone less than fifty yards when Rinna stopped short.

"I hear something," she whispered.

The two men nodded.

"Take Zarah back to the cave," Ross said.

"What's happening?" the pregnant woman asked.

"We're going to find out." Logan was already pulling off his shirt. He stepped behind a tree to finish undressing, and his cousin did the same.

As Logan climbed out of his pants, he thought of Caleb. Changing to wolf form was so much a part of who Logan was. What the hell would he do if he suddenly couldn't do it?

He grimaced as he imagined Caleb's mental anguish. He'd been angry at the guy, but at this moment, he felt sorry for him.

He closed his eyes, then began the chant that would transform him from wolf to man. The change always hurt, but today he welcomed the pain. It was a lot better than the alternative.

Two gray wolves started down the hill. It was too bad they couldn't speak to each other. But that was one of the inconveniences of being in animal form.

By mutual agreement, they slipped from tree trunk to tree trunk. When they caught sight of two men walking through the underbrush, they both stopped short.

One was large and balding. The other was smaller and more slender, with a nose that had been broken.

Logan had never seen them before, but they matched Quinn's description of the men who had buried the body. Both of them were holding guns as they walked slowly through the woods.

What did they expect? To find Caleb lying on the ground somewhere?

And what if they walked into the cave where Rinna and Zarah were hiding?

Logan's jaw clenched. He'd left his life mate exposed. He slipped over to Ross, giving his head a shake, pointing in the direction of the cave.

Ross nodded, then inclined his own head toward the SUV pulled up along the road.

Logan was pretty sure what Ross had in mind. He wanted to read the license plate before going back to the cave. He didn't like it. But he understood the reasoning.

They separated, Ross heading downhill and Logan making a circle around the men, before racing to the cave.

When he arrived, he saw the situation wasn't what he had expected. He couldn't see Zarah, and he had to assume she was inside.

His gaze went from the partially blocked entrance to the white wolf who stood guard. Her eyes were fierce and her front paws were planted firmly on the ground.

It was Rinna.

He put back his ears and growled at her. The wolf language was plain. But he wished he could tell her in words to get into the cave where she was out of sight. She growled back and stood her ground, and he knew that the woman he'd married hadn't changed all that much. She was going to do what she wanted. Sometimes that meshed with what *he* wanted. Sometimes not.

QUINN bent over Caleb, wishing she had brought more supplies with her into her own world. But she had dashed off in hot pursuit.

In the cave, Caleb had proved he was capable of escape—with no idea where he was going.

Seeing no alternative, she pulled the shirt over his head, cut it into strips with her knife and used the strips of cloth to bind his hands and feet. She hated leaving him that way—because if an enemy came along, he was helpless. But coming back and finding him missing would be a disaster.

After tying him up, she brought dry leaves to cover him, wishing she had a better alternative. Kneeling beside him, she kissed him on the cheek before saying, "Caleb, if you can hear me, try to stay calm. I'm sorry I had to tie you up. But I'll be back as soon as I can."

He didn't wake, and she knew she had to hurry. With one last look at him, she left the shelter of the woods and started toward Sun Acres.

She had come here with the vague idea of getting help, but as she hurried toward the city, she began to firm her plans. She knew of an old woman named Pamina who had been summoned to Griffin's house for deep healing sessions. That was the logical person to ask. She would explain the problem to her. And if Pamina couldn't help, hopefully she would know someone who could.

Quinn ran as far as she could. When the stitch in her side became too bad, she slowed to a fast walk, praying that she didn't encounter any slavers—or Baron's soldiers.

When she finally saw the city walls, she breathed out a small sigh. She had made it this far. But she had no idea what she was going to find beyond the wall. She'd kept telling Zarah that Griffin was all right. But he could be dead. And if so, then she was heading for disaster.

Shading her eyes, she studied the scene before her. It seemed peaceful enough, but that could be an illusion.

Last time she'd been here, soldiers disguised as thugs had stopped her. But she'd been able to show them who she was. This time, because she hadn't been summoned home, she didn't have her talisman. Worse, Griffin wasn't expecting her.

Could she get a message to Draden? Focusing on the link between them, she sent out a message, unable to tell if it had gotten through.

Feeling the hairs on the back of her neck prickle, she crossed the remaining distance to the gate. One lone woman.

Teeth clenched, she fought the impulse to call out and say she was coming to see Griffin. It made sense that he had someone out here—like last time. But if he wasn't in control of the city, using his name would be the worst thing she could do.

She was about eighty yards away when four men armed with swords and knives leaped out at her from a hidden hole in the ground. As they surrounded her, she saw that their hair was dusty and matted. Their clothing was rough. And none of them had shaved in days. They looked like outlaws from the badlands. But they could be soldiers—stationed in a different location from last time. Griffin's men. Or Baron's.

Unwilling to take a chance, she went for the gun in her fanny pack, but two of the men closed in on her, grabbing her arms and holding her immobile.

Another ruffian stepped forward. "Who are you?"

She raised her chin. "Who are you?"

"I'll ask the questions."

She had no choice now. She had to answer. Her heart was pounding, but she kept her voice steady. "Quinn. From Griffin's house. I have urgent business with him. He's expecting me, and he'll punish you if he learns something's happened to me."

"He didn't tell us to expect anyone. What are you doing out here?"

So they were his men. Or maybe not.

"I was on a mission for him. If you ask him, he'll vouch for me."

"You say you work for him. Who runs his household?"

"Philip."

"And who is in charge of the female slaves?"

"Branda."

The man looked at her with narrowed eyes. Intelligent eyes. He was dressed rough, but that appeared to be part of a pose. "You know some facts, but maybe somebody gave you the information so you can get close to him."

Quinn swallowed. "You're his soldiers? Keeping guard out here?"

"Like I have to tell you anything," the man snapped.

"I know you have to be cautious. I know about Griffin's household because I live there. I came back to give him information about his wife. Let me show you. I have something in my pack for him."

The man reached toward the pack and eyed the zipper, then stopped his hand. "How does it open?"

"I'll show you." Careful to move slowly, she pulled the zipper tab and opened the fanny pack.

The soldier reached inside, felt around, and closed his hand around the gun. Pulling it out, he turned it first one way and then the other.

Quinn winced. "Be careful with that."

"What is it?"

"A powerful weapon."

He smoothed his thumb along the barrel. "It's good quality metal."

Casually, he pointed it at her and she flinched back.

"So it is dangerous," he murmured.

"Yes. That can kill," she said, her voice deathly calm. "Point it at the ground."

"How does it work?"

"It has projectiles inside. They come out the front when you pull the trigger."

"This?" He looked at the pistol, slipping his finger inside the guard. It was a Glock, and there was no other safety catch.

"Watch out."

Ignoring the warning, he held the gun away from him and squeezed the trigger.

CHAPTER
TWENTY-THREE

THE BULLET HIT the stone wall of the city, making a twanging sound.

All the men around them clapped their hands to their ears, and one threw himself to the ground. From the walkway along the top of the wall, more guards watched in alarm, some notching arrows into bows.

One of the men next to Quinn screamed and rubbed his arm.

The soldier who had fired looked stunned. "What happened?"

"You shot off the gun. The bullet hit the wall, and a shell casing—the part that's ejected when you fire—hit your friend. But it's no worse than a bee sting. Lucky for you the bullet didn't kill someone."

The man held the gun away from him as though he had grabbed a poisonous snake and didn't know how to kill it.

"Get up," he growled to the man on the ground.

The soldier scrambled to his feet.

"Slip your finger out of the trigger guard so you won't fire accidentally," Quinn said.

He did as she asked, still looking shell-shocked.

"Give it back."

He balked at that. "So you can kill me with it?"

"I won't do that."

He kept the gun, holding it by the butt. "Where did you get this thing?"

"It's from the old times," she answered, her ears still ringing from the shot at close range.

"It doesn't look old."

"It's cleaned up. Griffin gave it to me—for protection," she added, lying through her teeth.

"I've heard of these. I've never seen one."

"Keep the gun for now," she said in a calm voice. "But let me prove I'm Griffin's friend."

When she reached toward the fanny pack, he pointed the weapon at her, and she flinched.

"What else in Carfolian Hell do you have in there?"

"Pictures. Let me show you. I can prove I've been with Griffin's wife."

Still holding the gun, he reached into the pack and pulled out the envelope of photos.

"I hope for your sake, this isn't another trick."

"The gun wasn't a trick! I told you it was dangerous."

A scream from the gravesite made the hairs on Logan's back bristle. When he whirled to look behind him, he saw nothing. Knowing that if he ran to help Ross, Rinna would follow him, he growled at her again. Seeing his dilemma, Zarah came forward, knelt down awkwardly and put her arm around the white wolf.

Rinna looked at her. She whined softly, but she lay down. Logan breathed out a sigh before turning and dashing down the hill.

He arrived on the scene in time to see Ross in hot pursuit of the men. But he was too far behind them to catch up, and they made it into their SUV. Then the engine roared, and the car shot out of the woods. Ross ran after it, snapping and snarling.

He couldn't catch them, but he'd obviously scared the shit out of them.

Both wolves waited to make sure the car wasn't coming back, then they turned and trotted back up the hill.

When they reached the cave, Rinna was still in wolf form guarding the entrance.

"What happened?" Zarah asked.

Logan lifted his head and nodded slowly. Then he and Ross returned to the trees where they'd left their clothing. When they came back again, Rinna had also changed to human form and pulled on her T-shirt and pants.

"Do you have to put yourself in danger?" Logan asked her.

"Do you?" she challenged.

"Yeah."

"Well, I had to defend Zarah."

Zarah cleared her throat, getting his attention—and Rinna's. "I could have stopped them with the lamp."

"Maybe you couldn't have stopped a bullet."

She winced, then asked, "Who were they?"

"I'm pretty sure they were the men who buried the body in the woods." Ross pointed down the hill. "They're gone, but I got their license number."

"Good going," Logan said.

"You scared them away?" Zarah asked.

Ross grinned. "Yeah. They weren't expecting to find a big bad wolf in the woods."

Rinna looked toward the road. "Did they see our car?"

"I don't think so. We were parked on the other side of the hill," Logan answered. "And they didn't get very far from their SUV."

"Thank the Great Mother," Rinna breathed.

"But we should go," Logan said.

"And I want to check the plate," Ross said.

As they made their way down the hill, Rinna looked back toward the cave. "I hope Quinn's all right."

"And Caleb," Zarah added.

They were all silent as they walked on.

Finally, Rinna said, "I can't imagine what it would be like—not being able to be a wolf."

Logan heard the tremor in her voice and slipped his arm

around her shoulder, holding her against his side. "Did you think of that when you changed?"

"Yes."

"So did I," Logan answered, his voice gritty.

"Yeah," Ross agreed. "He's got a hell of a life ahead of him."

"If he survives," Zarah murmured.

"You think he'll live?" Rinna asked.

"I wish I knew," Zarah answered. "He was very sick. And we don't know the conditions . . . in my world."

"Griffin is fine!" Rinna said.

"I want to believe that. I hope Quinn can bring me some news."

THE guard held up the envelope. "Open it."

Careful not to make any sudden moves, she pulled out the photos. Shuffling through the contents, she held up one to the man.

He gasped as he looked at her and Zarah standing together. Logan had taken it the day after they'd arrived. Probably he'd been having fun, showing Zarah the wonders of his world. Now it was coming in very handy.

"How did you get that?" the leader of the men demanded.

"It's a special process."

One of the men backed away from her. Several pointed at the photograph.

"I can show you how it works," Quinn said. "Can I reach inside my bag again?"

"Yes."

She brought out a small digital camera.

"Another weapon?" the leader of the group demanded.

"No. It's called a camera. I am an adept. I operate it with my brain waves," she lied because she knew they wouldn't believe her if she told them it had a computer chip inside.

She held it up toward the leader.

"Stop." He pointed to one of his men. "Do it to him."

"Okay."

She captured the soldier in the image rectangle and pushed

down on the shutter, then changed to viewing mode and turned the camera around so he could see the picture. "I can show you the image in here. But I do not have the equipment to make a copy on paper," she said.

The man drew in a quick breath. "That's me."

"Yes."

The leader craned his neck to see, and she turned the image toward him. He looked sorry that he hadn't been the one to have his picture shot.

Conscious of time ticking by, Quinn said, "Take me to Griffin. He will want to see the photographs of his wife."

BACK at Logan's house, Ross asked, "Can I use your computer to check that license plate?"

"Of course."

They all filed into Logan's office. Ross sat down, and Logan pulled up a chair for Zarah. She was fascinated with the computer, and Rinna was teaching her how to use the Web.

Ross called up a Web page and put in a password. "Don't tell anyone about this," he muttered. "It's illegal."

"Let's hope it works," Logan said.

Ross entered the number into the database of the Motor Vehicles Administration. But he came up with *nothing*.

"Shit!" He looked back at the women. "Sorry."

"We're used to it," Rinna said. "What's wrong?"

"It's not a valid plate."

Logan repeated the curse. "What does that mean?"

"That they altered it. You can do it with black electrical tape. Like you can turn an *F* or an *L* into an *E*."

"But there aren't a million combinations of the right letters," Logan asked.

"There are enough."

He wrote down the number. "It has an *E*. I guess I'll start looking at plates with *F*'s and *L*'s. But it may take some time."

"Do you want to talk to your friend, the cop from Montgomery County. What's his name?"

"Jack Thornton. Yeah, he'll be interested in a man buried

alive in the woods. But I think we need to find out who these guys are before we call in the cops."

QUINN held her breath. But the camera and the gun had turned the tide. The men looked at her with respect. They had treated her like a captive. Now they formed an honor guard around her as they escorted her to the gate. She had won a victory, but she might have lost the war. Caleb was still back there in the woods, and she still hadn't gotten him the help he needed.

Worse, she still didn't know if Griffin was all right. These men were acting as though it was true. But they could be putting on a show. Or they might not have the latest information.

She wanted to ask if there was someone who could receive messages among the group. But she decided it would be better simply to act confident.

"Give me the weapon back," she said.

"You must not use it inside the city."

"I won't—unless someone attacks me."

He returned the gun, and she put it back into her fanny pack, along with the camera. Then she let the soldiers escort her inside the city. It would be a half-hour walk from the gate to Griffin's house, and she looked over her shoulder, thinking about Caleb out in the badlands. Once again, military horses were waiting in a nearby stabling area.

Two of the men accompanied her as she headed for Griffin's house, still praying that she was going to find him there.

More guards were stationed at the gates that enclosed his courtyard. And more were inside, looking over the wall. The man at the gate let her and the soldiers through. Inside she dismounted and waited with her heart pounding while a messenger went into the house.

Draden came out.

"Did you get a message from me?" she asked.

"Yes. But it was faint. I thought you were still on the other side of the portal."

"No."

"You've worried Griffin. I'd better take you to him." The adept led the way to Griffin's office.

When she saw the expression on Griffin's face, she felt her throat clog.

"Come inside and close the door," he ordered. When she turned back to him, his expression was thunderous.

"You're supposed to be taking care of my wife! What are you doing back here? Is there some problem?"

"Zarah is fine. She's with Logan and Rinna. They're all fine."

"Then what are you doing here?"

"It's complicated."

"Spit it out!"

"First, I have some pictures and a letter for you—from Zarah." She reached into her pack and brought out the packet that her friend had given her.

Griffin's breath caught when he saw the photos of his wife. "This is from that camera thing?"

"Yes."

"She's well," he whispered.

"Yes."

He shuffled one more picture to the front and stared at it. "What is this?"

"In Logan's world, they can do something called a sonogram. It gives a picture of the baby—inside his mother's womb. That's a picture of your son."

He stared down at the black-and-white image. "My son! Is that possible? A picture?"

"Yes." She pointed to the fetus. "You can see his head, and his arms—and his . . . uh . . . male part."

Griffin made a strangled sound. "This picture blesses me."

"And Zarah will be blessed as well when she finds out that you are safe and sound here. When we went through the portal, you were leading Baron's soldiers away from us. We didn't know what had happened to you. She was very worried."

"I led them into a rock outcropping—and attacked them as a wolf."

"Thank the Great Mother." She looked out the window at

the guards in the courtyard. "Things are no better here than when I left, are they?"

"They're a little better. I was able to kill Baron before he killed me."

She winced.

"Assassination is a crude political tool. But he was the one who tried it first. In this case, it's no loss. Some of his followers are still making trouble. But I expect to end the mess soon."

He tipped his head to the side. "Zarah sent you back?"

She took her lower lip between her teeth. "She wanted to know you were all right, but I came here with my own problem. Something impossible to fix in Logan's world."

He was watching her closely. "Something that requires psychic ability?"

"Yes." She took a gulp of air, then began speaking rapidly, telling him about Caleb Marshall's ghost.

When she finished, he looked at her differently. "You want to save him."

"His soul will be nowhere if this body dies."

Griffin pressed his fist against his chin. "But a werewolf who cannot change may not want to live."

She swallowed hard. "I hope I can convince him that life can still be good."

Griffin nodded. "I will send a cart. And guards. And I will send for the woman, Pamina, who has healed some of my people."

"Thank you."

"She taught us some things. But I think she keeps many of her techniques secret."

"I understand."

"You might not like her method."

"I don't think I have a choice. And thank you so much," she whispered.

"Thank you for the pictures of my wife and my son," he answered.

"I'm glad I could bring them."

When she raised her gaze to his face, she saw his eyes

were moist. Looking away, she said, "I left Caleb tied up. Hours ago. I must go back and get him."

"I don't want to send my men out into the badlands until you speak to the healer and tell her the problem. We need to know if she thinks she can help your friend."

Quinn nodded, though she wanted to order men and a wagon outside right away.

Griffin called in the captain of the guards and made the arrangement. Quinn started to pace back and forth while she waited. But Griffin had a tray of food sent in.

"Sit down. Eat. Rest. You already walked here from the portal. You have a long trip there and back again."

"I wish I could take the healer there."

"Too dangerous. She's old, and if she were attacked, she might be killed."

"I'm sorry. I'm being selfish."

She sat down at the table and ate a few bites, but the food tasted like dust in her mouth, and she had trouble swallowing. She couldn't help wishing that they had a motorcar. Then the trip would be a million times faster. But that wasn't an option back in this universe.

She was pushing food around on her plate when the door opened and a slim woman with long dark hair walked in. Griffin was behind her.

"Quinn, this is Pamina. She's the healer I told you about."

Quinn stared at the woman's smooth face and dark hair. "But you don't look old," she blurted, then felt herself blush. "I'm sorry. I mean, I was expecting an old woman." She feared the explanation didn't help.

Pamina gave a laugh that sounded like the tinkle of small bells. "I *am* old. But I use my talents on myself."

"Thank you for coming so fast. But we can't get Caleb back here for several hours."

"Tell me what happened to him."

As Quinn gave a quick account of the problem, she felt the woman's assessing gaze on her.

"The body is rejecting his soul?"

"Yes," Quinn breathed, glad that the woman grasped the problem so well.

"I do not know if I can cure him. But if the treatment is to be successful, I will need your help," Pamina said.

"I'll do anything!"

"A quick answer. But you may not like what I ask of you."

Quinn gulped. "Whatever it is, I'm willing to do it."

"We will see."

Quinn couldn't keep a shiver from traveling over her skin. What was this woman going to make her do? *Tell me now,* she silently screamed. But she knew this was not the time to press for answers.

Pamina reached inside the leather bag she was carrying and sorted through several dozen small cloth packets. She pulled out one and handed it to Quinn. "Mix this in water and have him drink it. It should help stabilize him—until the two of us can work on him."

"Thank you so much!" Quinn sniffed the small packet. It smelled pungent but not unpleasant.

"A special herb blend that I make," Pamina said.

She thanked the woman again and tucked the mixture into the fanny pack. Griffin handed her a military canteen with a strap and a leather cup attached, which she slung over her shoulder.

"Can one of your men ride ahead of the wagon with me?"

"How will they find you?"

"Do they know the approximate location of the portal?"

Griffin stroked his chin. "That is a secret."

"Oh."

"But I can give them some landmarks along the way and near the portal."

"Thank you. When we find Caleb, I'll send my escort back to tell the driver of the wagon."

"All right," Griffin agreed. "Steph can go with you. He's a good man."

Steph turned out to be the leader of the group that had ambushed her outside the city walls. They left at once. After the wagon trundled out of the gate, she made sure the driver knew which direction to go in. Then she and Steph rode off toward the portal. It was a faster journey than the one she had completed earlier. But her heart was pounding as they approached the area. She wanted to call out to Caleb, but she knew that was dangerous. So she kept silent as she dismounted and led her horse into a small stand of stunted trees. The shadows had lengthened, and she hurried toward the half-standing house where she had left Caleb. At first she thought she had made a mistake. Then she found the makeshift ropes she had used to tie him up. They were lying on the ground.

CHAPTER
TWENTY-FOUR

"HE WAS RIGHT there," Quinn said, pointing to the spot that was now empty of anything but the dry leaves she'd piled there. "I tied him up, but he got free and wandered off."

"Or somebody cut him loose. Slavers, maybe," Steph said helpfully.

She struggled to damp down the sick feeling rising in her throat. "We have to look for him."

Steph glanced around. "We should split up. But be careful that nobody scoops you up."

"I will. And watch out. In his current state, Caleb's dangerous."

Steph snorted, and started off to the left. He had gone only a few yards when a figure leaped out from behind a wall and landed on the soldier's back.

It was Caleb, and he wrapped his arm around Steph's neck in a choke hold.

Quinn ran toward them.

"Caleb, no!"

He grunted and brought Steph to his knees.

She whacked him across the shoulder. "Get off. You're going to kill him."

"No. I'm here to help you," he panted. "The colonel's going to kill you."

She didn't have time to figure out what that meant, she only knew she had to save Steph's life.

She grabbed Caleb by the hair and gave a mighty yank. He cried out and whirled toward her.

Steph reared up.

"Don't hurt him," Quinn screamed.

But the soldier had already brought his fist down on the back of Caleb's head. He went limp.

"Great Mother, no!" Quinn cried as she ran to Caleb. He was breathing, but his face had turned pale. "You hurt him!"

"He was going to kill me."

"Yes. I'm sorry, but he doesn't know what he's doing."

Steph ran back to his horse, opened his saddlebag and returned with a shirt and rope. First they put the shirt on Caleb. Then Steph tied him up again. This time, Quinn was sure he wasn't going to get away.

"You stay with him. I'll go back for the wagon."

"Yes. Thanks."

She sat down, propped her back against the wall, and gathered Caleb to her so that his head rested in her lap.

Tenderly, she stroked his face.

"Caleb. It's me. It's Quinn. You're going to be all right."

She kept her gaze on him. "Wake up. Tell me you recognize me. Caleb, I love you," she whispered.

He didn't speak, and she fought back tears. But at least there was something she could do for him. With blurred vision, she pulled the canteen strap off her shoulder, then poured some of the herb packet into the cup. After adding water, she used her finger to stir the mixture, then sniffed. It didn't smell too bad. And maybe Caleb wouldn't care, anyway.

She eased him up a little. "Can you drink this?"

Once again, he didn't answer, but when she held the cup to his lips, he swallowed a little.

"That's good. Drink a little more. We're going to cure you." Or she hoped so. She still didn't know what Pamina would ask of her. But she would do it! She had to.

Her total focus was on Caleb. She was laboriously giving him the herb-laced water when she heard a noise in the underbrush and looked around. The wagon couldn't be here this quickly. Could it?

Two men in rough tunics stepped out of the shadows, one coming from the left and one from the right. With her back against the wall, that left no escape route.

"We'd better get you out of here," the taller one said, "before that other guy comes back. That horse will come in handy, too."

She looked at them warily. Both had long straggly hair and a month's growth of beard. Neither was the kind of man she'd want to meet out here in the badlands.

"Who are you?"

The man who had spoken laughed. "A friend."

"Oh, sure."

He gave her an assessing look. "You're in good shape. I'd say you haven't missed many meals. You'll fetch a good price. But we'll leave the man here. He's too sick to be worth anything."

Quinn set the cup down. Her hand dropped to the fanny pack hidden by Caleb's shoulders. Quietly pulling back the zipper, she eased the gun out, thankful that Steph had given it back to her. Odds were, these men had never seen a gun.

"Best get away from me," she said. "Before you get hurt."

"You can't take the two of us."

"No more warnings." She raised the pistol, and aimed for the speaker's chest, then fired.

He looked astonished as he went down.

Caleb's eyes blinked open, and a look of horror crossed his features as he struggled to sit up, the ropes preventing him from using his hands.

"Jesus! We're under attack."

When he got in her line of fire, Quinn tried to push him aside. "Caleb, down," she cried.

He lunged toward the weapon, and she was forced to smack his hand away.

The other man saw her problem. With a snarl, he leaped toward her.

Quinn's only choice was to rear up so she could raise her arm over Caleb and fire.

But the position was so awkward that the first shot went wild. And the slaver was almost on top of her when she pulled the trigger again and hit him in the shoulder. He screamed, his face a mask of fury as he reached for her throat with both hands. And now Caleb was in the way of her getting off another shot.

Still encumbered, she tried to shove the attacker away, just as a horse galloped toward the house.

She cringed back, but it was Steph. He slid out of the saddle and ran toward her, a knife in his hand. With a quick jab, he stabbed the slaver in the back, then pulled him off Quinn and threw him to the side.

Caleb had quieted again.

Quinn watched Steph walk to the first man she had shot and inspect the wound.

"Carfolian Hell," he muttered. "You used that weapon on him?"

"Yes."

"It is powerful."

"I told you it was lucky you didn't hit anyone. And it's lucky for me you returned it."

He laughed. "Yeah. I came back when I heard the explosion."

"It's a good thing you did."

She leaned back against the wall, tempted to close her eyes.

"I should stay and guard you."

"You have to tell the wagon where we are."

His expression darkened. "Yes. But I hate to leave you again. It's dangerous out here."

"Do it! The sooner you go, the faster you'll get back here. I'll lay Caleb on the ground and keep the gun in my hand."

Steph looked unhappy, but really, there was no alternative. He dragged first one man then the other away to the far side of the wall where Quinn couldn't see them. Then he helped her put a heavy shirt on Caleb to keep him warm.

"I'd better hurry. This isn't a good place to be after dark."

Quinn looked up at the sky, seeing she didn't have many hours of daylight left.

"I'll be all right," she answered, hoping it was true. She looked down at the spilled water. Caleb hadn't gotten much of it before the men had come out of the woods. Could she give him more?

She mixed more of the herbs into the water. But this time when she tried to get him to drink, he wouldn't cooperate.

Mother, was he getting sicker?

Exhausted and frustrated, she closed her eyes, then snapped them open again when she realized that dropping her guard was dangerous.

So she leaned back against the wall, resting and praying that the wagon would arrive soon.

Luckily, it had traveled faster than she'd expected, and the sun was still a yellow ball in the western sky when the soldiers loaded Caleb into the wagon.

She sat in the back with him, trying and failing to get him to drink any of the medicine.

By the time they arrived at Griffin's house, Caleb was pale as death, and she wondered how long he could hang on.

Griffin greeted them, then directed the soldiers to carry Caleb inside to the ground floor of the family quarters—to a small, candlelit room where Pamina was waiting. After they'd laid Caleb on a comfortable bed in the center of the room, Griffin said, "I'll leave you alone."

The way he said it made her wonder what Pamina had told him.

"Yes. Thank you for doing this."

"Close the door," the older woman said.

Quinn did as she was told. When she turned back, Pamina was beside Caleb, one hand on his chest and one on his forehead. Her eyes were closed, but she asked, "Did he drink any of the herbs?"

"Only a little."

"Then we must hurry."

Quinn's stomach clenched. "What are you going to do?"

"You'll see in a moment." The old woman stepped away, and Quinn saw she had brought a piece of equipment with her. It was a wooden box with a crank on the side and a long funnel-like tube sticking up at one end. The box was decorated with faded gold scrollwork.

She reached into her bag and took out what looked like a can of food from Logan's world. But it wasn't metal, and when she opened it, she took out a cylinder, which she fitted into a slot in the machine.

"This machine was invented by a man named Thomas Edison," she murmured.

"A record player? I've heard of it." In fact, Logan had told her about Thomas Edison, and she realized he must have existed in both universes before her world had changed.

"This uses a wax cylinder."

She turned a crank on the machine, and low, haunting music filled the room.

"What does that do?" Quinn whispered.

"Gives him auditory stimulation. He needs as much stimulation as possible. Incentive to come back to this body."

"What else?"

"Physical sensations. And enticements. We must lure him with the things we know he wanted. Things he cannot have unless he returns to this body."

"He wanted revenge," Quinn said.

"That may not be his strongest need. Each case is different. If he were a child, I would make him want to nurse again at his mother's breast. That is a primal need for the young. But he is not a child. We must use other channels. What does he like to eat?"

"Meat, and bread with jam," she answered, wishing they had shared more than one meal so she could give a better answer.

Pamina went to the door and called for a servant. In less than two minutes, she had bread and jam sitting on a small table and a piece of meat roasting on the fire. The aroma filled the little room.

Turning back to Quinn, she said, "Smear some jam on his lips so he can taste it."

She did, smelling the aroma of strawberries. When he licked his lip, she felt a little spurt of hope.

"Help me undress him. His shirt first."

Quinn unbuttoned the shirt Steph had given her. Standing on either side of the bed, she and Pamina pulled Caleb's arms out of his sleeves, then she lifted him up a little so the other woman could slip the shirt over his head. When they had laid his head back on the pillow, they worked on his sweatpants.

His body lay absolutely still—pale and naked on the bed.

Pamina brought a basin and a sponge. "Wash him," she said. "So he can feel that sensation."

Quinn dipped the sponge into the water and washed the front of him. As she did, the other woman unfolded a fan, waving it over his damp body, making him shiver.

"The body is responding," she murmured.

"Yes. But is that enough?"

"Not nearly enough. Dry him off."

Pamina's gaze was like the blade of a sword as she peered at Quinn over the naked man who lay between them. "Something you neglected to tell me in your account. Did you make love with him?" she asked.

Quinn flushed. "Yes."

"Very good. Then you have a connection to his body. That will help bring him back. If he wants to come back."

"What if he doesn't?"

"You must use your wiles. You must pull him back to this world." She took the top off a small jar and handed it to Quinn. "Rub this on him."

Quinn looked inside and sniffed at the top of the jar. The container held an orange-colored salve with a pungent odor that made her cough.

"What is it?"

"An irritant."

"Oh."

"Use your fingers. Start with his face, then work your way downward."

She dipped her fingers in. The stuff made her skin tingle and she wanted to wipe it off. Instead she began to rub the salve on his face, then down his body, across his chest.

He coughed and turned his head away.

"He doesn't like it."

"But he feels it and he smells it and it brings him back to this reality."

She moved to his belly, then did his thighs, his legs, and his feet.

"You skipped something," the old woman said. "Put it on his penis, too."

"But . . ."

"Do it."

Keeping her head bent so Pamina couldn't see her face, she did as she was told. When she started to pull away, her guide said, "Circle his cock with your fist. Hold him there."

Quinn's hand jumped. "Why?"

"I think you can guess. But you don't want to say it. We're hoping that he wants to come back and make love with you. But you must remind him of how it was between you. Was it good?"

"Yes," Quinn choked out.

"Then connect with him that way again."

Quinn made a small sound in her throat as she took his penis in her fist. Holding on to him. Despite the strange circumstances, she felt a tug of sexual arousal, and she hoped Pamina couldn't tell. Or maybe that was part of the process, her own arousal fueling Caleb's, but she didn't want to ask.

The healer bent over him.

"Who are you?"

His lips moved and he spoke for the first time in hours. "Caleb Marshall."

"Caleb!" Quinn cried.

His body jerked. "No—Wyatt Reynolds."

Quinn shook her head. "Is that the other man, the one who owned the body?"

"He is dead. They killed him. The bastards," he spat out.

"But you have some of his memories inside your head?" Pamina asked.

His shoulders rose off the bed. Pamina pushed him back, and Quinn started to take her hand away.

"Stay as you are," the healer ordered. Maybe she was giving the order to both of them.

Caleb was speaking again. "I was spying . . . have to . . . to stop them . . ."

"From what?"

"An attack . . ." His voice trailed off.

"An attack on what?" Quinn gasped out.

"Shush!" the old woman ordered. "That's not important now."

Quinn snapped her mouth shut.

Pamina leaned toward him. "You made love with Quinn. You feel her hand on you now. Do you want to come back and make love with her now?"

"God, yes."

"Caress him," Pamina ordered.

Never in a million years could Quinn have imagined this scene. Doing this in front of another person. And if she hadn't wanted Caleb back so badly she would have leaped up and run out of the room. But she wanted him—heart, soul, and body. So she fought off her embarrassment and did as the woman told her, stroking Caleb, feeling him harden in her hand. And when she looked down, the sight of him made her breath catch. His penis had grown as hard and stiff as a tree limb.

He was aroused. She was making him feel the connection to her. Making him want her. Making him come back to her—she hoped.

"Return to this body, and you can make love with Quinn again," the old woman said, her words staccato bursts.

He made a gasping sound. "I want to."

"You have to bridge the gap."

"But I am . . . damaged. . . . I cannot change to wolf form . . . what good am I?" he said in a broken voice.

Quinn's heart squeezed.

"I am less . . ." Caleb turned his face away from Pamina.

"No. Do not think that way. Think of Quinn. Your body making sweet love with hers."

"My love. My life mate." He moaned.

"Yes!" Quinn gasped. "I am your mate—for life."

"It's not enough," he answered.

Quinn heard a sob rise in her throat.

"Be strong," the old woman ordered, then switched tactics,

going back to something else Caleb clearly wanted. "Then think of the men who killed Wyatt Reynolds. You want revenge on them."

"I want revenge on Aden Marshall."

"No!" Quinn breathed. "He's dead. Long ago."

Pamina gave her a warning look, and Quinn closed her mouth again.

"You want revenge on those men," the old woman said. "The ones who buried you alive. That was a horrible thing to do. Who were they?"

"Colonel Bowie's men."

"Colonel Bowie?" Quinn asked.

Caleb's eyes were closed. "I have to report what they're doing. They're going to attack . . ." His voice trailed off.

"Then you have to let Caleb Marshall do it," Pamina whispered. "He is the only one who can. But first you want to make love with Quinn. You want that so much."

"Yes." His face contorted and he went back to his self-destructive theme. "If she still wants the thing I've turned into."

"Not a thing. A man!" she shouted. "My man. My mate."

He made a snorting sound.

"Of course I want you!"

"Let him feel you."

Quinn caressed him, sensing that they had almost won. She had connected with him physically. And the healer had used his desire for revenge to strengthen his need to return to this body.

"You can have Quinn. You want her. Your body and your soul tingle with wanting. Every nerve ending is screaming for her. And after you make love, you can attack those men."

"Yes."

Quinn's eyes brimmed with unshed tears. He wanted her. And she wanted him to come back to her. So much.

It looked like he was almost there. They trembled on the brink of something magical. Then in the next breath, he dashed her hopes as he came back to his own despair.

"But she won't want me like this. Who would want this pitiful excuse for a werewolf?"

CHAPTER
TWENTY-FIVE

QUINN LEANED OVER Caleb. "You're wrong. I want you. More than anything I've ever wanted in my life. Not just the sex. That was so good. But I want you for my life mate. I want to live our lives together. I will be like a walking dead woman if you don't come back to me."

When he tried to speak, she hurried on. "I've gone through Carfolian Hell to save you. I crossed the badlands alone. I was stopped by soldiers who thought I was trying to invade the city."

She gulped in air. "Slavers almost picked me up, and I had to shoot them. Please—don't make it all for nothing. Don't turn away from me now. Please."

He made a moaning sound, his head swinging back and forth on the bed as though he were trying to escape from some awful nightmare.

"He's almost here. Don't let him draw back. Make him feel you. Make him want you. Tell him how much you want him in this body."

"Caleb, please. Come back to me. I want you the way you are. I want to make love with you. I want to live with you and grow old with you. Don't take that away from me."

"No."

Somewhere in this strange encounter, Quinn had passed beyond embarrassment to desperation. She turned Caleb loose so she could rear up and pull her shirt over her head. When she was naked from the waist up, she slid onto the bed, her legs wedged against his as she rubbed her breasts against his chest, the salve she had spread over him prickling against her own skin, making her nipples tighten and throb.

Caleb cried out and his eyes blinked open.

"Quinn!"

"Yes. Make love with me."

She took him in her hand again, sliding her fist up and down, feeling him harden even more. And she felt the power of their connection like a psychic spark jumping back and forth between them.

"You're very close. But you must finish it—to anchor him here," Pamina said.

The woman drew back, and the music stopped. Then, to Quinn's profound relief, she heard the door open. A shaft of light knifed in. And then the door closed, leaving only two people in the room. Her and Caleb. Thank the Great Mother.

Her own need made Quinn clumsy as she wiggled out of her pants and kicked them off the bed, then clasped Caleb's shoulders, pressing her body against the length of his.

The salve that transferred itself from his skin to hers made her nerve endings jump as arousal coursed through her blood.

She slid herself against him, rocking him in her arms. And when his arm tightened around her, she moaned.

His eyes blinked open again, and he stared at her in puzzlement. "Quinn? Where did you come from?"

"I've been here all the time. Except when I had to leave you in the badlands."

"I don't remember."

"It doesn't matter."

Lowering her mouth to his, she devoured him, drinking his essence and the taste of him as she slid her hands over his slick body.

When she finally raised her head, they both gasped for breath.

"Quinn! God, you've made me so hot."

"Thank the Great Mother."

"I've got to have you."

"Yes!"

He reversed their positions, pressing her down into the bed with an urgency that made her head spin.

Clasping her tightly, he ran his hands over her arms and shoulders. "Where was I?" he asked, his face pressed against her neck.

"Does it matter?" she answered as she touched him everywhere she could reach.

"Not now." He gave a harsh laugh. "Jesus, open your legs for me before I explode."

Gladly, she did as he asked, guiding him to her, crying out as his cock slid inside her.

The salve was in her, too, inflaming her beyond endurance, and as he began to thrust, she matched his movements, frantic for release.

Nothing so intense could last for long. And when he cried out, pouring himself into her, she slid her hand between them, pressing against her clit so that she could follow him.

Climax rocked her, and she clung to his slick body, gasping out her thanks that he had come back to her.

CALEB collapsed on top of Quinn, breathing hard, then rolled to his side, taking her with him, stroking her face, her shoulders.

She snuggled against him, stringing little kisses over his hot skin.

He had come back because he wanted her. She had pulled him back to the world. And now he wondered if he had made a mistake. Was this right? For her? And for him.

"I can hardly believe I'm here—with you," he whispered.

"Believe it."

"I should be dead."

"Don't say that!"

"I would be . . . nowhere . . . without you," he said in a gritty voice.

But he was still struggling with reality. He had satisfied his overwhelming sexual need, but when he thought about the future, he felt a kind of desperate blackness stretching endlessly ahead of him.

"Nothing's changed. I'm still . . . damaged goods."

She sat up and looked down at him. "Your life will be different from what it would have been. You have to come to terms with that."

He clenched his jaw, then made an effort to relax the muscles. "What if I can't?"

"I'll help you."

He didn't like her looking down at him, so he sat, making himself taller than she. A petty assertion of power? Yet what he had to say was important. "I could have gotten you pregnant."

Her face softened and she laid her hand on his arm. "I don't mind."

"But whose child would it be?" he spat out.

She kept her gaze steady. "Don't keep looking for excuses to turn away from me. I love you. It would be a child we created—making love together."

His hand clenched as he struggled with too many emotions all at once.

"Do you love me?" she asked.

He wouldn't lie. Couldn't. "Yes. But I should not."

She looked sad, and he braced to hear some kind of argument from her. To his surprise, she changed the subject.

"Where did you go . . . when you weren't here?"

His gaze went unfocused as he struggled to answer the question. "I was somewhere else. A place with no light. And no feeling." He shuddered. "Nowhere." Honesty forced him to add, "I could have stayed there forever—if you hadn't pulled me out."

She slid her arm around him, holding him to her. "You're here now."

He nodded, still thinking about that empty place. "I talked to Wyatt Reynolds."

Her breath caught. "You did?"

He ran a hand through his hair. "Well, I think I did. But

it's like a dream now. Or maybe it was just the memory of him—in my brain. Neither one of us had a body. But somehow we recognized each other. I wonder now . . . why wasn't he in heaven, or whatever the afterlife is?"

"Maybe he came there . . . to meet you."

"Maybe."

She pressed her face to his shoulder. "What did he say?"

"The most important thing to him was why he left his body. He wanted to die. That's why he didn't try to come back after you dug him up."

"Why would a perfectly healthy man want to die?"

"His wife, Beth Ann, had . . . something called an aneurysm. It's a place where . . . a blood vessel in the brain is weak. It can break, and you bleed to death inside your skull. One day she was perfectly fine. Then, suddenly, she was dead. He missed her so much."

"I understand that," she whispered.

She lifted her head, and he looked into her eyes.

"No. You are strong," he said. "You could go on. But he couldn't endure life without her. That's why he took a dangerous assignment. Maybe he was *hoping* they'd kill him. Maybe he was even careless."

She winced.

Something else was nagging at him. Slowly, he began to speak. "But then he realized he'd made a mistake. He was sneaking around the farm, and he found something out. He knew he should have stayed on earth and . . ."

"What?"

"He had to tell the . . ." He stopped and made a frustrated sound. "I don't know!"

She pressed her hand over his. "Maybe it will come to you."

"It's important. I know that much. An attack on . . . something important. A lot of people are going to die, if I can't remember."

ROSS Marshall turned away from the computer and looked at his cousin.

"I may have found something."

"What?"

"I've been putting in license plates where an *L* or *I* could have been altered. And I've come up with something interesting. A car registered to a Colonel Jim Bowie."

"You mean, like the guy they named the bowie knife after?" Logan asked.

"I think that's right." He laughed. "There's a singer with that name, too. But it's David Bowie. I looked the Jim Bowie character up. He's got a place called Flagstaff Farm outside Frederick, Maryland. And he's gotten into trouble with the law."

"Like how?"

"Disorderly conduct. Assault. Nothing too big. I did a little digging. He doesn't do any farming. But he has a lot of men out there, and they've been seen doing military training. It sounds like he's got a paramilitary group."

"Nice."

"So maybe the guy who used to have Caleb's body was one of his men."

"It might be time for a couple of wolves to prowl around Flagstaff Farm."

"Or maybe not," a voice said from the doorway.

They both turned to see Rinna standing with her arms folded and watching them with narrowed eyes.

"How long have you been there?"

"Long enough to hear that you're planning something dangerous."

"We'd be careful," Logan said quickly.

Rinna looked from Logan to Ross and back again. "If he has a military organization, they have guns. Maybe they even like to shoot wild animals for fun. I don't want you anywhere near there. This isn't your problem."

"Maybe it is."

"How?"

"Maybe they're planning something big," Ross said. He'd been careful not to step on his cousin's toes, but he felt he needed to make that point clear.

"But it's not worth putting my life mate in danger. Or Megan's," she added, giving Ross a pointed look.

Logan sighed. "You may be right."

"Of course I'm right."

"So why did they kill the guy?" he asked.

"Because he stepped out of line? Like, he's one of the colonel's men, and he got to be too much trouble."

"I don't think so," Ross mused.

"Why not?" Logan asked.

"Because they could have just shot him. But they wanted him to die a slow, terrifying death."

"Yeah." Logan agreed. He tried to put the pieces of the puzzle together. But he was missing too many key elements.

"I'd like to know his name," Ross said. "Then we could look him up, too."

"At least we can drive out there," Logan said.

"If you do, I'm going along," Rinna said.

"To help us spy on them?"

She crossed to Logan and laid a hand on his shoulder. "To make sure you don't get into trouble."

CALEB watched Quinn stand up.

"Where are you going?"

"To take the roast off the fire." She moved the meat from the fireplace and laid it on a plate.

He sniffed. "Beef. Yeah. It smells good. I'm hungry."

"That's good. We can eat. Then we can talk about how to jog your memory."

"Okay."

He nodded and stood. She cut him some meat, and he ate a few bites, then rubbed his hand over his chest, making a face. "Um, what is this stuff all over me?"

She laughed. "Do you remember the other woman who was here?"

"Yes."

"She had me smear it on you. It's kind of like itching powder. She wanted you to have as many sensory experiences as possible."

"And she had you ... give me a ... uh ... intimate

massage?" he asked, unable to keep a little teasing tone out of his voice.

He saw color come into Quinn's cheeks. "Yes."

Turning, she crossed to the basin in the corner, dipped a cloth in the water and rubbed soap on it. Then she started washing. In the warm light from the oil lamps, she looked very sultry, and he told himself not to get trapped into wanting her again. He had to think through what had happened to him—before he could put her into the equation.

He joined her at the basin, washing off the sticky stuff.

"That woman was a witch?"

"An adept. With a skill in healing."

He laughed. "She knew what would lure me back to earth."

Quinn nodded, then dipped her head away.

"Are you embarrassed?"

"Yes. But I would have done anything it took to get you back."

He should thank her. But he couldn't quite do that yet. Here in this room, he felt comfortable. He wasn't sure what would happen when he had to face the world.

So he went on washing the salve off his skin. It felt good to get clean. Really, it felt good to be back in this body. But should he feel that way? What about the next time he got into a fight and tried to change to wolf form? He turned away so she wouldn't see the flash of pain on his face.

They washed in silence, and finally he felt the need to ask, "What are you thinking? And why are you keeping it to yourself?"

"I'm thinking that you told me something bad is going to happen, and we need help stopping it. And I'm keeping it to myself because I know you aren't going to like talking about it."

"You've got that right. If you're planning to ask your friends . . . the Marshalls."

"They'll help us."

Outrage came roaring into him. "Over my dead body."

CHAPTER
TWENTY-SIX

CALEB FELT QUINN grip his arm. "Stop thinking that way."

"Aden Marshall killed me! I hung around for seventy-five years to even the score with him. Do you expect me to just let that go?"

Her face took on a beautiful intensity in the flickering light from the lamp. "And the blame doesn't fall on his grandchildren. You're picking the wrong fight. If you want to get revenge on somebody, get it on the men who killed Wyatt Reynolds. They're within your reach. Aden Marshall isn't."

She was right. But he couldn't let it drop. "Yeah. But what if I can't work with the Marshalls?"

"They have the same heritage as you. They've managed to stop fighting among themselves."

"But I was born long before any of the ones living now. Into a different world. Maybe I can't stop fighting. And maybe I can't deal with . . . my condition."

"You can!"

"How do you know?" he asked, his breath shallow as he waited for her answer.

"Like you told me, you're resilient."

He turned so that he didn't have to meet her eyes. "What if I can't stand them looking at me and feeling sorry for me."

She spoke in a firm, confident voice. "If you go back there, they'll welcome you. You'll have a family and friends." Then she caught her breath.

"What?"

"I promised them I wouldn't take you back to their world. That was how I got them to bring Zarah to help me take the . . . blinder off the portal."

"That's an interesting problem."

"Yes. But you said their world is facing some kind of attack. The Marshalls will welcome your help in figuring out what it is."

"You hope." He muttered, then walked to the plate by the fire and cut off a piece of meat.

"ATTEN . . . shun," Colonel Jim Bowie called out, his voice hard as steel.

The men in the barracks snapped into position, standing with their feet together, arms at their sides and eyes forward.

As he walked down their ranks, he could smell their raw nerves. They feared these surprise inspections. And that was good. It kept them on their toes.

Discipline was the key to a successful military operation. Reward for a job well done was also important, but it was definitely secondary.

He began his inspection, walking slowly around the twelve-man barracks, opening lockers, checking the tightness of the blankets that covered the narrow cots, and the spit and polish of the shoes under the cots.

Half the squad was in the next building. Their turn would come tomorrow, or the next day or the day after that. He didn't want them to know exactly when it would happen. That kept the men on edge.

And he would be especially exacting when he inspected Portland's and Spencer's areas. Maybe a punishment session would get one of them to come clean.

There was something going on with the two of them. Something he didn't like and couldn't figure out. He'd sent them off to the woods with an assignment. And when they'd come back, he'd been sure he was rid of Wyatt Reynolds.

But as the days went on, he'd started to worry. He was a leader of men, and their behavior had set his soldier's intuition jangling. So he'd been keeping an eye on them.

His mind had been on automatic pilot as he inspected each man's area. Now he spoke to Sergeant Caldwell. "Hamilton, demerit for the condition of his bed."

"Yes, sir."

He moved on to the next man's footlocker.

"Prager, what the hell is chewing tobacco doing in your trunk?"

"Sorry, sir."

"Chewing tobacco is a filthy habit."

"Yes, sir."

Bowie looked at his sergeant. "Special punishment for Prager."

"Yes, sir."

Prager drew in a quick breath, but he knew better than to protest. One peep out of him, and the punishment would be worse.

Bowie ignored him for the moment, continuing his tour around the room.

He gave special privileges to two men—Winston and MacFarland. They'd be given overnight passes into town, where they could get drunk and get laid, if they wanted. The only requirement was that they be ready for duty in the morning.

He finished with the barracks, then he turned to Caldwell. "Escort Prager to the punishment ground."

Prager's complexion paled, but he said nothing.

The other men lined up in formation, and they all marched outside to the grassy area where two thick vertical posts had been set in cement. They would wait until Caldwell had brought the group from the other barracks. No point in public humiliation unless everyone witnessed it.

Bowie detoured to his quarters, where he opened a

wooden cabinet and took out the bullwhip he kept there. One of the things wrong with the United States today was that discipline had broken down. The current president was a wimp—afraid to do what needed to be done to beat the terrorists.

And most senators and congressmen were no better. They were a bunch of ineffective cowards, and they needed a jolt to wake them up and get them going in the right direction.

Every time something egregious happened, it proved how ill-prepared this once-great country was. Hurricane Katrina showed that the government was incapable of dealing with a large-scale emergency. Incidents like that guy with TB, Andrew Speaker, sneaking back into the United States showed our miserable border security.

The whole government was ineffective and rotten to the core. And they were pandering to terrorist countries when they should be bombing them to a pane of glass.

It would take a jolt of reality—from a superpatriot—to make the crybabies in Washington enact new, more stringent laws and carry them out effectively.

Bowie meant to administer that jolt.

Too bad about Prager. But every man at this compound had pledged to obey the rules. And one weak link could bring the whole operation down.

When he arrived at the punishment grounds, Prager had already taken off his uniform shirt and pants and folded them over the sawhorse that stood beside one of the restraining posts.

"Step forward," Caldwell ordered.

Wearing only his boxers, Prager did as ordered, and the sergeant attached his hands to rings fixed to the posts.

Colonel Bowie wrapped his hand around the handle of the whip, pleased with the familiar texture of the leather.

"Eight lashes," he announced to the men who stood in formation along one side of the square.

Then he turned and snapped the whip, listening to the sound as it whistled through the air.

When it landed sharply against Prager's back, the man gritted his teeth but made no sound.

Bowie smiled to himself. He'd wring a scream from the miscreant before he was finished.

And then there would be no more problems with discipline for a long while.

BY mutual agreement Quinn and Caleb finished washing and dressing. Then Quinn did her best to neaten her hair by finger-combing it. She was starting to feel shy again. Was Pamina still out there, waiting to see how the two of them were doing now? And what would Griffin think?

But when they stepped out, he wasn't hanging around. And the guard told her that Pamina had left.

Quinn breathed out a sigh, then asked if it would be okay to take Caleb on a little tour of Griffin's house.

When the man asked them to wait until he could arrange an escort, Quinn wondered if the political situation was really all that much better.

Trailed by an armed guard, they toured the household, and she showed him the kitchen where she had once worked.

"This place is like a little town," Caleb commented.

"Yes. It's pretty self-sufficient."

"And all the servants are slaves?"

"Not everybody. But in this world, many of them are." She gave him a direct look. "I was a slave, until Griffin freed me."

"Why did he?"

"Because I saved Zarah's life."

"And now you're her equal . . . in status."

"She's the mistress of this house. And a noble. I can never have that status."

"Are you ashamed that you were a slave?" he suddenly asked.

"No," she answered vehemently.

"You shouldn't be. You have guts. And determination. And talents most people would envy."

"Thank you," she whispered.

Maybe he realized he'd given his feelings away, because he switched to a less personal topic.

"This world is more primitive than the time I came from back home."

She explained about the sudden appearance of psychic abilities over a hundred years ago and how it had disrupted society.

Caleb's expression sobered. "I guess I wouldn't fit in real well."

"Why not?"

"I used to be a werewolf. Now I don't have any psychic abilities."

"Maybe you do, and nobody brought them out. We go to schools to maximize our talents."

"So I've missed a window of opportunity."

She fought to keep her voice even. "Not everyone here uses psychic talents."

"Yeah, I'm sure they need a lot of truck drivers."

She was saved from having to answer when Griffin called out to them. "I've tracked you down."

He and Caleb shook hands stiffly.

"You're feeling better?" Griffin asked.

"Yes, thank you," Caleb answered, polite but guarded.

Quinn was feeling that way herself. "Pamina spoke to you before she left?"

"Yes. She was pleased with what you accomplished. She said you were the key to success."

"Mmm," Quinn murmured and studied her hands. She hoped the woman hadn't given too many intimate details about the treatment.

"The two of you should take a few days to relax," Griffin said, "before you go back through the portal."

"We can't," Quinn answered. "The man who owned this body gave Caleb some vital information. There's going to be an attack. Something that will kill a lot of people. We have to stop it."

"Do you know what it is?"

"Not yet."

Griffin gave Caleb a critical look. "Maybe a psychic treatment could help you recover the memories."

"I'm hoping I can do it on my own," he bit out.

"Yes. All right," Griffin answered, catching the other man's tone.

"We should leave soon," Quinn said. She was feeling shaky about their return, and she wanted to get it over with. She had promised to keep Caleb here, but the situation had changed. She hoped Logan and the others would understand that.

Griffin eyed them with concern. "Tonight?"

"Yes."

"Then you should rest. And eat. I'll have soldiers go with you." He turned to Caleb. "Can you ride? I mean . . . ride a horse."

"Yes."

"That will make the trip faster."

They all ate a meal together in the private courtyard inside the family quarters. Caleb asked questions about this universe, and Griffin answered, telling him how the government had broken down into city-states and how powerful men still jockeyed for position in each city.

"Franklin Delano Roosevelt was president when I was killed," Caleb said.

"We never got that far with presidents," Griffin said. "What were the key things happening in your time?"

"We had a World War. It was supposed to be the war to end all wars. After that, in the twenties, there was great prosperity—and a lot of speculation in the stock market."

"Which is?"

Caleb thought for a moment. "Companies sell stock to raise money. And people were buying stock with money they didn't have but expected to get when the company made a bigger profit. But it all collapsed. Banks went out of business. Rich men killed themselves because they lost their fortunes. Ordinary people lost their jobs and lost their homes. And at the same time, in the Midwest, there was no rain and farms turned to dust. Franklin Roosevelt was trying to get the country back on its feet again."

"So this isn't the only place where something bad happened," Griffin mused.

"But Roosevelt was holding the country together."

"Lucky for you. He must have been a strong leader."

"He was." Caleb laughed. "A lot of people hated him for it."

"I know the feeling," Griffin muttered.

Caleb shifted in his seat. "I have a question. In my world, Christianity was the main religion. My mother was a Christian. But I've heard Quinn ask for the blessing of the Great Mother."

"When the bad times struck, people felt they didn't get protection from the old religions. They turned to sects and cults—many of them very ancient. The Great Mother was an important deity before the Jewish and Christian view that God was male."

Caleb blinked. "I always assumed that God was a *he*."

"Because that's what you were taught."

"Religion wasn't very important in my family. Well, not to my father. My mother used to go to church on Sundays sometimes. She took me when I was little. Then I followed my father's way."

"But you absorbed the cultural norms," Griffin said, "because your society was much less fragmented than ours."

Caleb nodded.

Quinn joined in a little, but she was mostly enjoying the give-and-take between the two men. Maybe Caleb and Griffin could be friends.

There was only one awkward moment—when Griffin talked about how much he missed his wife, recalling that Zarah had cured him of a disease werewolves sometimes get. "I couldn't control the change. I was running around the city out of control. And I'm lucky I didn't get killed."

He looked up to see that Caleb's face was white. "Sorry. I forgot . . ."

"I guess I'd better get used to it."

Quinn wanted to reach for Caleb's hand under the table. But she didn't do it because she didn't know if he'd welcome the contact. It seemed like every few days, she had to get to know him all over again.

"Can I use my old room?" Quinn asked at the end of the meal.

"Of course. It's still yours."

"And I'd like a room where I could rest as well," Caleb said.

"Not with me?" she asked before she could stop herself.

"We need to sleep."

She felt her throat tighten. So what was he really thinking? That he wanted to avoid getting her pregnant? In Logan's world, she could go on contraceptive pills—or they could use a condom. But not here. And would he walk away from her when they got back to the other side? She honestly didn't know.

"Okay," she managed to say.

"How long will it take to get to the portal?" Caleb asked.

"An hour—on horseback."

"Then someone should wake us at five in the morning," Quinn said. "That way, we'll get back just before dawn."

She left the men talking and went back to her old room, where she even managed to get a little sleep, probably because she was exhausted. When a soldier knocked on her door at the appointed time, she got up and washed, then came back to the courtyard, where servants had laid out bread, fruit, and meat.

Griffin was waiting for them.

"You didn't have to get up," she said.

"I wanted to wish you Godspeed. And I seem to have acquired a . . . dividend." He held up an old clock that she had seen in one of the rooms of his residence. She had never heard it ticking, but it was ticking now.

"Caleb fixed this for me."

She turned to him. "You did?"

"Yeah. It wasn't so hard. I'm good with my hands. When my truck broke down, I could usually get it going again."

"Maybe fixing the clock wasn't hard for you," Griffin said. "But nobody else in this world could do it." He turned to Quinn. "Please take this letter to Zarah."

"Or course." Quinn put the letter into her fanny pack. Four horses were waiting in the courtyard.

She embraced Griffin, then mounted. As they rode out into the city with two soldiers escorting them, she saw that

Caleb wasn't entirely comfortable in the saddle. But by the time they reached the gate, the ability seemed to have come back to him.

To Quinn's relief, the journey back to the portal was uneventful. She and Caleb dismounted several hundred yards away so the soldiers wouldn't know the exact location.

They thanked their escort, left the horses with the soldiers, and waited until the men started back to the city before walking into the cave.

Quinn stopped short when she saw the opening was stuffed with branches and brush. And she sucked in a breath when she realized she could tip her head and see through the membrane between the worlds.

Wondering what she would find, she made her way through, pushing the obstruction aside as she went.

They emerged into a gray dawn. And as they walked down the hill toward the Marshall house, a wolf that Quinn didn't recognize stepped into their path, bared its teeth, and growled at them in warning.

CHAPTER
TWENTY-SEVEN

QUINN STOPPED SHORT, staring at the wolf, wondering who he was. Not Ross or Logan.

Caleb stepped in front of her, making his own growling sound deep in his throat in response to the challenge. He could do that. But because he couldn't change, he'd just made the situation a lot more dangerous for himself. What was he going to do if the other wolf attacked?

She caught his arm. "Don't!"

"It's one of them."

"Yes. But he doesn't know us. Let me handle this."

"No." He kept his gaze firmly on the wolf. "I am Caleb Marshall, the cousin Aden killed. I assume you heard about that?"

The wolf nodded.

"Probably you're thinking, 'Funny he doesn't look like one of us.' But you also know I'm in another body—of a man who was buried alive in the woods."

The wolf pawed the ground and nodded again.

"When I was detached from the body," Caleb continued, "I was able to communicate with the previous owner. He gave me some information you need to have."

The wolf nodded once more, then backed away and disappeared behind a nearby tree.

"He's going to change," Quinn said.

"I know what the hell he's going to do!"

"Yes," she murmured, then more softly, "Sorry."

Moments later, a dark-haired man wearing only a pair of sweatpants stepped back into view.

"I'm Jacob Marshall, Logan's younger brother." While he spoke, he kept his gaze on Caleb as though he expected trouble.

Caleb stood stiffly beside Quinn, but he didn't make any threatening moves, and she was thankful for that.

"What are you doing here?" Caleb asked.

"I should ask you the same question. I thought you promised not to come back."

"Quinn brought me because I agreed not to try and rip out anyone's throat."

Quinn winced. Was he hoping to start a fight?

"Your turn," Caleb challenged.

"We've been guarding the portal to make sure nobody came through—except you. We were getting ready to send Rinna and a team in to look for you."

Quinn sucked in a sharp breath. "Rinna! I can't imagine she wants to go back there. Even though she knows Falcone, the man who raped her, is dead."

"She knows her way around. And Zarah can't do it."

"I'm sorry you were even thinking of it. You were worried about us?" she asked.

"Yeah. And we've got another problem, too."

"Oh yeah?" Caleb said.

"Give me a minute. Let me get my shoes and shirt," Jacob said, walking back to the tree where he'd left his clothing.

When he was dressed, Quinn said, "You don't have to stay here guarding the portal. Nobody but us is coming through."

"How do you know?"

"Because Baron—the guy who was challenging Griffin—

is dead, and his men have enough problems without looking for the portal."

Jacob nodded. "Then I can go back with you. The others will be glad you're here."

"Okay," Quinn answered, relieved for the moment.

"Why?" Caleb asked.

"Let's wait until we get there."

They walked quickly down the hill.

Caleb was silent.

Quinn said, "We haven't met before."

"I came to help," Logan's brother answered.

Quinn gave him a sidewise glance. Like the rest of the Marshalls, he was tall and dark and trim.

When she saw Logan's house, Quinn felt her stomach clench. She had broken her promise. But Jacob had made it sound all right. She hoped it was.

She wanted to tell Caleb to wait outside, but she cut him a glance and saw that he looked as tense as she felt. If she went in without him, he would only stand out here stewing. So when Jacob opened the front door, she followed him inside . . . with Caleb right behind her.

Everybody was in the kitchen, and she wanted to warn them to go easy on Caleb. But there was no chance of saying anything now.

As soon as they stepped into the room, Zarah's body went rigid, her total focus on Quinn.

"Is he all right?" she breathed.

"Yes. Griffin's fine."

Zarah jumped up and crossed the room, hugging her tightly. "Thank you. Thank you so much," she said in a choked voice.

"He loved the pictures of you—and the sonogram of the baby."

"That sonogram is a miracle," Zarah said, her voice cracking. She waited a moment, then drew back. "I'm being so selfish. How are the two of you?" She looked from Quinn to Caleb and back again.

Caleb shifted his weight from one foot to the other.

"We're fine," Quinn answered. "And I have a letter for you—from Griffin."

Zarah took it in her trembling hand. "Would you excuse me? I need to read it."

"Of course," Rinna said, then swung her gaze toward Caleb, who looked like a statue that had been hit with a hammer and was going to shatter into a thousand pieces. "Welcome to our house."

He gave her a doubtful look. Quinn watched as she crossed to him and embraced him. As she did, Logan looked like he was ready to spring across the room if Caleb made any threatening moves.

He stood stiffly for a moment. Then his hands came up and clasped Rinna.

When she stepped back, his eyes were bright. After a moment, Logan came over and held out his hand. Caleb shook it.

Jacob and Ross did the same.

"I'm glad you made it here," Logan said.

Caleb nodded tightly. Probably in a million years, he hadn't expected anything like this from the Marshall family. No, make that seventy-five years.

Taking a step closer to him, Quinn reached for his hand and clasped it. Maybe this really was going to work out okay.

"We're glad to meet you," Ross said. "It took guts to walk into this situation."

Caleb answered with a little nod.

"We're hoping you can help us," Ross said.

"With what?"

"We need information about Colonel Jim Bowie," Ross said. "He's running some kind of militia group out in Frederick County."

She felt Caleb wavering on his feet. He looked like he was about to fall over, and she clasped his hand more tightly—knowing why he was reacting. She'd heard him say that name when Pamina was trying to forge the connection between his mind and body. And now Ross was asking about the same man.

Caleb braced his shoulder against the wall, breathing

hard. Sweat had broken out on his forehead. "Actually, he's the bastard who ordered me killed. Well, not me. Wyatt Reynolds."

Ross watched him closely. "How do you know?"

"Because Wyatt Reynolds told me."

"You're talking about the man who was murdered?" Ross asked.

"Yes."

"You have his memories?"

"Some. Sometimes." As he spoke Caleb crossed the room and sat down heavily at the table.

Rinna ran water from the tap and handed Caleb a glass. He took a gulp. "Thank you."

"Bowie must be an assumed name. There are no records of the man before two years ago. What else do you know about him?" Ross asked.

"He was a . . . monster," Caleb answered. "Strict with his men. If you joined his organization, you conformed to his rules. And he's planning some big operation—soon."

"What the hell is he going to do?" Logan pressed, then softened his tone. "Sorry."

Caleb shook his head. "I wish I knew."

"Too bad," Ross muttered. "We'd like to know why he killed Reynolds."

"He was a spy," Caleb said. "I remember that much."

"Who was he working for?" Ross asked.

Caleb's brow wrinkled. After a long moment, he said, "I don't know."

"We need to jog your memory."

"How?"

"Maybe I can help," Zarah said from the doorway.

Caleb looked up, seeing the anxious faces around him. He had said he didn't want to have a psychic work on him, and Quinn waited tensely to see what he would say now that he saw how much these people needed him.

"If you give us a little privacy," he said in a low voice.

"Of course," Rinna answered.

"We can use my bedroom," Quinn offered, then wondered if he'd ask to do it somewhere else.

But he only nodded.

She let out the breath she was holding, but she was worried enough to ask, "Can I come with you?"

"Yes," he answered, his voice barely above a whisper.

While the others waited in the living room, she, Zarah, and Caleb went downstairs.

"Lie down and get comfortable," Zarah said to Caleb, then went to fetch her lamp.

Caleb stretched out on the bed, and Quinn brought in an extra chair from the family room. Then she sat on the side opposite the door.

Caleb lay with his body rigid, his hands clasped across his middle, as though he needed to hold on to something. Quinn wished he'd reached for her hand instead, but she wouldn't force him to turn to her.

When Zarah came back, she sat down in the chair on Caleb's other side and lit her lamp.

Quinn tried to quiet her own nerves. But she was worried about what was going to happen now. Surely nothing like what Pamina had done.

She stole a look at Caleb's rigid face and wondered what he was thinking.

Zarah looked down at him and smiled. "I'm going to lend you my energy and the energy of the flame—to strengthen your memories." She flicked a look across the prone man. "It will help if you have Quinn's energy, too."

Quinn thought that was probably true. She also thought Zarah had felt the strain between herself and Caleb and was trying to bring them closer together.

She waited with her breath frozen in her lungs, then heard him swallow hard before muttering, "Okay."

She closed her eyes, telling herself his reluctance wasn't a rejection. Then she heard Zarah's voice again,

"Quinn, take one of his hands." Grateful to be included, she did as her friend asked and felt Caleb's hand quiver. She wanted to ask him what he was feeling, but she kept the question locked behind her lips.

Still holding the lamp, Zarah took his other hand with her free one. She made a humming sound, but didn't speak for several moments. Finally, she murmured, "I feel the man who was in this body. You said his name was Wyatt Reynolds?"

"Yes," Caleb said in a strained voice. "Is he still . . . inside me?"

Quinn's breath caught as she waited for the other woman's answer.

After a few moments, Zarah whispered, "No. He is like a flickering shadow, dancing on the walls of a cave in the firelight . . ." Her voice trailed off, then she exclaimed, "Oh!"

"What?" Quinn gasped.

"He lost his wife—and lost the will to live. That's so sad."

Quinn heard the emotion in her friend's voice, and her stomach clenched. What if Zarah had learned that Griffin was dead? Would she give up? No, she couldn't. She had his child inside her.

"He told me that," Caleb said.

"You talked to him?"

"A little. When I was . . . separating from this body. I know he took a dangerous job because he didn't care what happened to him."

"He was spying on a militia group," Quinn said, then clamped her lips shut as she wondered whether she was supposed to butt into the dialogue.

Zarah leaned over Caleb. "Can you tell me who Wyatt Reynolds was working for?"

When Caleb didn't answer, she began to hum again in a low voice. Was that part of the process in this kind of ceremony?

"Concentrate. It's very close to the surface of your mind," she whispered.

Caleb squeezed his eyes shut, his focus turned inward as his body moved restlessly on the bed.

When his lips parted, Quinn tensed. "Jerry . . ." he said in a faint voice.

"Jerry who?" Zarah asked.

Quinn felt her heart pounding. She could see that this probing was taking its toll on Caleb. Was it going to hurt him? Make his body and his mind separate again?

But Zarah pressed on. "Jerry who?" she asked again.

"I don't know!"

Quinn could feel energy flowing around the room, pumping itself into Caleb, and she knew he could feel it, too—by the way his body shifted on the bed and he swung his head back and forth.

She knew Zarah was directing the flow of the energy. And she suspected it was hurting him. Physically and mentally.

She glanced across him at Zarah, and her face was a study in concentration.

Caleb made a strangled sound; his fingers tightened painfully on Quinn's. Beads of perspiration stood out on his forehead, and his shirt stuck to his chest.

"Stop," she begged, addressing herself to Zarah. "You're hurting him."

His breath was coming in gasps now.

"Stop," Quinn said again, this time more urgently. "He can't take any more."

On the bed, Caleb's body jerked, and then he went absolutely still.

WHILE the men were having their noon meal in the mess hall, Colonel Jim Bowie ate alone in his quarters. He was living in the old farmhouse that had come with the property, but he'd fixed it up so that it was a very comfortable retreat from the pressures of his job.

He had a plate of the same food. But he didn't want to be distracted by their conversation. He had so many responsibilities during the day that he needed this downtime to unwind.

As he ate, he was reading one of his favorite passages from Thomas Jefferson. The one where he said that the tree of liberty is nourished by the blood of tyrants and the blood of patriots.

That was part of Bowie's personal creed. He could see what was wrong with this damn country. And see how to cure it. The government needed a jolt, and he was going to give it to them.

Sometimes, when he was in a reflective mood, and he

thought about the important men who had shaped history, he imagined that he had been one of those early patriots who had prodded the colonies into separating from the tyranny of George III. He could imagine himself back then, in 1776, shouting down the pussies who wanted to stay tied to England.

And maybe he'd even been there in 1787 when they'd crafted the Second Amendment, the one that prohibited the government from infringing on the rights of the people to keep and bear arms.

A lot of modern liberals and conservatives both had forgotten all that. Or maybe they were too scared to act. Well, he'd force some steel into their spines, then he'd fade into the background—ready to do it again if need be. A lot of his men were going to die soon. But they were expendable. He'd find new recruits for the cause, even if they didn't have the intellect to follow his logic.

He already had his new identity picked out. Sam Houston, another patriot in another war.

He would . . .

The barking of the dogs interrupted his thoughts and he went very still, listening.

Since finding out Wyatt Reynolds was a traitor, he'd been on the alert.

Unholstering his Sig Sauer, he stood up, ready to see what had disturbed the animals.

CHAPTER
TWENTY-EIGHT

QUINN CLASPED CALEB'S fingers as she bent down, cupping her other palm over his damp forehead.

She looked accusingly at Zarah. "What have you done to him?"

"It wasn't me. It was him. He was trying really hard, and I knew he didn't want to stop."

"But he should have. What if he . . . what if he left the body again?" She heard her voice rise as she said the last part. With her heart blocking her windpipe, she hovered over Caleb, clasping his fingers. For a long moment, he lay still as death, his skin pale and clammy.

Zarah touched his cheek, murmuring something low and urgent.

At first, nothing changed, and fear clawed at Quinn's insides. Then he dragged in a shuddering breath.

"Caleb!" she exclaimed.

His eyes blinked open and focused on her.

"Quinn." He looked like he was glad to see her, and her heart turned over.

Heedless of what Zarah might think, Quinn bent to him,

held him tightly, and his arm came up to wedge her against his chest.

She felt a surge of hope. He might say that he didn't think their relationship could work. But when his mind was unguarded, he reached out to her on a very basic level. That was something. And she would build on it.

In the next moment, she wondered if he would give her the chance. Easing away, he sat up and ran a hand through his hair. He looked like he was concentrating really hard.

"Jerry," he said again. Then, "It's Jerry Ruckleman."

"You got his name!" Quinn breathed.

"But that's all. I still don't know what Bowie is planning to attack."

JACOB glanced down the hall for probably the sixth time. The bedroom door was still closed.

Too restless to sit and wait for a message from the psychic world, he said, "I'm going to see if I can get onto Flagstaff Farm."

Ross gave him a sharp look. "That could be dangerous."

"But with no life mate, I'm the logical one to do it."

His cousin nodded, and Jacob couldn't stop himself from resenting the gesture. He could go out there if he wanted. He didn't need Ross's permission.

"Can I give you some advice?"

Jacob considered the offer. He didn't like taking advice from another werewolf. But in this case, it made sense because Ross was a private detective. "Okay," he allowed.

"Wait until dark. And park at least a quarter mile from the farm."

"Yeah. But I'll start out now. Maybe I can get some information in town before I invade the militia compound. The troops may have rubbed some of the residents the wrong way."

Ross nodded. "Keep in cell phone communication—so we know you're okay."

"I will, until I change to a wolf."

* * *

CALEB swung his legs off the bed and stood up as Quinn hurried from the room. Bracing himself, he watched her return with Ross.

"I understand you came up with the name of Wyatt Reynolds' boss," the private detective said.

"Yeah. But what good does that do?" Caleb asked, hearing the harsh quality of his own voice. "What are we supposed to do, look him up in the phone book?"

"Not the phone book. The Web."

"Which is?"

"The greatest source of information since the smoke signal was invented."

Was this guy putting him on? "Smoke signal?" he asked. "Do they use them now?"

"No. I was just trying for dramatic effect. Come in the other room and I'll show you."

Everyone crowded into Logan's office. Ross sat down at a very strange machine. It had a keyboard that looked something like a typewriter. The numbers and letters were the same, only all the keys were on the same horizontal surface instead of being raised in tiers. And they were square instead of round.

But there was no roller at the top. And Ross didn't put in any paper. Instead, when he typed, words appeared on something like a little movie screen.

"Like a television?" he asked. "I saw one at the hunting lodge where we were hiding out. They had a lot of stations."

"With television, they're called channels. But you're right, it's like your radio. Companies broadcast programs— or send them out on cable channels, using underground wires." He paused and thought for a moment. "Let me see if I can give you the short course in a couple of minutes. This is a computer, and it's connected to other computers in the United States and around the world."

"Connected? Like a telephone exchange?"

"Something like that. But there's no operator. You do it yourself. And it's also like going to a library catalogue and looking up a book, then taking it off the shelf. And you can search in ways that you couldn't with a book or a catalogue. You can put in a name or a word and go right to the information you want. I'll show you." He laughed. "It's like the post office, too. You can send a kind of mail called e-mail that comes to your machine. Well, to your address. I'm using Logan's computer now, but I can use my own accounts."

Caleb's head was spinning. Struggling not to sound overwhelmed, he asked, "One machine does all that?"

"Yeah. And more. Let me type in my name and password. The password will show as a bunch of dots, so nobody else can use my account."

When he had done what he called "login," he said, "What's the guy's name?"

"Jerry Ruckleman," Caleb supplied.

"Not a common name. That should help. Of course, his real name could be Jerome."

AN afternoon in Frederick had yielded little information about the group at Flagstaff Farm—except that they weren't well liked.

After driving past, Jacob kept going to a patch of woods, where he climbed out of his car, then stepped into the shadows and began to say the chant that his ancestors had said back into the dawn of time.

In moments, he was down on all fours—a wolf in his element, the woods. He sniffed the air, taking in the scents of the night, then started off at a fast trot for the militia compound.

He easily climbed through the rails of the wooden fence. Fifty yards farther on, he found out why access to the property was so easy.

Two large Rottweilers came bounding toward him, barking loudly, ready to tear the intruder to pieces. They were both wearing what he recognized as electric collars. So if he beat it back to the fence, he would be safe.

JIM Bowie had seen a T-shirt once with the legend, "The United States—conceived by geniuses to be run by morons."

That was how he felt about it. The current government leaders weren't even up to the moron level. They were idiots. And they needed shaking up to put them back on the right track. He was going to do it in just a few days.

He was contemplating the feeling of power and glory when he realized that the dogs had started barking again.

He stood in his quarters, listening intently.

As abruptly as it had started, the barking stopped.

Earlier, the handler had said they'd gone after the vegetable delivery truck from town. Maybe this time it was a deer. There were plenty of them in the area, and it was hard for even a well-disciplined dog to resist chasing fresh game.

After a moment, he reholstered his sidearm, then sat back down in his easy chair, took another bite of his ham sandwich, and shuffled through the books on the table next to him.

The Founding Fathers had always been a source of wisdom. But he also liked to read the autobiographies of the modern generals. Patton was especially inspiring. He had a sense of history. And he knew how to rally his men to give that last full measure of devotion.

He'd inspired them with the ancient Greek battle of Thermopylae—without telling them that all of the Spartans had been killed defending the pass. The Spartans had been prepared to die. His men weren't. But that didn't make their demise any less glorious.

The analogy was so perfect. He knew his decision was the right one, yet he felt a sliver of uneasiness working its way through his skin, like an infected splinter.

He'd set his timetable for Operation Eagle's Flight weeks ago.

And he'd decided to do the unexpected. Hit right before a day when the D.C. police would be on high alert.

But maybe the universe was giving him a message. Maybe he'd better not sit here reading history books.

Standing, he walked to the door of his quarters. His room was on the first floor. When he reached the porch, he looked around at his domain.

Across the quadrangle, lights blazed in the recreation

hall. Most of the men were there—except the two who were on guard duty with the dogs.

He'd just take a tour around the grounds, then go back inside.

Were the men ready for the big day?

He couldn't believe otherwise. They'd been training for this one mission for months. They functioned as a well-oiled machine.

Most of the time.

But perhaps he'd better increase their readiness over the next few days.

JACOB went very still, making a soothing sound low in his throat, like a song.

The two dogs cocked their heads to the side, staring at him. He kept making the sound, sending out a signal to the two animals, telling them that he was no threat, that he meant them no harm, that he was their friend.

It was a talent he had discovered years earlier—even before the first time he had changed from frightened teenager to wolf. On the way to school, he'd had to walk past a yard with a chain-link fence. And inside the fence was a Doberman that scared all the kids. Everybody ran past that yard. But one day, when someone left the driveway gate open, the dog got out and cornered a little girl named Katie on the steps of the next house.

Jacob could have run. But he couldn't leave the girl. The problem was, he didn't have an idea in hell how to save her. Still, he ran toward the dog, calling at him to leave the girl alone. And the dog changed its focus, turning and rushing toward him, teeth bared.

He yelled at Katie to get out of there, but she only crouched on the steps, whimpering.

Jacob started talking to the dog, telling it that he was a friend. That he meant it no harm. That they were brothers. And to his astonishment the dog slowed down, cocking its head to the side and looking at him.

By that time, the dog's owner had come running, shouting, "Klingon, stay. Klingon, stay."

The man grabbed the animal by the collar and snapped on a leash. The dog went home quietly. And after that, Jacob stopped every day at the chain-link fence, talking to his new friend, trying to understand Klingon.

That had been the start of his knowledge that there was something inside him that allowed him to communicate with animals. He'd used that skill many times in the years since. In fact, it was now his job. He evaluated animals being held at shelters and animals being considered for special training. Sometimes he also helped with the training.

He could reach out to animals as a man. And he could do it as a wolf, although not as effectively, because he had no spoken words as a wolf. But even without real words, his message of brotherhood got across to other species.

He trotted along beside his two new friends, still humming his song of fellowship. And the two Rottweilers stayed on either side of him, allowing him free access to the militia compound.

Just as he figured he was home free, something moved to his right.

A guard—with a machine gun.

His eyes fixed on the weapon, Jacob froze in place.

CALEB clenched his fists at his sides as Ross typed in both variations. He didn't know how this was going to work, but he could see Ross had faith in the method.

"There are only two hits," he said after a few moment.

"Hits?"

"I found two men with that name. There's a Jerome Ruckleman who's an art museum director in Pennsylvania." He pointed to several lines of writing on the screen. "There are articles and biographies on him. But he's probably not the right one, unless Wyatt Reynolds was investigating a bunch of militiamen who are also art forgers."

The observation earned Ross nervous laughter around the room.

"The other is Jerome Ruckleman who works for the Department of Homeland Security."

Ross switched to another screen. "Apparently, he runs an elite counterterrorism unit."

Logan whistled through his teeth, then looked at Caleb. "Counterterrorism. Does that ring any bells?"

A sudden sick feeling shot through Caleb as a piece of information zinged into his head. "I think I know what the colonel is planning to do," he said, his voice hoarse.

THE guard walked past, and Jacob let out the breath he was holding, then moved cautiously toward a cluster of buildings, noting their locations. He could see a farmhouse and long low structures ahead of him. Barracks?

Wary of more security forces, he crept closer to the hub of activity, coming to what must be a recreation room, where he heard the sounds of men's cheerful voices. He inched toward the light spilling from the doorway, listening to the conversation. It was ordinary, and he gathered from the relaxed atmosphere that they would be there for a while.

When he looked toward the farmhouse, he saw a man standing under the porch light. A man with gray hair cut short, a lined face that matched the mug shot Ross had showed him on the Web, and a neatly pressed camouflage uniform.

Colonel Bowie. In the flesh.

From the shadows, Jacob watched him walk down the steps and head toward the recreation hall.

He'd left the door open a crack. Was there time to get inside the farmhouse and look around? Or was that taking too much of a chance?

Making a split-second decision, he ran across the open space, then through the door. He was in a comfortably furnished living room or lounge. He saw a kitchen off to his right. And down the hall, a light burned. He headed for the back of the house and stepped into a bedroom.

The blanket on the single bed was so tightly tucked in that you could have bounced a coin on it. The desk blotter was clear of everything—not a paper or even a paper clip. In the entire room, nothing was out of place, except a pile of books and papers beside an easy chair in the corner.

Jacob spotted a calendar hanging above the desk. A date was circled in red.

After looking at the calendar, he took a step closer to the table, scanning the top page of the papers. It seemed to be some kind of political statement that the colonel wanted to deliver to the U.S. Government.

He was pawing at the top page, trying to move it aside, when he heard footsteps in the hall.

CALEB felt all eyes on him. Moistening his lips, he said, "Colonel Bowie is planning to set off something called a dirty bomb in Washington, D.C. I assume that's something bad."

Around the room, some of the people drew in a startled breath.

"Yeah, a dirty bomb is bad. Very bad," Ross muttered. "Do you know about radioactive elements?"

"You mean like radium? Didn't Madame Curie discover it?"

"Right. She was excited about the medical applications. Radium is only one of the radioactive elements, and she didn't know they were dangerous. Military men were more interested in the weapons applications. Uranium and plutonium are also radioactive, and they're used in certain kinds of deadly weapons. What we call weapons of mass destruction because they kill a lot of people at once."

"Something they developed after the world war?"

"Yeah." Ross made a harsh sound. "The leaders of countries around the world hoped World War One would be the last war. But it didn't work out that way. We had another world war about twenty-five years later. Only there were big advances in killing ability. What ended the war was one of those weapons of mass destruction. An atomic bomb. It explodes when radioactive elements are slammed together so that they reach critical mass."

Caleb nodded slowly, although he didn't understand perfectly.

Seeing his expression, Ross said, "You don't have to

know how it works. You just need to know that radioactivity in large amounts is extremely damaging to animal and plant life. Depending on how much you absorb, it can kill quickly or cause illnesses like cancer and leukemia years later."

"He's got *that kind of bomb*?"

"Not exactly. Atomic bombs and hydrogen bombs rely on sophisticated technology. But it's possible to put radioactive material into a conventional bomb. When the explosives go off, the radioactivity is spread over a wide area. And it lingers there for a long time. So if Bowie's gang set off a bomb like that in Washington, D.C., it would be horrendous."

"You mean thousands of people could die?" Caleb asked.

"Yes. And part of the city would be contaminated—and unusable, because it takes a long time for radioactivity to decay."

Ross let that sink in, then looked at Caleb. "Do you know where they're going to do it?"

Caleb closed his eyes, trying to bring back words that Reynolds had spoken to him. "The Kennedy Center . . . or the Capitol."

He heard Rinna draw in a quick breath.

"Or both," he added, then clenched his teeth in frustration. "It's not clear which."

"But doing both makes sense," Ross said. "If they started with the Kennedy Center, rescue efforts would converge there. Then when they did the Capitol, it would be a very nasty surprise. You have a time frame?"

Again Caleb closed his eyes, desperate to dredge up the information. But all he could confirm was, "Soon."

"Too bad we can't just phone 911 and tell them about it," Logan muttered. "Because we don't have enough information to be credible."

"You mean the emergency number?" Quinn asked.

"Yes," Ross answered. "The phone number you dial when you need the police or the fire department."

"We could raid the militia compound," Logan said.

"Kind of risky to try and take them on their own turf," Ross answered.

They were silent for several moments, then Logan cleared his throat. "Homeland Security could stop them. An anonymous tip? Like when those guys wanted to bomb JFK airport and someone in the neighborhood turned them in?"

Caleb didn't get the reference, but he didn't interrupt the exchange.

"No. They couldn't just charge into the compound on the strength of a tip. They'd have to investigate. And then it might be too late—if the framework is tight," Ross said.

Logan looked at Caleb. "But what if Wyatt Reynolds went to his boss and told him he knew for sure that an attack was in the works?"

"You mean have Caleb impersonate Reynolds?" Ross asked.

"Yeah."

Quinn immediately looked upset. "That's too risky. Caleb doesn't know enough about Reynolds' boss—or about Reynolds, either."

Caleb silently conceded the point, but he wasn't going to let her dictate what he did or didn't do. In fact, while he was standing here, he had been working his way into a startling conclusion. He had stayed on earth for seventy-five years after he'd died because he thought he had a mission—to avenge his own death. Now he was starting to think there was another reason. He had stayed on earth because he had a more important mission—to prevent the deaths of thousands of people. When he turned it over in his mind, it sounded highfalutin. Something he couldn't say aloud to anyone else.

But he felt a commitment deep inside himself. He took a moment to catch his breath, then gestured toward the monitor. "If you can find out things about Jerome Ruckleman, you can find out about Wyatt Reynolds, too."

"Maybe not enough," Ross said.

CORNERED in the bedroom, Jacob looked wildly around. The closet door was slightly ajar. He could hide in there. But then he'd be trapped in the room. And what if the guy decided to hang his clothes in the closet? Or conduct a search of the room?

The only other option was the double-hung window. It was open, but a screen covered the opening.

Hoping it wasn't fixed too tightly in place, Jacob leaped for the window, tucking his head as he bashed into the screen. His weight sent it blasting outward.

"What the hell?" someone called behind him.

Without stopping to find out what happened next, he made for the fence, his two canine friends running alongside him.

CHAPTER
TWENTY-NINE

"SEE WHAT YOU can get on Reynolds," Caleb said. "And maybe more will come back to me."

"I don't like it," Quinn said.

"But you don't have to do it," Caleb reminded her.

Quinn started to speak, then clamped her lips together, and he was glad they weren't going to argue about it in front of a crowd of people. Even if he couldn't change to wolf form, he could do something else important.

Zarah hadn't spoken in several minutes. Now she joined the conversation. "But it's still dangerous."

Quinn looked like she wanted to hug her friend.

"Why?" he challenged. "Jerry Ruckleman's not going to attack Reynolds. Reynolds works for him."

"But he's going to wonder where he's been for the past few days," Ross said.

"Not necessarily. Not if he's supposed to be in deep cover," Logan argued.

Quinn glared at him.

"The militia was holding him captive. He escaped," Caleb said.

"I think if you want this to work, you're going to have to

spend some time getting your story straight," Ross said. "Let's hope Jacob comes back with details about the militia camp.

"And you'll have to do some studying. Not just about Reynolds. You need to know about Colonel Jim Bowie and his militia. Because we don't know how much Reynolds has already told his boss."

Caleb shifted his weight from one foot to the other. He didn't have much experience working in a group. But if these other guys could do it—he could, too. "Then we should get started. I need information from that computer thing."

Quinn's gaze shot to Zarah, but the other woman gave a tiny shake of her head. She was a healer, but she apparently didn't feel comfortable asserting herself now.

Caleb thought he understood why. Zarah was a guest in this world, and she would be going back home as soon as her husband sent for her. Still, the look on her face told Caleb that she had no faith in his abilities.

Quinn was the one who spoke. "At least get some rest before you get to work. You had a hard day yesterday."

Caleb looked at Ross. "We're trying to prevent an attack on the capital of the United States, right?"

"Right."

"And we don't know how much time we have?"

"Yeah," Ross agreed.

"Then I think we'd better get on with it. I hope you can find me the information I need."

"Okay. The way I see it, Ruckleman will expect Reynolds to know about computers and the Internet. So we might as well get started with a Web surfing lesson." He thought for a moment. "We have to assume Reynolds was held for a day or two before they killed him. That means we have to move quickly because the longer he's out of contact with his unit, the more explaining he has to do."

Caleb nodded.

"We don't know about Reynolds' mannerisms. Or much personal information. So we need to research that, too." He looked toward Logan. "Actually, maybe we'd better divide up the search. Can you use my laptop to get background on Reynolds while I focus on Ruckleman?"

"Sure."

Ross turned to Caleb and gestured toward the chair beside his. "Sit here. I'll take you through some of my search procedures. Then when we get information on Jerry Ruckleman, you can start studying it." He sighed.

"What?"

"The problem is, we don't know how much Reynolds knew about Ruckleman. You could slip up if you know what college he went to. And you could slip up if you don't."

"Yeah, but I have to try it."

"I'll do whatever I can to help," Ross offered.

"Thanks," Caleb answered. His head was still spinning when he thought about himself working with the Marshalls. But they were different from what he'd expected. And, to his astonishment, it seemed to be possible to cooperate with them. Especially with Ross.

JACOB ran straight for the fence, slipped through and kept going into the woods, stopping to listen for sounds of pursuit.

It seemed like no one was following him, but he waited for fifteen minutes in the woods before changing back to his human form. As soon as he'd pulled on his clothing, he climbed in his car and drove away. Ten minutes up the road, he called Ross's cell phone.

"Thanks for checking in," his cousin said. "Let me put this on the speaker."

"Sure."

"Were you on the farm?"

"Yeah. They have guard dogs—but I handled them."

"Good."

"I have some information. But maybe I should wait to tell you when I get there."

"Right. But we know what he's planning," Ross said.

"Well, I can give you a time frame. He had a calendar over his desk—with a date circled."

"You were in his office?" Ross asked sharply.

"His bedroom."

"That was taking a chance."

"Do you want to know the date or not?"

"Yeah."

"July third."

"Good work. I'll tell you what he's planning when you get here."

"Got ya." Jacob hesitated for a moment. "One thing you should know. He came back while I was in his room. I had to leap out the window—and I knocked out the screen when I went out."

Ross waited a beat before asking, "So what does he think happened?"

"Maybe that one of the guard dogs was in his room. He'd left some food there. And maybe the dog went after that."

"Yeah, maybe," Ross muttered.

CALEB watched Ross click off and put the phone back in the holster on his belt. "I'm thinking he's planning to set off his Fourth of July fireworks early."

"But why not wait until the actual day?" Logan asked.

"Too many people on the streets and too many police on crowd control," Ross answered. "He'd be running too much of a risk. But now we have a target date. And we know we have a few days to get ready."

THREE frantic days later, Caleb stood in the hot sun on a downtown Washington street waiting for the traffic light to turn green. *No, not the green light*, he corrected himself. *That was the old way.* He was waiting for that lighted picture of a man walking. When it flashed on, he and several other pedestrians hurried across the intersection. He saw a woman give him a quick inspection, then look away.

He was careful to keep his eyes straight ahead and his face expressionless. But he knew she was wondering what a guy who looked like he'd spent the night in Lafayette Square was doing in this part of town.

He and the Marshalls had debated what he should wear. Finally they'd decided that if he was supposed to have been in detention and then escaped through farm country, he should look disheveled. So he was wearing a pair of grimy blue jeans and a gray flannel shirt with a rip in one sleeve. Since he'd already neglected to shave for a few days before he arrived at Logan's house, the blond stubble on his face added to the picture.

It was ten in the morning—and he knew he wasn't ready for his acting debut. But, given the July third deadline, they'd waited as long as they could. And he had a lot of things going for him.

Nobody could really doubt he was Wyatt Reynolds. If they took his fingerprints, they would match Reynolds. His medical and dental records would match. And, of course, he looked exactly like the man. Now he just had to remember to respond when somebody addressed Reynolds.

Not such an easy task when he'd been Caleb Marshall for over a hundred years.

A van with the name of a pastry shop on upper Connecticut Avenue turned the corner. He and the driver made eye contact for a split second, then both looked away.

Ross Marshall was driving the van. Over the past few days they'd been working closely together. Ross had been giving him pointers on fitting into this society. And Caleb had been trying to wrap his head around the idea of a world where the United States of America was under attack from foreign and domestic terrorist groups, where kids brought guns to school to murder their classmates, and where a private home might cost a million dollars or more.

When they weren't dealing with socioeconomic issues, he was memorizing facts about Reynolds, Ruckleman, and Bowie.

And Ross was treating him as an equal, which was a good feeling. He would have enjoyed the experience if he hadn't been so conscious that flubbing up could sink this entire mission.

On the other hand, there was an advantage to the frantic activity. He didn't have to spend a lot of time with Quinn.

He'd made sure that the two of them were on different schedules.

He was staying up late with Ross. And she was getting up early to work with Zarah. They'd only met when she'd insisted that he practice a technique he might need for his visit to Ruckleman's office.

Even then, he'd kept the personal relationship on hold, and he knew she was upset. He also knew he should talk to her about what he was feeling. But it was still too painful.

He loved her. But what good did that do either one of them? Sometimes, he'd think that maybe he could make a place for himself in this strange new world. Other times, he wasn't so sure. And he wasn't willing to talk to Quinn about the two of them until he could orient himself in time and space.

He'd basically shut her out, but he couldn't dwell on that now. He had to stay focused on getting into the office and convincing Ruckleman that they had an immediate crisis on their hands.

But at the moment, hundreds of details were whirling around in his head, like those little spinning seed pods that came off of maple trees when the wind blew.

Including the intelligence Jacob had brought back from the militia compound, grinning as he slapped hand-drawn maps onto the table, along with descriptions of the buildings and the information that there were twenty men and a shitload of weapons on the property. And when they'd told him about the bombs, he'd come up with an excellent guess about where they were being stored.

Working another angle, Ross had done some great detective work. He'd found out where Wyatt Reynolds lived in Silver Spring, and they'd gotten into his house. They'd brought back family photos and home videos of Reynolds as a kid with his parents and then with his wife. The visual details had helped him peg the Reynolds identity. So he could imitate how the man walked and how he moved his hands when he talked.

Of course, being able to watch the videos was just another sign to Caleb that this world was a million times more complex than the 1930s. It wasn't just the sociology. It was the technology. There were too many things here that he'd never even dreamed of.

But he'd have to worry about them later. Right now, he had to focus on Wyatt Reynolds and Jerry Ruckleman.

One thing they'd discussed was why Reynolds had gone on a covert assignment using his real name—and not an alias.

Ross had answered the question. Reynolds had been an Army sergeant serving in Germany when his wife had died back in the States. Apparently, he'd gone to pieces and started a brawl at a local beer garden. He'd ended up with a dishonorable discharge from the Army. Initially, he'd been angry with the government, which was supposed to be the rationale for his seeking out Colonel Bowie's militia.

But really it was the other way around. After his drunken outburst, he'd wanted to prove he wasn't a screwup. He'd volunteered to work with the Department of Homeland Security, and all his dealings with Bowie had been at the instigation of that agency.

Still, Reynolds had been a man at war with himself. And it looked like his underlying death wish had won out over his remorse. Caleb could understand that better than most people. Was his own death wish the reason he was here? Getting killed would certainly solve his problems with Quinn.

Once again, he pushed his own problems to the back of his mind and centered himself on the complications of the moment.

For one thing, Reynolds wasn't a regular employee of the department but had been hired on a contract basis. For another, there were still some questions about his relationship with Jerry Ruckleman. The department chief was a straight arrow, and he probably had trouble dealing with a man who'd messed up in the Army.

In addition to the background on Reynolds, Ross had also obtained a videotape of Jerome Ruckleman in a management course he'd taken at the FBI Academy at Quantico. So Caleb had an idea of how the man functioned as a boss. From what he could see, the guy was insecure and reinforced his own status by coming down hard on his subordinates. Caleb didn't much like the resulting picture, but he was stuck with it.

Maybe that was why he felt the back of his neck tingle as he turned the corner and walked up H Street to a three-story gray stone building at the edge of the George Washington University urban campus.

The office was rented by the Department of Homeland Security, and Ross had driven him down here the day before so he'd know what it looked like.

They'd even gotten some photos that had been taken by the real estate company when the property was for rent, although nobody knew whether the layout had changed since then.

Outside was a narrow strip of grass and a neatly trimmed hedge. Above the hedge was a brass plate on the exterior wall with the initials DHS. Building sixteen.

That was all, but he knew it was the headquarters for the covert surveillance unit run by Jerry Ruckleman.

When Caleb reached the building, he wanted to look up, but he kept his gaze down, not on the security camera that he knew was taking a moving picture of him. *No, a video.* He had to stop thinking in terms of movies. But that was part of the difficulty. He kept coming up with 1930s terms for things when this was the twenty-first century.

Well, too late now. He'd volunteered for this job because he knew it was important, and he had to pull it off.

Or what?

He tried to push any thought of failure out of his mind, yet the possibility of screwing up gnawed at him.

Hoping he looked like he had every right to enter the building, he opened the door and stepped into a cool, dimly lit, windowless lobby about ten feet wide and fifteen feet long.

He stopped short, glancing around. The space had been changed since the pictures had been taken. It was smaller now, with false walls along the sides. To the right was a counter with a blue uniformed guard and security monitors showing views of various hallways in the building.

Straight ahead he spotted a card reader that he now would

describe as looking something like a gate at a subway station.

He didn't have a card to put in the slot. And he knew what would happen as soon as he stepped through without identifying himself.

They'd discussed what he should do when he reached this point.

It could be bad either way. So he walked through.

In seconds, guards materialized from doorways and he was surrounded by four men in blue uniforms with their weapons drawn.

All their guns were pointed directly at him.

CHAPTER
THIRTY

"HANDS IN THE air," one of the guards ordered, his voice hard and commanding.

It could end right here, if I make a wrong move, Caleb thought as he stood in the tomblike twilight of the entry.

But he was prepared for the order and raised his hands. He hoped he looked cool when his stomach was tied up like an old-fashioned German pretzel.

"Wait a minute," one of the other men said. "I recognize him. He looks like a panhandler, but it's Wyatt Reynolds."

Caleb's gaze swung to the guard, a sandy-haired man wearing horn-rimmed glasses. He'd just been hit with his first curveball. He didn't recognize the guy. Were they friends? Or was this man usually on shift when Reynolds came in? What?

His colleague gave Caleb a closer inspection. "I don't know him. And he looks pretty scuzzy."

Caleb cleared his throat. "I've been in solitary confinement. And now I'm reporting in. I've got to talk to my section chief, Jerry Ruckleman."

"Not likely."

The guard who'd spoken crossed to the security desk,

picked up the receiver from a telephone, and started dialing—
No, punching in numbers. Ross had told him the dial had
gone out of use years ago, except for vintage phones.

"Connors here."

"Yes, sir. We have a situation at the card reader."

From his position several yards away, Caleb strained to
hear the rest of the conversation. But the man glanced at
him, then turned his back and hunched his shoulders so that
Caleb's line of sight and hearing were blocked.

"Yes, sir," he finished, then replaced the receiver.

Turning to Caleb he motioned with his hand. "This way."

"Can I put my hands down?"

"Yeah."

They could have cuffed him. Mercifully, they left his
hands free as they escorted him through the barrier, then
down a hall. But not to Ruckleman's office, as far as he
could tell. Instead, they ushered him into a windowless room
with gray walls and a couple of hard chairs.

Two of the guards stayed with him. Two more left the
room.

When he'd run over various scenarios in his mind, Caleb
had pictured something like this, and he'd decided it was
better to sit and look relaxed than to stand and pace.

Time ticked by like grains of sand falling one by one
down the narrow tube between two parts of an egg timer.

Did they still have them in this world? He should have
asked.

No. Not important. He had to keep his mind fixed on the
crucial things, starting with his expression. He had to look
like a man who had nothing to hide, because probably they
had a camera trained on him at this moment. They'd want to
see what he was doing now. And they'd review the tapes
later.

He kept his gaze straight ahead. But in his mind, watching
the picture of the egg timer helped keep him calm.

When the door opened he looked up, then stood as a slim,
balding man in his early fifties stepped into the room. He
had small, close-set eyes and a Roman nose that looked too
big for his face.

"Jerry!"

As soon as he saw the man's expression, Caleb felt his stomach twist. This guy might be Wyatt Reynolds' section chief, but he hated working with him. Probably they had some kind of history that hadn't come out in their investigation.

Ruckleman turned to the guards. "Wait outside."

The two men left and closed the door behind them, and Caleb was sure they were standing on either side of the doorway, prepared to keep him from escaping.

As soon as they were alone, the older man rounded on Caleb. "Where the hell have you been? You were due to report in six days ago."

"You know they watch all the guys out at the farm. I can't always stick to a regular schedule."

"Yeah. So what's your excuse this time?"

"I don't make excuses. I report what's happening."

The section chief folded his arms across his chest but didn't speak.

"The colonel suspected me of spying. I've been in a prison on the compound for the past week."

Ruckleman's eyes narrowed. "He's a hard case. He whips guys for not washing their hands after they piss. If he suspected you weren't being straight with him, why aren't you dead and buried somewhere out in the woods?"

Caleb fought not to wince, since that was exactly what had happened. "They've been trying to get information out of me."

"What did you tell them?"

"Nothing. You have to listen to me."

"Do I?"

Caleb ignored the question and plowed ahead. "You thought Bowie was a homegrown terrorist. But his motivation isn't what you think. He's convinced himself that he's a superpatriot. He's trying to force the government to take away more of our civil liberties—and strengthen their policies against terrorists."

The other man didn't seem to be getting it. Instead, he was giving Caleb a considering look. "I wouldn't say they worked you over too much."

"They can make sure it doesn't show."

Ruckleman tipped his head to the side, still looking like he was withholding judgment. "So, how'd you get away?"

"When they came back to get me for another session, I pretended I was in too much pain to get up off the floor. Usually, two of them came in when they opened the door. But this time there was only one. I jumped him, then lit out across the fields. They searched for me, and I tumbled off the edge of a cliff and landed hard. But I got up and crawled through a drainage pipe."

The section chief was looking at him skeptically. "You're not supposed to come here without the security card you've got hidden."

Caleb touched his head, getting ready to spout the lie that would explain what seemed like gaps in his memory—when they were real gaps in his knowledge of Wyatt Reynolds and his relationship with this very hostile man.

"I don't know where it is! When I went over that cliff, I hit my head. There are holes in my memory."

"Convenient."

"What are you trying to say, that I'm lying? Or maybe they sent someone here to impersonate Wyatt Reynolds? All you have to do is check my fingerprints."

Ruckleman stared at him. "I'm not doubting your identity, but you always were a little flaky."

Oh, great.

"Yeah, well, I came here to tell you something important."

"Something you conveniently remember?" the man asked, a sneer in his voice. "Then spit it out."

"Bowie had me in detention because he has a big operation ready to go. And he didn't trust me." He took a deep breath and let it out. "He's getting ready to set off a dirty bomb in Washington, D.C. Two bombs, actually. One as a diversion for the main event."

"When?"

"July third."

"Where?"

"The diversion is at the Kennedy Center. The real thing is at the Capitol."

"You have any proof?"

"You mean like a calendar circled in red?" he asked, thinking that was what Jacob had seen. "Of course I couldn't get out of there with anything written down. Maybe he doesn't *have* anything written down. But I risked my life to get you that information."

"Maybe. But right now I don't know if you've switched sides."

Caleb fought not to answer with a curse.

As he was still trying to rein in his anger, the section chief walked up to him, grabbed the front of his shirt and ripped the placket open, exposing his chest.

"What the hell?"

Caleb looked from his bare chest to the other man's smirking face.

"At least you're not wearing a wire."

It was all he could do to keep from wrapping his large hands around the man's neck. In as mild a voice as he could manage, he said, "Of course not. Why would I?"

"I wouldn't put it past you."

"Stop acting like I joined the militia. You know I took this job because I'm trying to protect my country."

Keeping his expression bland, Ruckleman said, "So you're saying the colonel didn't send you to deflect attention from what he's really planning?"

Caleb didn't have to struggle to sound outraged. "You've got to be kidding. I volunteered for this assignment because I'm against everything the colonel stands for."

"Uh huh." Ruckleman gave him a long, considering look. "I haven't been pleased with your performance for the past six months. You haven't come up with much new information."

Scrambling for an answer to the accusation, he said, "Maybe because they had me out of the loop."

Ruckleman ignored the interjection and kept talking. "Now you come to me with a crazy story about a bomb plot and holes in your memory."

"If you raid the compound, you'll find the bombs."

"How did you find out about them—if you're out of the loop?"

"I was sneaking around, listening and watching."

"Uh-huh. Well, I can't raid the place on your say-so. We're going to have to verify your story. And you're going to have to stay here while I see what I can find out."

"Don't dismiss this out of hand."

"I'm not. I told you, I'm planning to investigate."

"Sure."

"I never did like that smart-ass attitude of yours."

Caleb wanted to tell Jerry Ruckleman that he was being a jerk. But all he did was stand there, facing the man who should be thrilled that his spy had escaped and dragged himself in here with important information.

Too late he saw the fatal flaw in the scenario they'd devised. With all their careful planning, they didn't know that Jerry Ruckleman had never trusted Wyatt Reynolds. Maybe he'd been forced to work with him—under protest. Maybe all along he'd thought that Reynolds would get himself killed.

Ruckleman was at the door again, speaking to the two guards. They came back in, their gazes drilling into Caleb.

"Make Mr. Reynolds comfortable in room fifteen," the section chief said.

When the two men moved up on either side of Caleb, he looked at Ruckleman. "You're making a mistake. They're going to set off the bombs the day after tomorrow. You need to get out to Flagstaff Farm and disarm them."

"I'll give the orders around here."

Caleb felt a cold chill sweep over him. Ross had told him about 9/11. The same numbers as you called in an emergency. Only they meant something different, too. He'd learned that that was the day terrorists had blown up the Twin Towers of something called the World Trade Center in New York. Since then, Americans had been fighting a "war on terror." And they'd allowed some of their civil liberties to be taken away. You could be held indefinitely, with no formal charges and no chance to talk to a lawyer. Ross had given him examples that had curdled his stomach.

Technically, Wyatt Reynolds was a member of a militia organization bent on creating chaos in the United States. If

Ruckleman wanted to, he could have Caleb locked up under the same terms as anyone else suspected of being a terrorist. Meanwhile, the real terrorists would go about their business, getting their attack ready. And a lot of people would get killed.

It took every ounce of discipline he possessed to keep from wrenching away and running down the hall. But he knew if he did that, he'd end up with a bullet in his back.

His eyes darted to the left and right, as though he expected some kind of help to come oozing through the walls. But no help came, so he let the two men march him out of the room. Instead of heading into the back of the building, they walked toward the lobby area again.

As he looked toward the entrance and saw a figure enter the building, his heart leaped into his throat.

CHAPTER
THIRTY-ONE

THE TWO GUARDS on either side of Caleb had stopped moving and stood like the statues he'd once seen in a wax museum when he'd taken a trip to New York. Not just the guards. Everyone within sight had gone rigid.

Caleb's gaze flicked around the room, taking it all in. Then he focused on the doorway, where Quinn was standing. He knew it was her, although he couldn't see her face. She had on a thin rubber mask that adhered to her features, making her nose longer, her cheekbones higher, her lips thicker, and her chin heavier.

The change in appearance meant no one could recognize her from the security camera that was doubtless recording the scene.

And her fingerprints would not transfer to any surface because she was wearing surgical gloves.

Through the mask he could see a look of concentration on her face.

"Hurry," she said, her voice low and breathless. "Zarah and I can't keep them immobile for long."

He took a deep breath, struggling against the feeling that

his brain had melted inside his head and his body was wading through a vat of thick molasses.

"Hurry."

"I can't," he managed to say.

Panic flashed in her eyes, and he knew she and Zarah hadn't been prepared for this glitch, since he'd practiced resisting their suggestion.

He kept struggling toward her, each step feeling like he was lifting thousand-pound weights on his shoes.

And as he moved, he kept waiting for the sound of gunfire behind him.

This was the team's fallback plan, although it wasn't playing out the way anyone had expected.

Ruckleman had checked for a wire under his shirt and hadn't found one. That was because Ross had used a different location—a transmitter in the heel of Caleb's shoe. If they'd detained him and done a thorough search of his clothing, they would have found it.

But they hadn't gotten the chance.

Of course, a mike muffled by a shoe wasn't as sensitive as one right up on his chest, under his shirt. Probably, the transmission wouldn't stand up in court. But they weren't trying to get Ruckleman to say something to incriminate himself. They were just trying to find out if the interview turned hostile.

Which it had.

And the range of the transmission was good enough for Ross to pick it up out in the pastry van.

He'd waited until they were going to transfer Caleb to detention, then activated the other part of the equation: the two adepts. They'd been practicing together, reinforcing the facility they both had to control the minds of other people.

Although they'd both studied the skill in school, neither one of them had enough power for a full-scale attack on her own. But they were working together now, making everyone within range of Caleb stop in their tracks—with Zarah in the van and Quinn directing the process.

Too bad he couldn't quite filter out the command they

were broadcasting. Maybe because they were using more power than in their practice session.

Worse, Quinn had to put herself in danger, which wasn't helping him focus.

But there had been no alternative, except coming in armed. The guards would have responded, and then someone would have gotten killed. And that hadn't been their intention at all. They'd wanted to alert Homeland Security, not start a gun battle.

Caleb was the only one in the lobby moving. But he could still feel the command buzzing at the edges of his brain, trying to stop his forward movement.

Quinn's expression sharpened. "Focus on something else like you practiced," she called to him.

"I'm trying." He didn't bother telling her it was different under battlefield conditions.

"Think about how good that steak tasted back at the lodge."

The memory leaped into his head. He'd been a ghost for seventy-five years, and that was the first meat he'd eaten. It had tasted heavenly—once Quinn had cooked it enough. But no more heavenly than the taste of Quinn's sweet mouth.

He didn't want to think about that. But once he started, he was helpless to stop remembered sensations from bombarding him.

He didn't speak to her again. Couldn't risk breaking her concentration. Instead he put one foot in front of the other, each step feeling like he was lifting his shoe off of flypaper.

Centuries passed as he dragged himself across the room. Then he felt something change inside his head. He was about to offer a prayer of thanks when he realized that the change wasn't just affecting him.

Someone behind him made a strangled sound. And when he half turned, he saw that one of the guards who had been standing beside him was glancing around in confusion.

Behind him, Jerry Ruckleman was staring at the scene with a look of shock.

"Get him."

Caleb found he could speed up.

But the men around him were getting more of their faculties back, too.

"What the hell?" someone shouted.

"I don't know. Just get him," another panicked voice answered.

Other guards were moving, still slowly. But Caleb saw them picking up speed and knew that the mental suggestion had been broken. Now he and Quinn had only seconds to get away.

"Stop, or I'll shoot."

He kept going, pushing Quinn through the door, just as a bullet slammed into the woodwork too close to his head for comfort.

He grabbed her hand, dragging her outside and around a panicked-looking woman who was coming up the sidewalk. A group of students in track suits came jogging toward them. Caleb and Quinn dodged them as they sprinted for the van, which had pulled up in the no parking zone in front of the building. The back door was already open, and he flung Quinn inside, almost slamming her into Zarah, who was staring wide-eyed at the armed men behind them.

Caleb peered through one of the windows in the back door. He could see guards on the sidewalk, but they couldn't get off a shot at the van because too many people were in the way.

"Go, go!" Caleb shouted to Ross.

"I'm trying, dammit." As he attempted to make a getaway, a car pulled in front of them blocking their exit.

Ross pounded on the horn, then backed up, and started forward again, zipping around the car.

Beside Caleb, Quinn was pulling at the mask. She peeled it off her skin, then looked at it in disgust before stuffing it into a plastic bag. "Yuck!" She rubbed her face. "I hope I never have to wear something like that again."

"We've got to disappear before they can get to their vehicles—or call in the cops," Ross said as he turned down an alley, then into the parking lot in back of a gray stone church where Logan was waiting in his SUV. They all piled out, leaving the van—and no fingerprints because of the gloves they all wore. He saw Quinn also take the plastic bag with the mask. The cops would find the van, but they couldn't trace the people who drove it. Except Caleb. But Ruckleman's men had already seen him get inside.

The license plates were also a dead end—from a junkyard wreck.

Caleb breathed out a sigh as they pulled out of the parking lot, then turned down the alley, moving at a normal pace.

"So much for getting help from Homeland Security," Caleb muttered.

"That guy doesn't like Reynolds much," Ross observed.

"Yeah, I'd say Ruckleman hates his guts. I wonder why they ended up on the same assignment."

"Bad luck." Ross might have said more, but the sound of a police siren cut him off.

"I think the cops are on the case already," Logan said.

The van had been windowless, except for the back door and the driver's compartment. The SUV had tinted windows, but there was still some chance of being seen.

"Duck down," Ross instructed Caleb and Quinn. They both slipped to the floor behind the front seat, resting their elbows on the cushions.

"What do you think they're going to say happened in the lobby?" Quinn asked.

"Damned if I know," Ross muttered. "The security tapes are going to be interesting." He looked over his shoulder at Caleb. "They probably think you zapped them with something, which is further proof that you're on the wrong side."

"Yeah."

"Are you all right?" Zarah asked.

"Yes. Thanks to all of you," Caleb answered. Then his gaze shot to Quinn. "I didn't like seeing you in there."

"You mean with my clown mask?"

"No. You were in danger."

"So were you. The moment you stepped into that damn building. Only we didn't know it would happen that way."

He started to say something else, when she scooted toward him and slung her arms around his neck, pulling him to her. He couldn't stop himself. He hugged her tightly, even though he knew everybody in back was watching.

He'd kept trying to distance himself from her. But it wasn't working. Even when he'd been a ghost, he'd suspected that she was his life mate. And whether he liked it or not, they were tied to each other. When she slanted her mouth over his, he was helpless to hold back a surge of need.

Then Logan slammed on the brakes, and Caleb pulled away, muttering, "This is a dangerous place to kiss."

She kept her gaze fixed on him. "We'll find a better place later."

The way she said it made his temperature rise. And he knew she wasn't thinking only about kissing. The very private exchange in front of a carful of people made his face grow warm. He wasn't used to such openness about sex, which was another unsettling aspect of this society. In his time, married couples in movies couldn't even lie down in the same bed. In this century, you could see movies and TV shows with people doing everything imaginable.

Quinn reached for his hand, squeezing his fingers. And he squeezed back, silently admitting that it was impossible to fight what he felt for her.

But what about later? Five years from now, would she end up hating him?

A jangling like the ringing of an old-fashioned telephone made him jump. Would he ever get used to phone calls coming and going everywhere including the bathroom?

Ross answered, "Yeah?"

It was Jacob, who had stayed out at Flagstaff Farm to keep an eye on Bowie and the militia.

His voice came over the speaker—another modern feature.

"We've got a problem. There's considerable activity on the property. I think they're getting ready to make a move."

"But it's a day early," Caleb answered from the backseat.

"Maybe that wolf in the bedroom made Bowie nervous."

CHAPTER
THIRTY-TWO

AS THEY CONTINUED to speak, Caleb kept his gaze on the back of Ross's head, a sick feeling rising in his throat.

"How soon are they moving out?" the detective asked.

"I can't be sure. But probably tonight. I'll let you know if anything else happens."

"What the hell are we going to do?" Caleb asked when the call had concluded.

"You were entirely focused on trying to get help from Ruckleman," Ross answered. "But the rest of us have been making contingency plans."

"Oh, yeah?"

"They're not exactly fully formed," Quinn put in, her voice heavy with frustration.

That was one of the things he loved about her. She was always straightforward. Well, maybe she hadn't been when she'd been trying to get the Marshalls not to kill him. He wasn't real proud of his attitude toward them back then. But he understood it. He'd been operating out of werewolf anger—and misinformation.

Ross turned to look at him. "We've been calling in reinforcements. By the time we get home, Sam and Olivia Morgan should be there."

"Sam and Olivia?" he asked.

"Sam used to be Johnny Marshall, my brother. After he got framed for a murder in a bar, he took off for California. He's had a very colorful career as a thief."

Quinn goggled at him. "You're kidding, right?"

"No. He's going to be a big help," Ross answered. "And so will his wife, Olivia. Logan's brother Lance is already there. He left his wife, Savannah, home because she's pregnant."

He gave Caleb a direct look. "Are you going to be uncomfortable with so many of the pack on hand?"

"No," Caleb answered, hoping he could handle it. Hell, he had to handle it. He swallowed. "Did you tell them what happened to me?"

"Yeah," Ross answered. "They're all intrigued to meet a man who was dead for seventy-five years."

And what do they think about a werewolf who's stuck in human form? He kept that question to himself.

Logan looked at him. "Um, maybe you want to change your clothes before you meet them. I have a shower out back. And spare clothing in the shed."

"You do?"

"So I can clean up after work without messing up the house."

"Thanks for the offer."

When they pulled into the driveway, he headed around back. After showering and shaving, he changed clothes. Then he took a deep breath and went to meet more of his family.

When he stepped into the great room, the conversation stopped.

"Here he is," Ross said, then introduced him to Lance, Sam, Olivia, and his wife, Megan.

To Caleb's relief, everyone acted like he belonged there.

Now that he'd gotten past his murderous rage at Aden's descendants, he silently admitted that he liked these men—and their wives. Too bad he could never be their equal.

Later, he'd have to decide how much he could stand to be the impotent wolf among them. For now, they were all too busy working out a plan for keeping Colonel Jim Bowie and his men from leaving Flagstaff Farm with the bombs.

"Zarah and I can use the same technique on Bowie and his men that we used on the guards in Ruckleman's building," Quinn said. She turned to Zarah. "Why did it stop working?"

"Because we didn't have a visual link between us, I think. This time we'll stay where we can see each other."

"Outside the farm boundaries," Caleb said, his voice emphatic.

He listened to the conversation swirling around him. It was obvious that Ross was the leader of the pack, although nobody was stupid enough to say it out loud.

QUINN and Zarah went off into a corner to practice strengthening the control technique, since it was a key element in Ross's plans for the attack.

"Maybe we should go off where we have more privacy," Quinn murmured.

"We won't have privacy during the operation. We need to work under battlefield conditions," Zarah answered. "So let's stay here."

They built the link, focusing on each other's minds as the others worked out plans. Then, suddenly, Quinn felt the connection snap.

"What happened?"

"Sorry. I'll be right back."

When Zarah got up and headed down the hall, Quinn figured that probably the baby had kicked her in the bladder.

She came back a few minutes later, her face white as chalk as she stood in the doorway.

Quinn quickly crossed the room to her friend. "What's wrong?"

Zarah looked at her, her eyes large and panicked. "I . . . I'm bleeding."

"Great Mother. When did you find out?"

"Just now. I felt . . ." She flushed and lowered her voice, turning her back to the people in the great room. "A little wet. So I went into the bathroom to check." She looked at Quinn with brimming eyes. "It's much too early for the baby."

Megan, who was near enough to hear the worried conversation, rushed over. "Let's go into the bedroom where we can have some privacy."

Zarah gave her a grateful look, then turned to Quinn. "Will you come, too?"

"Of course."

As they walked down the hall, Megan said, "You know I'm a doctor."

"Like my obstetrician?" Zarah asked, hope in her voice.

"I have a different specialty."

Zarah's worried look came back.

"But we all have training in every field of medicine," Megan said.

When they'd stepped into Zarah's bedroom and closed the door, Zarah pulled off her panties and showed Megan the small bloodstain on them.

"You're not in any pain? No cramping."

"No," Zarah said.

"What month are you in?"

"The fourth."

"That's all excellent. I think it's just that a piece of the placenta broke off."

Zarah sucked in a sharp breath. "Is that bad?"

"No, not bad at all. But you should have your doctor examine you. I'll take you to the emergency room," she said.

"Would you?" Zarah asked, her gratitude shining in her voice.

"Of course."

Quinn went out to report what was happening. Then Megan and Zarah appeared.

"I'm sorry, I won't be able to help Quinn immobilize the men," she said in a low voice as she looked at the expectant faces of everyone in the group.

Quinn could feel the tension that suddenly filled the room, since their role had been a key factor in the assault.

Ross was the one who answered. "Of course not," he said. "You go make sure everything is all right with you and the baby."

Quinn turned to her friend. "I should stay here, so we can come up with something else. Will you be all right without me?"

"Yes," Zarah answered.

When she and Megan had left, Ross cleared his throat. "I guess we go to plan B."

"What's plan B?" Lance asked.

"I don't know yet. But we'll think of something."

Before anybody else could speak, Ross's cell phone rang, and he put it on speaker again. It was Jacob.

"Bad news," he said. "I think they're getting ready to leave the farm."

"Before dark?"

"Maybe they're moving to a staging area nearer D.C. They've got two vans and a couple of SUVs."

"Can you stop them?" Ross asked.

"I'm going to try. I'll get back to you as soon as I can. Meanwhile, maybe you'd better start driving out here."

Ross stood. "We'd better finish the planning session on the way out there."

JACOB took one more look through his binoculars. Then he headed back to the woods where he'd left his backpack. He'd come up with a plan. It was risky, but he couldn't think of any alternative.

First he got out a knife in a leather sheath. Then he changed to wolf form. Taking the sheathed blade in his mouth, he started back toward the fence that bordered the farm.

The two dogs he'd met the night before came trotting up when he slipped through the wooden rails. But this time they recognized him. And when he began humming to them the way he had the night before, they both gave him friendly greetings, then stayed with him as he headed toward the center of the compound. Men were moving around, and he waited until the area was clear to slip under one of the vans.

Now came the tricky part. As a wolf, he couldn't hold the knife tightly enough in his mouth to do what he needed to do. So he set down the knife, then, as he lay on the ground under one of the vans, he said the chant in his head that changed him from wolf to man. Moments later, he was naked, exposed, and praying that nobody was going to look under the vehicle.

One of the dogs growled at him, the hairs on its back bristling.

Jacob spoke to him in a low voice, telling him that everything was all right—that he was a man as well as a wolf.

In the middle of his speech, he saw booted feet approaching the truck and clamped his mouth shut.

He waited with the knife in his hand and his breath frozen in his lungs. When a man bent down to talk to the dogs, he clenched the knife, prepared to strike if the guy bent any lower and happened to see a naked arm or leg under the vehicle.

MINUTES after Ross had spoken to Jacob, they started getting ready to leave.

"Are we going in as wolves?" Lance asked, then glanced at Caleb before looking away.

Caleb struggled not to let his natural reaction show. "Maybe I can go in as a ghost," he answered.

"Whatever we decide, we're going to make sure we're armed," Ross cut in. "The colonel's men will have automatic weapons. So I brought along Uzi's."

"Which are what?" Caleb asked.

"Small Israeli-made machine guns."

"That's a company? Like Winchester?"

"No, a country. You'd call it the Holy Land."

"They make deadly weapons *there*?"

"I'll tell you about it later."

"Yeah, right." He shook his head. "I know guys who carried revolvers," Caleb said. "But I never used one." He started to say tooth and claw were his specialty but choked off the words before they reached his lips.

"With a machine gun, bullets come out in a rapid stream, meaning you have more chance of killing."

Ross looked at Lance. "Will you give Caleb a quick lesson in machine-gun handling? Then follow us out to Frederick?"

"Yeah," his cousin answered.

Caleb wondered if he was annoyed at being asked to stay back. But he knew why Ross hadn't asked Logan. He and Logan still rubbed each other the wrong way.

The others left in two of the SUVs, and Lance took Caleb and two of the Uzi's down to the firing range.

"In battle, you won't have ear protectors," he said. "But we'll use them now—to preserve your hearing."

After some instruction, Caleb took the gun and aimed at the target. But he wasn't prepared for the kick, and his first bursts of bullets went way above the bull's-eye.

QUINN kept stifling the impulse to glance over her shoulder as they rode toward Flagstaff Farm. She didn't like leaving Caleb back at Logan's house. But she wasn't going to protest. A firing lesson made sense. Caleb had never shot a modern weapon. He needed to know what it felt like.

Hoping to ease the tightness in her chest, she turned to Olivia, the wife of Sam Morgan, who was sitting beside her in the back of the SUV. They'd all talked about their special abilities at the planning session, and Quinn had been surprised to hear that everyone in Olivia's family had a psychic talent.

"Did you ever try to influence another person's thoughts?" she asked.

"Yes," Olivia answered, "when Sam and I were under attack from the man trying to kill him and dominate me. But that was only one man."

"Maybe together we could reach more," Quinn answered.

"If we had time to practice."

"Open your mind," Quinn said, "Try to be receptive to me." Then she flushed, thinking how presumptive she'd been. She was a former slave, and she was giving orders to a woman she'd just met. A woman who had grown up rich, from what she'd heard.

But Olivia smiled at her. "Yes, that's a good idea." She reached for Quinn's hand, leaned back against the seat, and closed her eyes.

Quinn did the same, searching for a link to the other woman. It was crazy, thinking they could do it under these circumstances, but she would try it. Because Caleb's life might depend on her success. Colonel Bowie had sent men to kill Wyatt Reynolds. And Caleb was in that body now. Bowie was going to react when he saw him again—and it wouldn't be to stretch out an arm and shake hands. When the colonel looked at Caleb, he was going to see his enemy.

So she strove to make a connection with Olivia. At first she felt nothing.

"Just let it happen," Olivia murmured.

"Yes," Quinn answered. She knew from the other woman's response that she'd felt *something*.

So she tried a more relaxed approach, pretending that Olivia was like Zarah—an old friend.

And in a few moments, she felt the tendrils of the other woman's thoughts reaching toward her.

Good.

She could feel Olivia smile, then hear her mental voice.

How much can we do? And how long will this last?

I wish I knew.

What orders should we give them, if we can reach their minds?

Nothing complicated. We've got to keep it simple.

AFTER what felt like centuries, the man moved away, and Jacob let out the breath he'd been holding.

Then he inched toward the right front tire and pressed the point of the knife into the black rubber.

Quickly, he made similar holes in the three other tires. Then he waited, listening.

The hiss of air escaping sounded like the roaring of Niagara Falls to him. But he hoped it wouldn't be quite so obvious to anyone passing by.

Of course, there was something he hadn't thought about. Now that the tires were deflating, the van was pressing lower to the ground, giving him a lot less room.

Would it come down far enough to crush him? He hoped not.

In a low voice, he murmured the chant that changed him from man to wolf again. The change never felt pleasant, but the pain was greater this time because he'd done it so recently and because he had to be in such an awkward position. All he could do was grit his teeth and ride above the punishment to his muscles and tendons. When the transformation was complete, he started to slither out and head for the other van.

But he ran smack into a man who had come pounding toward him from one of the buildings.

CHAPTER
THIRTY-THREE

THE MAN STOPPED in his tracks when he saw an animal he hadn't been expecting. Jacob used that moment of surprise to spring at him, knocking him to the ground.

Only half his mission was accomplished. He'd disabled one van, but he knew he'd just run out of options.

Hoping he could escape, he took off toward the fence.

"What the hell?" the guy shouted.

Then a bullet hit the dirt behind Jacob, and he sprinted ahead. The fence was in front of him. He'd wiggled under a split rail to get in here. But that took too much time.

Instead, he leaped higher than he ever had in his life, clearing the barrier by millimeters.

COLONEL Bowie strode across the compound. Every man had his job in the current operation.

"Give the order to move out," he said to Sergeant Caldwell.

Before the man could comply, the sound of gunfire broke out through the compound.

Eyes blazing, Bowie ran toward the staging area. He'd

given explicit orders that shooting around the bomb was
dangerous. So what the hell was going on?

Private Pinder was standing with his arms outstretched, a
Sig in his hands. Obviously, he'd been firing toward the
woods.

"Weapon down."

To his credit, the man instantly obeyed.

"What's going on?" Bowie barked.

"The tires on the lead van are punctured. I think a wolf
did it."

Bowie laughed, a harsh sound that held no mirth. "You're
kidding, right?"

"No, sir."

"How did a wolf get past our dogs?" he demanded. But
even as he spoke, an image flashed into his mind, an image
of a furry body leaping through the window of his quarters
and out into the night.

Pinder shook his head, then squatted down and pointed to
the closest tire.

Bowie squatted beside him, his eyes going from the
front tire to the rear. They were both flat. He cursed under
his breath, then lay down on the ground and looked under
the vehicle. Sliding forward on the blacktop surface, he
stretched out his arm and pulled out a knife, holding it up
to Pinder.

"You think a damn wolf was using this thing?"

"No, sir."

"There's a sheath under there. Get it."

Pinder got down and wriggled under the vehicle, no easy
task considering that the deflated tires had lowered the van a
couple of inches.

He emerged grasping a leather sheath, which he held up
to the light, his eyes narrowed.

"What?" Bowie snapped.

"There are teeth marks on it."

"And?"

He pointed. "Animal teeth marks."

Bowie stared at the marks. They definitely weren't human.

He heard an indrawn breath from behind him and saw Spencer standing there. His face had gone white.

"You know something about this?" Bowie snapped.

"No, sir."

"Then what the hell is the matter with you? Have you turned chicken on me?"

Spencer swallowed, then began to speak in a strained voice. "We saw wolves in the woods, where we left Reynolds."

"And you failed to mention that fact?"

"It didn't seem relevant at the time."

"But you noticed it."

"Yes, sir."

He'd like to march the man to the punishment ground, strip off his clothing, and give him enough lashes to make him faint. But he didn't have time for that now. He had to think. He was poised to pull off the greatest act of patriotism in the history of the United States—Operation Eagle's Flight—and he had encountered a setback.

Something had happened. Something he didn't quite understand. It had started a couple of nights ago. First the dogs had been barking. Then they'd stopped. And when he'd returned to his quarters he'd seen an animal go out the window.

Was someone using trained dogs to spy on him? A man with a German shepherd partner, like a K-9 team. Or could it be a man working with wolves?

He thought he'd prepared for every contingency. Everything was ready to go. And now they had a problem.

Pinder cleared his throat.

Bowie glared at him.

"Permission to speak, sir."

"Go ahead."

"I think I winged the wolf."

"Ah! Good work. Too bad you didn't drill the man."

PAIN stabbed through Jacob's right front leg. When he spared a glance at it, he saw that it was bleeding.

Damn! The shooter had gotten him.

He kept moving, making for the pile of clothing he'd left in the woods. But one of the colonel's troops had gotten there first and had picked up his T-shirt, shaking it to see if anything fell out.

Jacob turned and faded into the underbrush, listening to the man shout and another guy answer.

"Hey, over here. Look at this."

"Somebody stripped out here."

"Why the hell would he do that?"

"To change clothing?"

"Yeah. Maybe he has on a uniform like ours. Maybe he thinks he can blend in." The first speaker riffled through Jacob's belongings. "Here's a cell phone. And car keys."

"Radio the colonel."

"Yeah."

Shit, Jacob silently muttered. His wallet was hidden in a special compartment in the car. But the cell phone was bad enough.

He could hear the soldier talking, but not the answers.

"We've found a pile of clothing—with a cell phone and car keys."

"Yes, sir."

"Should we press redial?"

"Yes, sir."

Shit! What if they got Ross?

Jacob curled into the underbrush, wishing to hell he could contact the other Marshall men. That was out of the question now. But he had a pretty good idea of what they might try to do, and there was one way he might be able to help them.

Eyes closed, he sent his thoughts toward the two dogs still roaming Flagstaff Farm.

Could he reach them? He didn't know, but he had to give it a shot.

My friends are coming. My friends are coming, he said, over and over, praying that the message was getting through. The distance might be too far. But he'd already made contact with the dogs twice before. Maybe that connection would let him do it again.

IN the front seat, Ross stared at his cell phone. "I don't like it. Jacob hasn't called in."

"You think he's in trouble?" Logan asked.

"Yeah. Unfortunately. Otherwise we would have heard from him." Ross pulled off the road into the woods. Then he called Lance. "You on your way?" he asked.

"Yeah."

"I'm parked about a quarter mile from the entrance to the farm. Logan and I are going in as wolves."

"I'll join you," Lance answered. "But then what?"

"We look for Jacob. And we try to figure out how to disable Bowie's men."

In the back of the vehicle, Quinn cleared her throat.

"What?" Ross asked, and she could tell she'd broken his train of thought.

"I have an idea," she said. "Maybe it won't work. But I think I should tell you."

BOWIE clicked off. They were making progress. They'd found enough to identify the guy who'd left his clothing in the woods. And his vehicle had to be nearby.

They were also bringing his phone, which should give a list of incoming and outgoing calls.

But top priority was finding the intruder. So was he still on the farm? If so, he was either wearing a uniform like the troops had on, or he was hiding out.

Bowie pulled out his whistle and blew—two short blasts and a long one, summoning the troops to the parade grounds.

When they were standing at attention, he said, "Able team goes into the woods." He gestured in the direction where Pinder had been firing. "Look for a vehicle. Disable it. Shoot out the tires. Then look for a man and a wolf. I want them brought back here. Go."

"Yes, sir!"

Eight men moved off. He addressed the rest of the troops. "Grady and Hover will guard the vehicles. Maxwell, you change the tires. The rest of Baker team, search the area near the buildings and vehicles. Shoot any intruders you see. Shoot to wound. I want to interrogate the man."

THE phone rang, and Lance answered.

"This is Ross again. Put this on the speaker."

Lance clicked the button.

"Quinn has a suggestion, and I need you in the loop."

Ross told them the plan, and Caleb wanted to shout at him to leave Quinn out of it.

But he knew she wasn't going to back down, and he knew they needed her help. Quinn and everybody they'd brought along.

"We'd better get some details straight," Lance said, and Caleb felt his stomach clench as he listened to him making plans with Ross.

Werewolf plans. Well, that didn't apply to him, and he'd better stop wishing things were different.

CHAPTER
THIRTY-FOUR

QUINN WATCHED AS Logan, Sam, and Ross got out of the car and headed for the woods.

Just before he stepped into the trees, Ross turned and gave them a thumbs-up sign. She knew that was to say good luck.

Still, as he disappeared from sight, Quinn swallowed. She'd come up with this plan, but now she was wondering how well it was going to work.

She and Olivia moved to the front seat and Olivia drove up the road, closer to the edge of the farm. When they reached the fence that Jacob had described, they stopped. Olivia pulled the hood release, and both of them got out. After raising the hood, they both peered inside, then stood talking and gesturing and looking at the engine.

COLONEL Bowie pressed the redial button on the captured phone. The instrument called someone named Ross. Bowie could see the number, but nobody answered.

Well, he'd worry about the intruder's friends later. Right now, he had to figure out who was on the compound, screwing

up his plans. Slipping the phone into his pocket, he strode off
to search the farm.

QUINN and Olivia kept up the act for five minutes, and
Quinn was sure her plan wasn't going to work.

Finally, two men in uniform came out of the woods and
walked rapidly toward them.

"This is private property," one of them called.

Olivia eyed the machine gun slung over his shoulder.
"And it looks like you're on guard duty. I'm so sorry to . . .
uh . . . interrupt your work. But our car stopped. We don't
know what's wrong. Could you possibly help us?"

He tipped his head to the side, looking at them with a
smirk on his face. "Don't you ladies have Triple A or something?"

Quinn had heard of that. You paid a yearly fee, and they
helped you out if your car broke down. She smacked her forehead. "I knew I shouldn't have let my membership expire."

She was wary of the guns as the men came closer. From
their behavior, she assumed they didn't see two young
women as a threat. But she couldn't be sure.

"We'd really appreciate it if you could tell us what's
wrong with the engine," Olivia said.

One of the men gave his companion a look and rolled his
eyes. "If it will get you out of here."

She and Olivia were standing close together. Now they
brushed shoulders and sent the message that they had worked
out in the car.

*We are no threat to you. We're just two dumb women. The
other militiamen at Flagstaff Farm are the threat. We are no
threat. The militiamen at Flagstaff Farm are the threat. You
must eliminate the threat. You must shoot the other militiamen. You must go back and shoot them.*

One of the men looked at her and blinked. "What?" he
said, his voice puzzled.

Quinn glanced at Olivia. The man had heard something,
so the women sent the message again.

We are no threat to you. We're just two dumb women. The

*other militiamen at Flagstaff Farm are the threat. We are no
threat. The militiamen at Flagstaff Farm are the threat. You
must eliminate the threat. You must shoot them. You must go
back and shoot them.*

She held her breath, wondering if a message so contrary
to all their training was going to work.

She dared to give Olivia a quick look, but the other woman
was standing with her eyes staring straight ahead.

Maybe she was thinking the soldiers might turn their
weapons on *them.*

It could happen, if the message got garbled.

One of the men slid his hand toward the machine gun
slung over his shoulder, and Quinn tensed, ready to duck under the weapon and attack him.

Then, to her vast relief, both men turned and walked
stiffly away. She watched them until they disappeared into
the woods.

"Nice work," Olivia murmured.

"I hope so."

They drove slowly up the road again toward the other side
of the farm. If the trick had worked and they could pull it
again, they could get more of the militiamen shooting at
each other.

LANCE stopped a quarter mile down the road from the
farm. "I'm going to change to wolf form now," he said to
Caleb.

"Go on. I'll be all right."

They'd talked about Caleb's plan, and he knew Lance
thought it was too risky. But there wasn't a real alternative.
The other Marshalls had the advantage of the wolf. And he
had the advantage of already being dead.

Too bad there hadn't been a lot of time to coordinate their
efforts. But Bowie had forced them into attacking before
they were ready.

They both climbed out and headed for the woods. Caleb
found the fence that circled the property and ducked under
it. When a dog came racing toward him, he stopped short.

"Good boy," he called softly, holding out his hand.

The dog stopped and sniffed, then licked his palm. It recognized him. Well, not *him.* Wyatt Reynolds. But that was good enough.

Wyatt had gotten what he wanted—death. Once again, Caleb wondered if he'd inherited the man's goal. Or was he tempting fate on his own account?

Quinn had made him want to live. Yet he couldn't be sure that was the best outcome—for both of them.

And now he had the opportunity to let destiny determine if he lived or died. Whichever way it came out, he'd know he'd helped the Marshall family. That made him feel good. He'd started out hating them, then realized they were nothing like the werewolves of his generation. Well, that was going a little too far. They still harbored their animal aggressions. But Ross had pulled off a kind of miracle in getting them to work together.

His machine gun at the ready, he started toward the center of the compound—until the sound of automatic weapons fire had him turning quickly to his right and moving at a dead run. Ross and the others had gone in as wolves. So they weren't the ones shooting.

THEY'D gotten the bastard in the woods, Bowie thought. In the next moment, he wasn't so sure. The clattering sound of machine guns continued. What the hell was going on? It sounded like his men had encountered an invading force and were returning fire.

Was the guy named Ross coming with reinforcements?

From the corner of his eye, he saw a flash of movement and stopped short.

One of the dogs. No—not a dog—a wolf. It was coming toward him, a purposeful look on its face.

What the hell? He drew his sidearm, just as a voice to his right called out.

"That wolf isn't your enemy."

Bowie jerked toward the sound of the voice. His jaw dropped

open when he saw Wyatt Reynolds standing in front of him.

"You're dead," he managed to say. "Portland and Spencer buried you alive."

"That's right. But that doesn't do you much good."

Bowie raised his gun and fired, hitting Reynolds in the middle of the chest. He saw the bullet go through his shirt.

The man staggered back, but he didn't go down. Before he could fire again, a gray shape leaped forward. Then another. Two wolves brought him to the ground, and he fought to get his weapon into position.

GUNFIRE still sounded nearby, and Jacob had no idea what was going on. He'd thought they were looking for him. It sounded like they were after someone else, too.

Then he saw a man in a beige uniform coming toward his hiding place, gun drawn.

Oh, shit.

It looked like they'd found him. He gathered his strength, ready to spring. But before he could climb to his feet, a wolf leaped on the man's back, bringing him down.

Logan.

Jacob would have shouted his relief if he could have talked. He staggered up, forcing his injured body to function, but he could barely move.

Logan bit down on the man's shoulder, and he screamed but still held on to his machine gun.

Another soldier came running out of the woods, his own weapon in firing position. Jacob gathered the last of his strength, ready to go for the militiaman's gun hand.

Before he could leap, the newcomer shot his comrade, and the guy went still.

For a moment, the shooter's eyes registered confusion. Then he firmed his jaw, turned, and headed back the way he'd come.

Logan was wearing a pack and a whistle around his neck. He blew into it, making a call like a bluejay to tell the other wolves that he'd found Jacob. Then he trotted into the thicket and shrugged out of the pack.

Jacob grimaced before managing to silently say the chant that changed him from wolf to man.

He knew Logan was doing the same thing.

As soon as he could talk, he asked, "What the hell was that?"

"I guess the women's plan worked. Quinn and Olivia were going to try and lure a soldier to them by looking like they had car trouble. Then they were going to tell him to start shooting at his friends," he answered as he climbed into sweatpants and a T-shirt.

"Sounds like the guy is doing it," Jacob answered as he tried to pull on the pants Logan handed him. Finally, he gave up and lay back as Logan pulled out his cell phone. Again, he could only hear half of the conversation.

"Olivia?"

"We're fine, but Jacob is wounded," he said. "Bring a first aid kit. I'll use the bluejay whistle so you can find us."

"Mind putting on my pants before the women get here?" Jacob asked when Logan had finished.

"Yeah." Logan bent down and helped Jacob pull on the sweatpants. Then he blew the whistle, repeating the action again in a couple of minutes to signal their location.

Jacob was woozy, but he realized there was something he needed to say. "They got my clothes and cell phone."

"Not good," Logan muttered.

"They took the phone to Colonel Bowie, I think."

Finally, he saw a slender figure running toward him.

One of the women! But where was the other one?

Then another burst of gunfire made them all stop in their tracks.

BOWIE struggled with the wolves. Neither one of them had gone for his throat. One of the animals clamped down on his gun hand. The other crunched his left arm, and he screamed as he felt bone shatter. Then it did the same thing to his right leg.

The two wolves kept him cornered, until one of his own men came running toward him. It was Spencer—firing like his colonel was the enemy.

"Don't shoot. Don't shoot," he shouted. "The bomb's right in the van in back of me."

CALEB recognized the man running toward him. It was one of the bastards who had buried him in the woods. The one named Spencer.

His chest hurt like a son of a bitch from where he'd been struck in the bulletproof vest. But he slid behind the edge of the van where the two wolves had taken down Colonel Bowie.

The colonel was still shouting. "Stop. No. Stop. The bomb is in that van."

The two Marshall wolves sprang away from Bowie, one leaping to the right and one to the left, circling toward Spencer.

Caleb held the gun the way Lance had taught him, in a two-handed grip. As Spencer ran forward, firing, Caleb began shooting. And the satisfaction of hitting the man in the chest was sweeter than he could have imagined.

"You won't stay dead," Bowie gasped.

"You wish."

His eyes glazed with pain, the colonel looked from Lance to Ross. "Did those wolves save you?"

"Yes," he answered, his throat so tight he could barely speak. It wasn't literally true, not the way Bowie meant it. Quinn had dug him up, but the Marshalls had saved him from himself. "They're my brothers," he answered.

"Your brothers? I don't understand."

"You wouldn't."

Bowie looked at Ross and Lance, then back to him. "You have talents I never dreamed of. Help me," he begged. "The salvation of the United States depends on my mission."

"You're crazy."

"No! Please listen. My mission is vitally important!"

Before Caleb could answer, fire erupted inside the van, probably from a bullet that had struck the wiring.

"Fuck," the colonel shouted, sliding away as best he could.

Caleb pulled himself up, dashing toward the back of the vehicle.

He heard the colonel scream, then scream again, but he was too intent on opening the back of the van.

When the fire reached the explosives, it would act like a trigger mechanism. And Ross had explained what would happen. It wasn't just an ordinary bomb in there. It was full of radioactive material that would spray all over the area. And Quinn was here. It would get Quinn.

He couldn't let that happen. And if he had to die trying to prevent it, so be it.

CHAPTER
THIRTY-FIVE

SMOKE ENVELOPED CALEB. Racked with coughing, he fought not to black out as he pulled open the back door of the vehicle.

He didn't know how he was going to get the bomb out of there. A flash of movement made him whirl, expecting to see one of the colonel's militia. Instead, Ross and Sam Morgan had changed from wolves to men—then leaped to help him.

Sam climbed into the van, and Caleb blinked. He had expected to see some kind of cylinder with a rounded end. Like bombs he'd seen in movies.

Instead he found a large wooden box that looked like a shipping crate.

Sam pushed it toward the door. He and Ross tried to pick it up. But it was too heavy for the two of them.

Smoke was all around them now. Caleb ducked his head and struggled to breathe shallowly to keep from coughing. He knew that if the fire reached the gas tank, they were done for.

But none of them ran. They kept shoving at the box, which must have been lined with lead to prevent the radiation from escaping. At least he hoped it wasn't escaping.

Somehow he and Ross steadied the dead weight in their arms. Then Sam was on the ground, helping them hold it up.

He saw movement again through the smoke. And he gasped when someone else joined them. It was Quinn.

"Get back," he managed to say before a fit of coughing took him.

"No. You need me."

He didn't spare any more breath. Neither did she. But she stayed where she was, standing between the men and taking one corner of the heavy box as they all staggered away from the van and toward the shelter of a building.

She seemed to be taking more than her share of the weight. And in some part of his mind he remembered that she had run kitchen equipment with her mind. Was she doing something like that now, using her mental powers to help hold up the box?

Colonel Bowie was still on the ground, staring at them with a kind of horrible fascination. And Caleb was pretty sure he had seen the Marshalls change from wolves to men.

They staggered past the fallen man, away from the fire. And Caleb saw that he was trying to pull himself after them. But with a shattered arm and leg, he wasn't making much progress.

They angled toward the side of a shed. Behind them smoke surged. And just as they rounded the corner, a tremendous boom sounded.

The ground shook. And a wave of heat rolled toward them. Seconds later, debris rained down around them.

They set down the box, and the naked Marshall men crouched, covering their heads with their hands. But Caleb reached for Quinn, pulling her against him, curving his body around hers.

"Are you all right?" he gasped out.

"Yes. Are you?"

"Yes."

When the debris stopped falling she pulled his head down to hers for a savage kiss. And he kissed her back. Profoundly thankful that she was alive and in his arms.

When he heard someone running toward them, he tensed

and grabbed for the machine gun still slung over his shoulder. But it was Lance.

"Are you all right?" Lance gasped.

"Yeah," Ross answered for them, then he tried to suppress a fit of coughing. When he could speak again, he said, "And we got the bomb out of the van before it went up."

He pointed toward the box, then started to step out from behind the building.

"You might want to put some pants on," Lance murmured.

Ross looked down at his naked body. "Yeah, thanks."

When Lance handed out sweatpants, both naked men turned away and pulled them on.

"You got something to wipe away our prints?" he asked.

Lance pulled off his shirt, and Ross wiped their fingerprints off the box.

Then they stepped out from behind the building and looked toward the van. It was a charred hulk. And so was the man lying on the ground nearby.

Colonel Bowie was dead. And the second van stood forty yards away, untouched by the fire.

Ross pointed toward it. "I assume the other bomb's in there?"

"We'd better make sure," Sam said, striding toward the other vehicle and opening the doors. "Yeah, there's an identical box in here."

"Good." Ross said.

Lance looked around. "How much time do we have?"

"To be safe, we should be out of here in twenty minutes. If a neighbor reported the shooting, the cops could be on their way. Are there any of Bowie's men left?"

"If they survived, they've taken off," Lance answered.

Quinn looked at Ross. "We've got a casualty. Jacob was shot."

"Damn! How is he?"

"Logan and Olivia are with him. She says it's not serious. Let's hope she's right."

"She's got some ability with healing," Sam said as he headed for Logan's vehicle.

"Okay, good." Ross looked at Lance. "You have a phone?"

"Yeah." He handed it over, and Ross called Megan, who was back at the house. She told them Zarah's problem had turned out to be minor, as she'd assumed. And she said she'd wait for Jacob.

Ross's next call was to Olivia, to tell her to go on ahead with Jacob when Sam got there.

When that was taken care of, Ross and Caleb started entering buildings.

Ross returned a few minutes later. "If the bombs aren't evidence enough, I found those papers Jacob was talking about. I left them for the authorities to find. So let's get the hell out of here."

They headed toward the edge of the property.

When they were off the farm property, Quinn stopped by a fallen soldier and picked up the clothing lying beside him. Apparently, she wasn't squeamish about getting close to a dead man.

"Is this Jacob's?" she asked.

"I think so. Thanks," Ross said. He rummaged through the soldier's pockets and brought out Jacob's keys. "Logan said the colonel had Jacob's phone," Ross reported.

"Then it's burned beyond recognition," Lance answered. "Let's hope we didn't leave any more evidence."

"Wolf tracks," Ross said. "Let them make something of that."

They climbed in the two remaining vehicles and drove back toward Logan's house.

"Open the glove compartment," Ross said to Caleb. "There's a prepaid cell phone."

"Which means?"

"That nobody can trace the ownership. So you can call Ruckleman and tell him that the bomb is out at Flagstaff Farm."

"What if he doesn't believe me?"

"Then he's going to get in trouble. Don't let him keep you

on the phone for more than a few minutes. We don't want them sending the cops after us."

Caleb punched in the number he'd memorized several days earlier and asked for Jerry Ruckleman.

"Who is this?"

He almost said his own name, but managed to switch to, "Wyatt Reynolds."

"Where are you?"

"I'm not talking to anybody except Ruckleman. So if you want me to hang up, keep stalling."

"Hold on."

"Put him on now."

Seconds later, Ruckleman came on the line. "Where the hell are you?"

"I went back to Flagstaff Farm to stop the colonel's plot, since you didn't seem to have any interest in preventing him from setting off a couple of dirty bombs in D.C."

The Homeland Security man winced, and Caleb suspected that he was recording the conversation.

"It looks like Bowie's troops went crazy and shot each other. When you get there, you'll find the bombs. One's in a crate behind a shed near the burned van. Bowie's body is burned, too.

"The other bomb is in a second van, still in the shed. Both of them are stuffed full of radioactive waste. So be careful. Also, in his quarters, he has notes on his plans. I'm hanging up now."

"Wait!"

Caleb pressed the off button.

"Now call 911 and tell them there's been a mass murder out at Flagstaff Farm. If the cops aren't already on their way, I want them out there so Ruckleman can't do a cover-up."

"Yeah, right."

Caleb called the emergency number, gave the message, and hung up again.

After putting the phone back into the glove compartment, he asked, "You think he can't track me down?"

"We can give you a new identity. You just have to stay out of trouble, because your fingerprints are on record."

"Yeah."

"And there are certain jobs you can't take, because they'll print you."

He nodded, wondering exactly how he was going to make a living. He'd seen the trucks they had now. And the idea of driving one of those monsters didn't appeal to him.

Maybe Ross noticed the expression on his face. "Take some time to relax and think about your options. We'll help you."

"Thanks," he answered. "And thank you for coming out here with me. I couldn't have stopped Bowie alone."

"We wouldn't have missed it for the world," Ross answered. "Well, speaking for myself."

Quinn, who was in the backseat, leaned forward, and put her hand on Caleb's shoulder. "How do you feel?" she asked.

"Like I've done what Wyatt Reynolds wanted me to do. And that's a weight off my chest."

Quinn kept her hand on his shoulder, and he wished she were sitting beside him. They still hadn't settled anything. But he was coming to terms with the reality that she was going to be in his life.

Had to be. Because she was his life mate. He couldn't deny what they meant to each other. But they had to have a frank talk about the future.

When they arrived home, Megan, Ross's wife, was waiting for them with a piece of unfamiliar equipment.

"A Geiger counter," she explained. "I want to make sure you're not contaminated."

"Good idea," Ross said.

They stood by the cars while she pointed a wand at each of them. Caleb held his breath, waiting. He wasn't so worried about his own sorry ass. But if anything had happened to Quinn, he would run off into the woods screaming.

"You're all okay," Megan said.

Ross grinned. "Of course."

His wife's eyes narrowed. "I hate it when you take chances."

"That brings up the subject of Jacob. How is he?"

"Resting comfortably."

"I'll go in and talk to him."

Caleb got the feeling that Ross wanted to chew out his cousin for almost getting killed. But at the same time, he knew that slashing the tires had prevented Bowie from leaving the farm.

They all went into the house, where Zarah was waiting anxiously for them. She jumped up when she saw Quinn.

"I'm so sorry I couldn't go along to help," she apologized.

"It worked out okay. And I would have been afraid to get too close to the militiamen with you along."

"But you weren't afraid for yourself?"

"I was afraid. But Caleb and the other men needed our help."

"What did you do?"

"Pretended to have engine trouble. When two of the militiamen came over, Olivia and I were able to influence them," Quinn said with some pride in her voice.

"To do what?" Zarah asked.

"Shoot the others."

Zarah winced.

"It was either them or us."

"Yes. I know. But I hate all this violence."

Caleb knew she was talking about the situation in her own world—as much as anything else.

Because the house was crowded, Lance said good-bye to everyone and went home. Sam and Olivia stayed for a while, but they had booked a room in a nearby motel for the night before their return to California in the morning.

Caleb suspected that they were going to do some private celebrating as soon as they got away from the group. And he was hoping he and Quinn could slip away somewhere private, too. Maybe the woods. He wanted to make love with her—after they talked.

He was thinking of asking her to go for a walk when Megan approached them, a serious look on her face.

"Let's go out onto the porch where we can have some privacy. You, too," she said to Quinn.

"Okay," he answered, wondering what she wanted to say.

They stepped onto the screened porch, and Megan closed the door before turning back to them.

"Before all this started, I was thinking that gene therapy might work for you. I mean, it might make it possible for your new body to change to wolf form. What would you think about that?"

He hadn't had much time for his private problems, but he felt a spark of hope leap inside him. And he remembered the rush of joy he'd felt when he'd run through the woods as a ghost wolf. He had thought he would never experience that again. Maybe he'd been wrong.

"Is it dangerous?" Quinn asked.

"It could be," Megan answered honestly. "Nobody's tried to treat something like this. Usually it's done for a medical condition."

"Can you tell us something about it?" Caleb asked, wondering how much he was going to understand. In 1933, medicine had been far less advanced than it was now.

"You may not know it, but when I first did a genetic study of Ross, I found out that he had an extra chromosome that creates the werewolf trait. Do you know what a chromosome is?"

Neither of them did, so Megan went on. "It's complicated. Your body is made up of cells. Chromosomes in the nucleus of each cell contain the genes that determine how your body works. I own a biotech lab, and I've studied werewolf genes. They interact with male hormones in ways that are different from ordinary people."

Caleb nodded.

"In the Marshall family, all girl babies died at birth."

"I know," Caleb murmured.

"I was able to save my daughter's life."

Catching the emotion in her voice, he felt his own throat tighten. The death of his infant sisters had been one of the terrible sorrows of his mother's life—that and losing half her sons when they first changed to wolf form at puberty.

"I may be able to give you the crucial genes. I'd deliver them to you with a detoxified virus. Probably the virus for German measles."

"It sounds complicated," Quinn said.

"It is." Megan glanced at Caleb. "Ideally, I'd put you in the hospital, but I can't exactly tell the staff what I'm really doing. So I'd have to use a motel room near my clinic. If you want to try the procedure, I'd do genetic testing on you. And I'd get the gene from one of the other Marshall men."

"How long would it take?"

"A few days. But it will take me several weeks to get ready."

"And there's some risk?" Quinn pressed.

"Something could go wrong, yes."

Quinn reached for his hand and held on tightly.

Caleb swallowed. "Can I let you know what I want to do?"

"Of course."

They were about to walk back into the house when a scream made them freeze. Then Caleb leaped toward the door.

CHAPTER
THIRTY-SIX

THE WOMEN WERE right behind him as he rushed back into the house to find everybody in the living room. A large, dark-haired man dressed in jeans, a T-shirt, and leather sandals strode toward Zarah and caught her in his arms.

"It's Griffin," Quinn said to the room in general. "Her husband."

She rushed toward the couple, then stopped, not wanting to interrupt.

"How did you get here?" Zarah whispered.

He looked apologetic. "I put a psychic tracer into Quinn's clothing. She left the clothing at this house, and it gave out a signal."

Logan stepped forward. "You gave us all a shock. But welcome to our home."

"You have been sheltering my wife?" he asked, his voice thick with emotion.

"I have. I'm Logan and this is Rinna."

Rinna also stepped toward Griffin. When he hesitated, she hugged him. And he hugged him back.

"Thank you so much," he said, his deep emotion obvious.

After Logan had introduced Griffin to the others in the

room, Zarah asked in a shaky voice, "Why did you come here? Did you have to flee?"

"No. Things are much better." He looked at Quinn and Caleb. "They were getting better when you were there last, but I was afraid to take any chances, so I kept the city well guarded. But we've had a breakthrough since you came back. I've actually shown the members of the council the advantages of working together."

He laughed. "I mean I pointed out they might like getting to live their lives without someone trying to knock them off. And I've sent delegations to some of the nearby cities. I'm trying to get them to see the wisdom of signing a mutual defense pact. So far, White Flint and Eden Brook have sounded positive."

Zarah stared at him. "That's wonderful."

"I left a guard at the portal. But I'm feeling good enough about conditions in Sun Acres to bring you home."

"Thank the Great Mother," Zarah breathed.

Griffin turned to Quinn. "And you—if you want to come."

"I . . . don't know." She glanced at Caleb. "It depends on what he wants to do."

"I was hoping he would join my household."

"As what?" Caleb asked, wondering if he was being offered some kind of charity.

"I'm trying to modernize our world. And you were able to repair that clock. As I told you, we have lots of equipment we don't know how to run. If you could get some of it working and maintain it for me, that would be of great help. Have you worked with steam engines?"

"Only for fun," Caleb answered, feeling his throat clog. "I made myself a steam-driven motorcycle when I was a teenager."

"Fantastic. We have an old steam car that I'd like to get operational. I hope you'll bring us your talent for fixing things."

Caleb swallowed and gestured toward Megan. "Dr. Marshall offered me a treatment that might restore my ability to change to wolf form. If I went to your world, could I come back here for treatment?"

"Of course."

"What do you want to do?" he asked Quinn.

Her eyes met his. "I want to be with you. Whichever place you choose."

His chest tightened as he stared at her. He wanted that, too. "Yes," he managed to say.

"You're going to leave the portal open?" Rinna asked.

"Yes. But we'll keep it hidden," Griffin answered, then looked around at the modern conveniences. "I'd love to take some equipment from this world, but I think that would be a mistake. If people start wondering where we got it, there might be too much temptation to traffic back and forth."

"Yes," Ross agreed.

"But I was thinking that if we could find some old books on manufacturing processes, we could get some small factories going." He looked at Caleb. "And maybe we can set you up as an inventor. You might come up with some actual inventions. But you could also duplicate what other men have done in this world . . . well, at a more primitive level."

"Men and women," Rinna said.

"Pardon." He grinned at her. "Men and women."

"Good ideas," Ross answered. "If he sells the equipment in your world, he can get rich."

Caleb's mind was spinning. He hadn't counted on anything like that. But he could see the possibilities. Maybe starting with telegraph or radio. A reliable means of communication over long distances was something the other universe could use. And something faster than horses for travel. In this world that had been the railroad.

But that required a large industrial base. Maybe steam cars and trucks would be more practical in Quinn's world.

Griffin looked at Zarah. "If you are well enough, I'd like to take you back now."

"Yes," she breathed. "I've longed to be with you."

He turned to Caleb. "And if you wanted to come with us, I've taken the liberty of setting aside rooms for you."

"They've had a lot to deal with," Zarah said. "Not just them—the whole family. They just stopped a madman from setting off a deadly bomb in the capital city. It might have made the cable news channels by now."

She picked up the remote from the coffee table and pointed it at the television.

Griffin jumped when the picture came on.

A reporter on CNN was excitedly describing a plot to blow up the U.S. Capitol. Then the picture switched to Flagstaff Farm, where they saw the blackened wreck of the van—and then a picture of the crate that held the bomb.

Rinna sucked in a sharp breath and looked at her husband. "*That's* what you were doing?"

"Yeah. We got the bomb out of the van before it blew up and spewed radiation all over us."

"Radiation. I assume that's bad," Griffin said.

"Very bad," Ross answered. "You can't taste it or feel it or smell it, but it will kill you—either quickly or slowly, depending on how close you are to the source, and how much you absorb."

Caleb saw Quinn shudder.

Griffin gestured to the television set. "How do they do that?"

Ross laughed. "Nobody here has the technical knowledge to explain how it works. But we watch it. Sometimes it's an advantage to know what's going on all over the world. And sometimes it's too much information." He picked up the remote that Zarah had put down and switched to several other stations.

"From all over the world?" Griffin asked.

"Most of it's recorded. But a few programs, like that newscast are live. I mean it's happening right now."

He handed Griffin the remote, and while he ran through the channels, Zarah went to get her things.

She was back quickly, with a small rolling suitcase. "One thing I'm going to hate is the maternity clothes back home. What they have here is a lot more comfortable."

"Maybe you can start a new fashion," her husband said.

"If I don't scandalize half the city."

She thanked Logan and Rinna profusely.

Griffin pulled a pouch of antique coins and jewelry from

his carry bag. "I hope you'll take this in payment for letting Zarah stay here."

"There's no need to pay us."

"I want to. Don't deprive me of that pleasure."

Logan nodded.

"So I will expect you in a few days?" Griffin asked Caleb.

He looked at Quinn. When she nodded, he answered, "Yes."

After they had said their good-byes, Caleb took Quinn out into the woods. To a secluded glen he remembered from when he'd been a ghost.

That seemed like a thousand years ago. The memories of a different man. And in reality, that was actually true. He had been very different. More primitive in his thinking and focused on the wrong thing.

When he turned to face Quinn, he could see she was nervous.

"What's wrong?" he asked.

"Are you getting ready to say good-bye?" she asked.

"Lord no! How could you think that?"

"I . . ." She didn't get a chance to finish the sentence, because he swept her into his arms and covered her mouth with his for a long, greedy kiss.

When he lifted his head, they stared into each other's eyes.

"I love you. I want to spend my life with you," he told her, his voice strong and sure.

She clasped her arms around his back, holding on tightly. "Even if that treatment Megan talked about doesn't work?"

"Even if it doesn't."

"You were so . . . upset when you found out you couldn't change."

"Yes." He heaved a deep sigh. "All I could think of was what I'd lost. I still hadn't realized what a precious gift I'd been given." He swallowed hard. "Two gifts—actually. My life and you."

"Oh, Caleb."

"You are the best thing that ever happened to me."

"Yes. I feel that way, too."

He hitched in a breath. "Our children. They won't be Caleb Marshall's."

"They will be—if you're a good father to them."

"I will be. Better than my father ever was to me. Ross and the others have shown me what family can mean to each other. I never thought it was possible for werewolves to . . . help each other. Too bad Aden couldn't have seen it."

"You forgive him?"

"Yes. Because he made it possible for me to find you. Maybe that was why I hung around for all that time."

"Or maybe to save the world." She brought her mouth back to his for a long, deep kiss. And as he kissed her, he rolled up her T-shirt, unsnapped her jeans, and lowered the zipper.

She wasn't wearing a bra. And with a glad exclamation, he lowered his head to her breasts, pressing his cheeks against the inner curves, then claiming first one distended nipple and then the other with his mouth. At the same time, he slipped his hand into the pants he'd opened and found her pussy. She was slick and swollen for him.

"You're working pretty fast," she panted.

"Yeah. Because I'm going to explode if I don't get inside you. Open these damn jeans for me."

She did as he asked, pulled them down his hips and freed him from his undershorts. Because his pants still trapped his legs, he pulled her down on top of him.

She quickly shucked out of her own jeans, then straddled his body and brought his cock inside her. They both exclaimed at the joy of their joining. And when she squeezed her inner muscles around him, he clasped her hips.

"What?"

"Hold still for a minute."

She took a breath and did as he asked.

"I love you. I was crazy to think I could give you up. I want to tell you that now."

"Oh, Caleb." Her eyes turned misty. "I love you so much."

He held her still for as long as he could stand it—another few seconds. Then he slid his hand to her clit and she began to move with quick, jerky motions.

They both came in a firestorm of release. And when she collapsed on top of him, he held her tightly.

"I have so much," he whispered. "More than I ever dreamed possible."

"Yes," she answered. "That's true for me. I never imagined being this happy. Not in my most vivid dreams."

He held her to him, knowing how lucky he was. And knowing that whatever happened in the future, he would have this woman at his side.

Turn the page for a special preview
of the next book in the series,

ETERNAL MOON
BY REBECCA YORK

Available soon from Berkley Sensation!

"YOU ARE NOT crazy." Renata Cordona said the words aloud to the empty house because she needed to hear them. In the next second, she wanted to smack herself for being such a wuss.

She might be nervous about this assignment. But she'd been trained by the best PI in the business. She was armed with a Glock Model 28, designed for concealed carrying and with less recoil than the bigger models. And she was an excellent shot.

Still, as she stood without moving, listening to the sound of the wind blowing the branches of the trees outside the window, she couldn't stop a shiver from traveling down her spine.

She heard the wind like that sometimes when she woke up and found herself barefoot in the backyard of her rented Ellicott City, Maryland, house. Or in the living room, surrounded by natural objects she didn't remember gathering.

She'd been sleepwalking.

But sleepwalking wasn't crazy!

"Stop it!" she ordered herself. "You're not going to sleep now. It only happens after you've gone to bed for the night."

But why was it happening at all?

She didn't know. And she wouldn't discuss it with her boss, Barry Caldwell. Or the police liaison detective, Greg Newcastle, of the Howard County, Maryland, PD.

Newcastle was already acting like a pain in the ass, and she wasn't going to give him a valid reason to pull her off this assignment.

It was too important to let her own doubts stop her.

Three women agents, who all worked for Star Realty, had been murdered in the past nine months while showing houses to clients. And Renata was going to make sure it didn't happen again—to her or to anyone else.

She walked to the front of the house and looked out the window. But she saw no cars coming up the long driveway that led to the wooded property she was supposed to be showing to a man named . . . She pulled out the slip of paper again.

Kurt Langana. He'd contacted Star Realty a few days ago, asking to see properties with several acres of land around them. Because that fit the MO of the murderer, Dick Trainer, the owner of the company, had given her the job—with the proviso that if she actually did end up selling anything, the money would come to him.

Which was fine with her. She wasn't doing this for money. She hadn't gone to work for Barry for money. Her parents had left her enough so that she could sit back and collect interest and dividend checks for the rest of her life.

She was just determined to make a difference.

So here she was, in an empty house, dressed in a baby blue pantsuit and open-toed high heels, waiting for a man who might be a killer.

She ran a hand through her long hair, then flipped it back over her shoulder. Her nerves were too on edge for her to stand there in the living room like Andromeda chained to a rock, waiting for the sea monster to come and get her.

She wasn't sure why her mind had leaped to that image. But even as a child back in Costa Rica, she'd been fascinated by mythology and read and reread a lot of the old stories—from many different cultures. Today the Andromeda story was a dark vision, and she needed the sunlight.

So she stepped out the front door into the spring afternoon and looked up at the sunshine filtering through the leaves of the towering oaks and poplars that someone had planted sixty or seventy years ago.

With narrowed eyes, she checked her watch again. Where was the guy? Lost?

Well, he had her cell phone number if he needed directions.

Striding down the driveway past the house, she walked toward the detached garage. It was a little far from the house to be convenient, and she realized that she should have checked it out in case Mr. Langana turned out to be a legitimate customer.

That thought made her firm her lips. She was focusing on the murder part of this assignment and forgetting that she also had to play a convincing real estate agent, one who would obviously have paid more attention to the house.

Let's see. She'd taken a good look at the kitchen. It had been updated, but maybe not recently enough to go with the $800,000 asking price for the property.

She was almost to the garage when movement in the woods made her stop. With a jolt, she turned. Had she and the police totally misread the killer's method of stalking his victims? Was he coming on foot to isolated locations where female agents were showing houses?

All that ran through her mind in a split second. Then she saw it wasn't a man at all, but a dog. A Rottweiler, she guessed.

He looked large and dangerous, and her blood ran cold when she realized he wasn't alone.

Behind him, five more dogs stepped out of the underbrush. They were all about his size. One looked like a Shepherd mix. Another was a Doberman. And the remaining two appeared to have at least half pit bull genes.

But what they mostly had in common was the threatening look in their eyes.

Did they belong to someone? Or were they a feral pack? Peering at them more closely, she saw that none of them appeared to be wearing collars—which wasn't reassuring.

Bent on getting out of their way, she took two quick steps to the side door of the garage and twisted the knob. Unfortunately it was locked, and she realized that the key was lying on the counter in the kitchen, along with the key to the house.

The Rottweiler, who appeared to be the leader of the pack, started barking. The others followed suit.

Then they broke off as quickly as they had started.

Somehow, that abrupt silence was more threatening than the previous noise.

The leader bared its teeth and snarled at her. The others did the same.

They were maybe sixty feet away, but she could clearly hear them growling.

Instinctively, she knew they were out for blood, and that she was no match for them.

She drew the gun hidden in a holster below her suit jacket at the small of her back. She'd never shot a dog in her life, and the idea of doing it now made her sick. But that might be her only chance to get out of there alive.

Would a warning shot scare them away—or send them charging toward her?

Her mind scrambled for what she remembered about canines. You weren't supposed to challenge a dangerous dog by looking him in the eye. And you weren't supposed to show fear.

Yeah, right.

Should she try to run back to the house? Or should she walk? And should she turn her back?

No, that had to be a mistake. Then she wouldn't know what they were doing.

She took a step back and then another, keeping her gaze slightly to the side of the pack.

But she saw the leader raise his head as the snapping and snarling become more furious.

And she knew in that moment that they were going to charge her.

Just before the leader could charge, another dog came dashing out of the woods. A bigger dog with gray fur. Her gaze took in the details. The pointed ears. The long, upturned